VERY IMPORTANT CORPSES

VERY IMPORTANT CORPSES

An Ishmael Jones mystery

Simon R. Green

This first world edition published 2016
in Great Britain and 2017 in the USA by
SEVERN HOUSE PUBLISHERS LTD of
19 Cedar Road, Sutton, Surrey, England, SM2 5DA.
Trade paperback edition first published
in Great Britain and the USA 2017 by
SEVERN HOUSE PUBLISHERS LTD

British Library Cataloguing in Publication Data
A CIP catalogue record for this title is available from the British Library.

ISBN-13: 978-0-7278-8671-2 (cased)
ISBN-13: 978-1-84751-774-6 (trade paper)
ISBN-13: 978-1-78010-842-1 (e-book)

All Severn House titles are printed on acid-free paper.

Severn House Publishers support the Forest Stewardship Council™ [FSC™],
the leading international forest certification organisation.
All our titles that are printed on FSC certified paper carry the FSC logo.

*C*all me Ishmael. Ishmael Jones.
      There is a hidden world, of the strange and unnatural.
      A shadowy world, of aliens and monsters and men who
have monsters in them. I operate in the darkest parts of the
hidden world, dealing with things that shouldn't exist but
unfortunately do. And if I've done my job properly, none of you
will ever know I was there.

I came into this world in 1963. An ordinary-looking man
in his mid-twenties, with a face you wouldn't look at twice. A
face that hasn't aged one bit in all the years since. I live
among you, but I'm not one of you. Because back in '63 a
star fell from the heavens and landed in a field in south-west
England. Or, to put it another way, an alien starship came
howling down out of the upper atmosphere with its super-
structure on fire and crashed in the middle of nowhere. Killing
all of its crew but one.

The sole survivor was made over by the ship's transformation
machine, given a human face and form so he could move
unnoticed in this hostile new world. But the machine was
damaged in the crash, and all the survivor's previous memories
were wiped clean.

I don't even remember where my ship is buried.

It's become increasingly difficult for me to stay hidden, in
this surveillance-heavy society; so these days I work for the
Organization. They protect me from the world's overly inquisi-
tive eyes, and in return I deal with the problems they set me;
protecting Humanity from things that don't officially exist.

I have a partner now; a delightful young lady called Penny
Belcourt. Together we solve mysteries and track down killers.
We love each other as best we can, given that one of us isn't

entirely human. She holds me in the night when the bad dreams come, and I catch glimpses of what I used to be before I was me. She believes in me; and I would too, if only I could be certain there's no one else in my head but me.

ONE

Someone Has Already Died

Most people have at least heard of Loch Ness and its monster. What most people don't know is that monsters can be real, and in the hidden world there are all kinds of monsters.

The hired car's engine roared enthusiastically as I sent it racing along the narrow road that skirted Loch Ness. The dark waters were placid and calm, untroubled by boats or people or wildlife; or anything even a little bit monstrous. 'But then, Penny and I were probably the only people who'd come to the loch in that late-autumn evening who weren't interested in its famous creature. The Organization had something else in mind for us.

They hadn't told me what, as yet. Just instructed me to get from London to Loch Ness as fast as possible because something bad had happened. And when the Organization says that, it means something really bad has hit the fan; and all sane people should be heading in the opposite direction.

Gnarled twisted trees crowded together on the opposite side of the road, as though desperate for comfort in the cold, bleak setting. They stood firm and tall, like so many watchmen standing a guard that would never end, keeping a stern eye on whatever lurked in the depths of the loch. No leaves, or colour, or any other sign of life: just a dark heavy presence. The road was thankfully free of other traffic this late in the tourist season. I hadn't seen another car go by in ages. It was starting to feel like driving through an area that had been evacuated because of some unnatural disaster. I glanced at the loch, half expecting to find something staring back at me, and kept a wary eye on the cloudless iron-grey skies. The weather forecast said serious snow was on its way, and I really hoped I would be done with my business and gone before the storm started. When snow falls in Scotland, it does so with a vengeance. As if to remind people they only live there at the weather's sufferance.

I'd booked our passage to Scotland on a sleeper train, all the way up the spine of the country. Several hours crammed into a tiny compartment with Penny; which wasn't nearly as much fun as you might think. So neither of us was in the best of moods when we picked up the hired car waiting for us at Inverness. A deathtrap on four mismatched tyres, with frankly suspicious mileage on the clock and far more character than was good for it; but it was all I could arrange at such short notice. The accelerator liked to stick, the brakes only responded to brute force, and you had to catch the gears by surprise. The best you could say about the car was that it wasn't actually trying to crash; it just encouraged you to drive in such a way that some kind of disaster was inevitable. I was having a great time. I like a car that likes to be driven. I goosed the accelerator again, just for the hell of it, and the car jumped forward like I'd found another gear.

I laughed out loud, and Penny smiled dazzlingly at me from the passenger seat. Resplendent in a cute black dress and broad-brimmed hat, she seemed entirely unperturbed by the car or my driving. I was always happy to see her smiling. The hidden world may contain wonders and marvels as well as threats and terrors, but it's not the kind of place where you stop to smell the daisies. They might bite. Penny was a bright young thing with dramatic features, lots of dark hair and a fine figure, and enough nervous energy to scare off any man with an interest in a quiet life. She beat a happy tattoo on the dashboard with both hands as the car took a bend in the road with more enthu-siasm than control, and then shot me a frankly sceptical look.

'You are sure of where you're going, aren't you, sweetie? Only I can't help noticing this car doesn't come with satnav . . . or a heater that works . . . And you haven't so much as glanced at a map since you got behind the wheel. Have you been this way before?'

'No,' I said. 'I memorized a map of the area before we left London.'

'What? All of it?'

'Of course,' I said.

'Alien!' Penny said cheerfully. She looked out over the loch. 'You know everything there is to know about the weird and the wonderful. Does something ancient and frightfully monstrous live in Loch Ness?'

'I don't know everything,' I said. 'I've just been around for a while and talked with a lot of people experienced in the kind of things most people have the good sense to avoid. I know the original legend, of how a monster rose up in the loch to face off against St Columba, back in AD 565. And I know that modern sightings only started in the 1930s, when the first main road was built alongside the loch. But apart from that, your guess is as good as mine.'

'I like to think there's a monster,' said Penny. 'Just because it pleases my romantic soul to believe such things exist. Of course, if there is a creature in the loch, it's probably better off staying a legend. If it ever stuck its head above the surface during a live television broadcast, how long do you think it would be before hunters started turning up from all over the world, just so they could be the first to kill it and enjoy a lifetime's bragging rights?'

'Wouldn't surprise me,' I said. 'Back in the twenties a London museum offered a really good price for the creature's carcass, just so they could stuff it and put it on display. Until they were shamed into withdrawing the offer.'

'You see, you do know everything! And if it wasn't hunters it would probably be businessmen, looking to put it in a theme park so they could charge people to see it. No, you stay out of sight, Nessie dear, and stay safe.'

'I know the feeling,' I said.

When we finally reached our destination the last of the light was dropping out of the evening, as if someone had hit a dimmer switch. I eased the car through a series of unlit narrow lanes until a sudden side turning brought us at last to the Purple Heather inn, a squat stone structure with weather-stained walls and an unevenly tiled roof, and a battered satellite dish hanging from the gutter. The inn perched precariously on a promontory looking out over the loch, bright lights shining from its windows and loud music blasting out of the open door. The car park was

only half full now the tourist season was almost over, and I
brought the hired car to a juddering halt with a definite feeling
of relief. Riding a headstrong stallion can be fun, but you know
the end result is always going to be a pain in the arse.

I got out of the car and closed the door carefully, because I
had a feeling slamming it could have unfortunate consequences.
And I'd had to put down one hell of a deposit before they'd
even let me have the damned thing. Penny came bustling round
the car to join me, one hand holding her big hat in place despite
the determined attentions of the gusting wind. She studied the
Purple Heather inn and then gave me a look that clearly said
'Is that it?'.

'When you work for the Organization, it's first class all the
way,' I said blithely.

'That's a laugh!' said Penny.

Once we got inside, the bar was crowded and no one paid
us any undue attention. The noise level was painfully high, with
a whole bunch of shouted conversations trying to make themselves heard over the music (mostly popular Scottish songs
written by people who had never lived there). I approved of the
general hubbub. A noisy crowd is always the best place to hold
a private meeting when you don't want to be overheard. I
elbowed my way to the bar to get the drinks, while Penny laid
claim to one of the few remaining empty tables at the back of
the bar.

As the barman sorted out my large brandy and Penny's g & t,
I took in the many monster-themed drinks on offer. Including
the Nessie cocktail ('It's big and green with one hell of a bite!')
and Nessie Whisky ('Made with our loch's very own peat-rich
waters. Guaranteed to have almost no distressing side effects!'),
neither of which appealed to me. Neither did the Nessie burger
('For those with a monstrous appetite!') or the Nessie Vegetarian
Surprise (the surprise in question almost certainly being that it
didn't contain anything a vegetarian would want to eat). I paid
the barman rather more than I'd expected, and carried the drinks
over to the table Penny had bagged. A middle-aged couple tried
to sit down with us, complaining loudly about how packed the
place was, only to change their mind when I gave them a cold
stare. I do a good cold stare. Not far away, some local youths

were playing an electronic game that seemed to involve many different ways of catching and killing the monster. Penny gave me a significant look, and took a solid gulp of her g & t.

'Have you seen the overpriced rubbish they're trying to palm off on the tourists?' she said. 'Fluffy Nessie toys and cartoony T-shirts, mugs with the legend WORLD'S BEST MONSTER, and sealed cans claiming to contain fresh air from the loch . . . They're selling people empty cans!'

'Like all souvenirs, it's not what you buy it's where you buy it,' I said wisely. 'It's just memories, like postcards.'

Penny sniffed, and looked disdainfully around the crowded bar, as though just by being there she was lowering her standards to a dangerous level. 'No sign of our contact. Why do you always come running when the Colonel calls?'

'Because that's the deal I made with the Organization,' I said. 'The Colonel is our only point of contact, and both sides prefer it that way. I take care of business for them, and they help me remain invisible. And of course both of us think we're getting the better end of the deal.'

'They do work you hard, Ishmael.'

'It's work that needs doing,' I said. 'Which comes as something of a relief after some of the things I've had to do down the years.'

She considered me thoughtfully, then put her drink down so she could place one gentle hand on mine. 'You don't like to talk about the other groups you've worked for.'

'No,' I said. 'The price of my survival has sometimes been higher than I'm comfortable remembering.'

'How does the Organization stand up, compared with the other groups you've worked for?'

'More consistent than most,' I said. 'And they've never asked me to do anything that troubled my conscience. So far . . .'

'You think they might?'

'Secret organizations often have good reasons for being secretive.'

'You don't trust anyone, do you, Ishmael?'

'No. Apart from you, of course.'

'Nice save, darling. I barely had time to raise an eyebrow. How many secret groups are there?'

'I've at least heard of most of them,' I said carefully. 'The subterranean societies and the ancient conspiracies, all with their own special areas of interest. The secret agents and the private contractors, the shadow people and the press-ganged heroes. Trading in under-the-counter information, obscure objects of power and second-hand souls. All of them a bit tainted, a bit shopworn, but still valuable merchandise. It's not always about good and evil. Or at least not as often as it should be. Whoever we work for, we all go our own way; and our various patrons are careful not to look too closely at how we get things done. Just like you with Nessie, there are things I choose to believe in and others I hope are just legends. Down the years I have bumped into odd individuals – some of them very odd – who have told me things . . . But people in my line of work lie like they breathe. It's part of the job.'

'You don't talk much about your past,' said Penny. Not making any particular point, just letting the comment lie there in plain sight. 'I know you used to work for Black Heir, cleaning up after alien contacts and salvaging whatever tech they left behind. But I only know about them because my family was involved.'

'A lot of my past I don't care to remember,' I said. 'Sometimes . . . a man on the run doesn't have much choice when it comes to finding shelter.'

And then I looked round sharply as the Colonel came striding through the crowd to join us. A tall, upright figure with an ex-military bearing and a general air of disdain, shoulders back to show off his classic tweed suit. The crowd seemed to naturally part before him without even realizing it was doing so, responding unconsciously to his air of innate authority. It made me feel like throwing things at him. The Colonel was handsome enough in an inbred aristocratic sort of way. The second son who goes into the army because he knows he's never going to inherit, and ends up in security because the army hasn't given him enough opportunities to be ruthless and underhanded. He slammed to a halt before our table, nodded briefly to Penny and just barely to me. Up close, I could smell the Turkish tobacco he'd been smoking earlier, the aftershave that isn't nearly as distinctive as he likes to think it is, and traces of the urine the crofters had used to fix the colours in his tweeds. He sat down opposite me without waiting to be asked.

'Mister Jones, Miss Belcourt. On time, for once. I trust you had a pleasant journey.'

'Not really,' I said. 'But that's what happens when you're called from one end of the country to the other at a moment's notice. From your calm, relaxed and almost unbearably smug manner, I deduce the Organization flew you up here. Why do I always have to make my own way everywhere?'

'Because I'm the Colonel, and you're not,' he said crushingly. He bestowed a brief smile on Penny. 'Good to see you again, Miss Belcourt. I don't believe we've spoken since that unfortunate business at your old family home.'

'You mean when all my family were slaughtered,' she said unflinchingly. 'You did a good job of cleaning up afterwards. I heard there was a very convenient gas explosion to explain why no one got to see the state of the bodies.'

'The simplest cover stories are always the best,' said the Colonel.

'Can we talk about why we've had to come all this way in such a hurry?' I said. 'And why you couldn't even hint at what's happened until now.'

'And why we had to meet here,' said Penny. 'I've gone drinking in after-hours Soho lock-ins with a less distressing ambience.'

I looked at her. 'You have?'

'I've lived,' said Penny.

'If we could stick to the subject . . .' said the Colonel.

'Is it something to do with the monster?' Penny said hopefully.

'No,' said the Colonel. 'You're here because this year the Baphomet Group are holding their annual meeting on the banks of the loch. At Coronach House.'

And having dropped that particular bombshell, he sat back and studied me carefully to see how I was taking it. I kept my face studiously calm, while I thought hard. Penny looked at both of us blankly.

'What's the Baphomet Group?' she said. 'I've never even heard of it.'

'Not many have,' I said. 'That's the point. Think of the Bilderburg Group, only more so. The Bilderburg and all the other famous big-name meetings are just distractions. Something to hold the public's attention while the really influential people get on with their own special meetings, tucked safely away in the background. So no one will ever know as they make the financial decisions that affect the fate of nations.'

'Exactly,' said the Colonel. 'The Baphomet Group hold their extremely secret gatherings in a different location every year. Just the knowledge that so many economic movers and shakers were all in one place, talking together, would do very unpleasant things to the world's financial markets. For reasons of their own, which are of course none of our concern, the Group decided to come here this year.'

'To Coronach House?' I said. 'With its reputation?'

'I might have known you'd have heard about it,' said the Colonel. 'Perhaps the Group chose the House in the hope its unhealthy reputation would keep people away. If so, their stratagem would appear to have backfired on them. We need you to go there and take over as Head of Security.'

'Why do they need someone like me?' I said. 'What's happened at Coronach House?'

'The first agent the Organization sent has been killed,' the Colonel said flatly. 'Jennifer Rifkin. A first-class operative, but not good enough. She'd barely been in the House twelve hours before she was found dead in her room.'

I sat back in my chair and frowned. Penny put a hand on my arm.

'Did you know her, Ishmael?'

'I've heard of her,' I said. 'I didn't know she was working for the Organization.'

'We don't talk about our agents,' said the Colonel. 'Even to other agents. You of all people should appreciate that, Mister Jones.'

I gave him my best cold glare. 'I'd work better if you weren't always keeping things from me.'

'I could say the same of you,' said the Colonel. 'Unless you're finally ready to tell me your true name and background?'

I kept looking at him until he shifted uncomfortably in his chair.

'You could always ask your superiors about me, Colonel,' I said calmly.

'I have. Repeatedly. But apparently I don't need to know. You have no idea how much that irritates me.'

'Good,' I said. 'Now tell me how Jennifer Rifkin died.'

'Badly,' said the Colonel. 'And in a somewhat unusual manner. According to the reports, it seems some kind of creature was involved.'

'Did anyone see it?' I said.

'No. No one saw or heard anything. How a wild animal could have got into Coronach House past all the layers of security, kill one particular person and then leave, all without being noticed, remains a mystery.'

'Which is why you're sending me,' I said.

'Hold everything!' said Penny. 'Your agent was killed by a creature in a house on the banks of Loch Ness . . . Are you sure the monster isn't involved?'

The Colonel looked down his long nose at her. 'Unless it's a lot smaller than has always been supposed, I really don't see how, Miss Belcourt. The Loch Ness monster has been gifted with a great many unusual qualities, but sneakiness is not one of them.'

'Oh, pooh!' said Penny.

'Couldn't have put it better myself,' I said. 'Still, of all the houses the Group could have chosen . . .'

'Why?' Penny said immediately. 'What's wrong with it?'

'Coronach House is centuries old,' I said, 'with a celebrated history. Though not in a good way. It was home to two infamous clan massacres, and the family had a disturbing preoccupation with the occult. The House was even a meeting place for the original Hellfire Club when their members were driven out of London after one unfortunate scandal too many. More recently, Coronach House was the setting for quite a famous disappearance. Some fifty years ago, a very well-thought of family rented the place for a vacation. They moved in quite happily, looking forward to a pleasant weekend of hunting and fishing . . . And then the whole family just vanished. No signs of violence, or even of a struggle. The servants just arrived one morning to find the front door open and the House deserted. People who've stayed there in the years since have reported bad dreams and noises in the night. And a feeling of never being entirely alone.'

Penny batted her eyelids at me admiringly. 'Oh, Ishmael, you do know everything!'

'Did you also know that back in the thirties Coronach House was briefly home to the Most Evil Man in the World?' said the Colonel.

I looked at him. I hadn't known that. 'Crow Lee lived there?'

'Briefly,' said the Colonel. 'Apparently he saw something that frightened him and he left in a hurry.'

'What could be bad enough to scare the Most Evil Man in the World?' I said.

'Exactly!' said the Colonel.

'I know the name,' said Penny, frowning. 'But that was all just . . . publicity, wasn't it? To help sell his books on the occult?'

'No,' I said. 'Crow Lee really was everything they said he was. I ran into him once. Back when I was still working for Black Heir. We were bidding for the same item at a very specialized auction house.'

'What were you bidding for?' said Penny.

'Almost certainly not what it was supposed to be,' I said. 'You come across a lot of fakes in our line of work.'

'What was he like?' asked Penny.

'Appalling views, but surprisingly good company,' I said. 'I was supposed to make him disappear, but at the last moment the kill order was rescinded. I'm still not sure whether I should have ignored the reprieve and done the job anyway. Just on general principles.'

Penny stirred uncomfortably. She doesn't like to be reminded that I used to kill people. Even if they were people who needed killing.

'If we could return to the subject of Coronach House,' said the Colonel. 'Another part of its unsavoury history might have a connection to our agent's death. The Coronach creature.'

'There's another story?' said Penny. 'I'm amazed anyone will go near the place.'

'It's the stories that attract the tourists,' I said. 'And this one predates everything we've discussed. Supposedly, a horribly misshapen child was born to the family in the House. An abomination. Too monstrous to be allowed to live, it was taken down to the loch, thrown in, and left to drown. But somehow it survived, and grew up alone and abandoned. In the depths, in the dark. Becoming something terribly powerful . . . an undying thing, with an undying hatred.'

'How is that even possible?' asked Penny.

'Legends aren't strong on details,' I said. 'Though some versions hint there was a reason why the child was what it was, something the family did . . . Anyway, apparently once in every century the creature emerges from the loch and comes ashore to take its revenge on whoever happens to be living in Coronach House at the time.'

'Has anyone ever seen this creature?' said Penny.

'It's just a story, Penny,' I said. 'Superseded in the public imagination by the Loch Ness monster. Probably because that's less disturbing.'

'But some animal is supposed to have killed Jennifer Rifkin,' said Penny. 'Could it be the creature in the story?'

I looked at the Colonel.

'Unlikely,' he said carefully. 'Rather more likely is that someone is using the old story as a cover for their own purposes.'

'What is the mission, exactly?' I asked. 'Solve Jennifer's murder? Or protect the Baphomet Group?'

'Both,' said the Colonel. 'On the one hand, no one kills one of our agents and gets away with it. On the other hand, the members of the Baphomet Group must be kept safe until they have completed their deliberations and left the country. After which, their safety can be someone else's concern. However, there are . . . complications.'

'Somehow, I just knew you were going to say that,' I said.

Penny nodded solemnly.

'All the members of the Group – usually referred to as "the principals" – will have their own security people, in addition to those provided by the House.'

'Because they don't trust each other?' said Penny.

'Precisely,' said the Colonel.

'What are they afraid of?' I asked. 'Hostile takeovers?'

'Oh, at least,' said the Colonel. 'Technically, all the security forces will answer to you, Mister Jones. But given that the principals are all very powerful and very private people, it's entirely possible their security people will be reluctant to give up any of their authority. You might have to bang a few heads together to get everyone to play nicely.'

'How far am I allowed to go in disciplining these people and still have the Organization back me?' I asked.

'You must rely on your own judgement,' said the Colonel. Which we both knew wasn't really an answer.

'And if I should happen to get a chance to . . . listen in, while these very important principals are having their private discussions?' I said.

'The Organization would be happy to learn of anything you might happen to overhear,' said the Colonel. 'As a bonus. But . . . discreetly, please. And do try to keep as many of them alive as you can, for a change. The Organization would prefer it if at least some of them were in a position to owe us a favour afterwards.'

'Got it,' I said. I paused, as a thought struck me. 'If I'm there representing the Organization . . . what are the chances of some other subterranean group being represented at Coronach House?'

'World finances aren't really their territory,' said the Colonel. 'It wouldn't normally be ours, but . . .'

'Yes,' I said. 'I was expecting a "but" at some point. Why did the Organization send Jennifer, in the first place?'

The Colonel considered his words carefully. 'It seems there is a possibility . . . no more than that, you understand . . . that one of the principals has already been abducted and murdered, and replaced by a double. We don't know who or why, and we don't dare point a finger without hard evidence.'

'Who told you this?' I said. 'Someone at the House?'

'Someone,' said the Colonel. 'What matters is that the Organization cannot risk any internal threat to the Group's deliberations while they're on British soil.'

'All right,' I said. 'That's the real reason I'm there, but what's my cover story? Why will the Baphomet Group think I'm there? Why was Jennifer there, officially?'

'The Baphomet Group requested extra security,' said the Colonel.

'Because they don't trust each other?' said Penny.

'Got it in one, Miss Belcourt. Apparently there were some

. . . unfortunate incidents at last year's meeting. Bad enough that the principals felt the need for an outside agent to be placed in overall charge.'

'What happened?' I said.

'No one is talking,' said the Colonel. 'Or at least not to us.'

'How did the Organization end up with a plum job like this?' I said.

The Colonel pretended he hadn't heard me. 'It's up to you to observe the situation, decide whether a substitution has taken place, and then take whatever actions you deem necessary.'

'Including killing the impostor?' I said.

'Whatever you deem necessary,' said the Colonel.

'Protecting the Group and finding Jennifer's killer could turn out to be two different things,' I said. 'Which mission has preference? What am I supposed to do if there's a conflict of interests?'

'I'm sure we can trust you to make the right decision,' said the Colonel.

Meaning, of course, that it was down to me. And God help me if I got it wrong.

'I have authority over the security people,' I said. 'Do I also have authority over the principals?'

'Of course not,' said the Colonel. 'These are all very important people.'

'Then how do I get them to do what I need them to do, when it's almost certainly going to involve them doing things they're not going to want to do?'

'You could always try charm.' The Colonel looked at me for a long moment. 'I did argue against you being given this assignment, but I was overruled. It calls for tact and diplomacy, neither of which have ever been your strong points. If you antagonize any of these people, there could be serious repercussions for the Organization.'

'Why?' I said.

'I asked that,' said the Colonel. 'I was told I didn't need to know.'

'Ishmael can be very charming,' said Penny. Just to show she wasn't being left out of the conversation. 'In his own way.'

'I am relieved to hear it,' said the Colonel.

'Have you brought us any special weapons?' asked Penny.

'I mean, if there is some kind of creature lurking around the House killing people . . .'

'I prefer not to use weapons,' I said. 'If you've got a gun, you often feel obliged to use it.'

'Then what about special equipment?' Penny said stubbornly. 'Secret agents always have a technological ace up their sleeve.'

'I don't use those, either,' I said. 'They tend to attract attention.'

'Couldn't agree more,' said the Colonel. 'However; you can't turn up at Coronach House in that awful little hire car of yours. So I've arranged for you to make use of one of our official vehicles. It's outside in the car park. A Rolls-Royce Phantom. Because you only get one chance to make a first impression. Please take good care of the car, I had to sign for it.'

'Ooh!' said Penny. 'Can I be the chauffeur? In a proper uniform, with a peaked cap? I've always wanted one of those.'

'No,' said the Colonel. 'Here are the keys to the car, Mister Jones, and here is your security ID.'

The ID card turned out to have a number on it, but no name or photo.

'Don't I get an ID?' said Penny.

'No,' said the Colonel. 'Burn the ID after use, Mister Jones. I've also placed a change of clothes in the back of the car for you.'

'What's wrong with what I'm wearing?' I said. 'It's good enough for fieldwork.'

The Colonel looked at my jacket and jeans, and didn't quite curl his lip. 'Coronach House is not the field. You will be representing the Organization, and you need to look the part if you want people like the principals to accept your authority.'

I frowned. 'I'm not comfortable with being in the public eye.'

'Outside of the House, you won't be.' The Colonel allowed himself one of his thin smiles. 'Everyone will remember the outfit, not the man wearing it. Now, I really must be going. I think I've enjoyed about as much of the local ambience as I can stand. Don't contact me until the case is over, one way or the other.'

'What if I decide I need backup?' I said.

'Don't!' said the Colonel.

He got to his feet, nodded briskly to Penny, then to me, and left. People in the bar stared vaguely after him, recognizing that someone important had just passed by. Penny scowled at the Colonel's departing back, and then looked at me.

'Why do you always go out of your way to antagonize him, Ishmael?'

'Because he's worth it.'

Penny sighed, recognizing a lost argument before it even started. 'OK . . . Coronach House. What does the name mean?'

'A coronach is a Scottish lament,' I said. 'A death song.'

'Ah,' said Penny. 'Not at all ominous, then. How well did you know Jennifer Rifkin?'

'Not well,' I said. 'She used to work for Black Heir. Not as a field agent, like me. Jennifer was in charge of internal security, investigating information leaks and the like. She had a reputation for getting to the bottom of things, no matter how many obstacles were put in her path. And she specialized in uncovering the kind of secrets people didn't want other people to know. If the Organization sent her to Coronach House, it must have been because they thought there was something there worth uncovering.'

'About the possible double? And about the Group itself?' said Penny.

'Almost certainly,' I said.

'If someone killed her, she must have found out something.'

'Or someone thought she had.'

'What do you know about the Baphomet Group?' asked Penny.

'Not much,' I said. 'Not really my field.'

'But are they human?' said Penny. She leaned forward, her eyes shining. 'I mean . . . you do hear stories about the Bilderburg Group and others like them. That they're all secretly Lizardoids, or Alien Greys, or Secret Ascended Masters. Running the world from behind the scenes, manipulating the economic fortunes of nations for their own nameless purposes . . .'

'You've been reading those weird magazines again, haven't you?' I said. 'Most conspiracy theories only exist to comfort people. The idea that there's some group of evil masterminds in charge of everything is actually preferable to the idea that there's no one at the wheel. That all the world's governments are just bumbling along, doing the best they can, and screwing up because the job is too big for them is a much scarier prospect than some inhuman secret cabal.'

'But . . . if there was such a cabal, human or otherwise, would you know about them?' Penny said craftily.

I sighed. 'I have heard things . . . but rarely anything I could verify. There are all kinds of secret groups operating in the shadows, but they've got more important things to worry about than world finances.'

'But are any of them aliens?' said Penny. 'Have any of them made contact with aliens and struck secret deals with them?'

'Don't ask me,' I said.

'Ishmael . . . Have you ever met another alien?'

'Not as such,' I said. 'I've met some people who weren't strictly speaking human; you can't avoid them in this line of work. Like the Immortals. Now they really were out to rule the world. Nasty bastards. Shape-shifters, too. But there were never enough of them to make a real difference. And you don't have to worry about them, because they're all dead now.'

'What happened?'

'They annoyed someone even worse than them. The Droods.'

'Yes! I've heard about them!' said Penny, bouncing eagerly on her seat. 'An ancient family, dedicated to fighting monsters and protecting Humanity! I thought they were just an urban legend.'

'You believe in ghosts,' I said, 'but balk at the Droods?'

'Are they real? I mean, are they everything they're supposed to be? Have you ever seen one?'

'Only from a distance,' I said. 'Which is always the safest way to see a Drood. I don't think they approve of people like me.'

'Who else?' demanded Penny. 'Who else have you met?'

I knew I shouldn't indulge her, but it was hard to deny her when she was so enthusiastic.

'Well,' I said. 'There's the Spawn of Frankenstein . . . All the various people – some of them only technically people – created by the Baron.'

'Oh, you are kidding me!' said Penny, her eyes wide. 'They're real? He's real?'

'Yes,' I said. 'The living god of the scalpel. Most of the

stories that have grown up around him aren't nearly as bad
as what he really got up to. The terrible things he created in
the butcher shops of his laboratories. The Baron's still out
there somewhere, hiding from his many enemies and selling
his awful secrets, in return for privacy and enough funding to
continue his work.'

Penny sighed happily. 'You've led such an exotic life, Ishmael.
Why do you never want to tell me about all the amazing things
you've done?'

'Because mostly you're better off not knowing.'

'What about . . . people like you?' said Penny.

'Nothing I could ever prove,' I said. 'No one I believed.'

'What about Roswell?' said Penny, like a card player slapping down an ace. 'Were there really aliens at Roswell?'

'Yes,' I said. 'And a great deal nastier than most of the stories
would have you believe. But they're all dead now.'

'Why? What happened?'

'They came up against something worse than them.'

Penny's eyes widened. 'The Droods again?'

'They do get around,' I said. 'Change the subject, please.'

'All right,' said Penny, reluctantly. 'Answer me this one. Why
is the Baphomet Group called the Baphomet Group? What does
the name mean?'

'Supposedly, a mysterious creature the old Knights Templar
used to worship in a stone labyrinth carved out under their
castle in France.'

Penny looked at me, until she realized there wasn't going
to be any more. 'But what does that have to do with world
economics?'

'Good question,' I said. 'I suppose it's always possible that a
long time ago the original Group made a deal with this Baphomet.
Or it could just be another piece of misdirection to make the
Group seem more powerful and mysterious than it actually is.'

Penny frowned. 'Could this Baphomet, whatever it is, still
be alive somewhere? Still connected to current members of the
Group?'

'Another good question,' I said. 'Think about it, there's a
creature connected with the Group, a creature connected with
the House, and Jennifer was apparently killed by some unseen

creature. All of which leads me to suppose that there's a creature involved in this case. Unless, of course, that's what someone wants me to think.'

'You don't trust anybody, do you?' said Penny admiringly.

'All part of the job,' I said. 'In our line of work, paranoia isn't just a way of life. It's a survival skill.'

'OK,' said Penny. 'Let's start with what we can be sure of. The Baphomet Group doesn't actually run the world?'

'Almost certainly not,' I said. 'The world is simply too big and too complicated. There are various groups who like to say they do, but a lot of that is just whistling in the dark to make themselves feel better. The members of the Baphomet Group are certainly rich enough to influence things, but that's as far as it goes.'

'Who are the principals?' said Penny. 'Would I recognize any of them?'

'I doubt it,' I said. 'They won't be anyone you'd know from the financial pages or the celebrity magazines. They don't represent governments, or even countries. They'll be members of old financial families; long-established money. People with power, but no responsibilities and no accountability. That's what makes the Group so dangerous. There's no one to tell them they can't do things.'

'How does that make them different from the Bilderburg Group?' said Penny.

'Because the world doesn't know the Baphomet Group exists,' I said patiently. 'Apart from some of the more feral conspiracy sites – who tend to view the Group through their own particular beliefs and interests. Alien Infiltration, New World Order, the Great Satanic Conspiracy . . . The usual. I wouldn't be at all surprised to find a few of the more dedicated fringe journalists trying to sneak into Coronach House. Looking for evidence of the truth; to prove they're right and everyone else is wrong.'

'Would you kill them?' said Penny. 'For being in the wrong place at the wrong time?'

'Of course not!' I said. 'Why would I want to do that?'

'You talked about killing whoever's replaced the dead principal.'

'Only to see what my orders were,' I said. 'I'm not going to throw some poor journalist in the loch just because he's got a bee in his bonnet.'

Penny smiled dazzlingly. 'So, off we go to Coronach House. Where we will solve the mystery, catch the killer, keep the Baphomet Group safe, and look good doing it!'

'Damn right!' I said.

We finished our drinks, and got ready to leave. Penny looked at me thoughtfully.

'Which conspiracy theories do you believe, Ishmael? Which ones do you know to be true?'

'I believe in all of them,' I said. 'It saves time . . .'

'Even when they contradict each other?'

'Especially then. Because the only truth behind all the stories is that the world really is very complicated.'

TWO
House Rules

Out in the Purple Heather's car park, a great gleaming silver-grey beast was waiting for us. The Rolls-Royce Phantom stood alone, a discreet distance from all the other cars, so it could look down its long bonnet and intimidate them. Penny made happy 'Oooh!' and 'Aaah!' noises while I walked around the car, studying it suspiciously from every angle. Beware Colonels bearing gifts. I hit the remote, opened the front door, and then crawled all over the interior, checking every inch with a practised eye. Penny watched me for a while, then cleared her throat in a meaningful sort of way.

'Ishmael, what are you doing?'

'Looking for hidden cameras and microphones,' I said.

'You don't even trust the people you work for?'

'Today's friend can be tomorrow's enemy,' I said, feeling around inside the glove compartment, because it looked bigger than it had any right to be. 'Better safe, than ending up in a Black Heir petting zoo. Or stuffed and mounted in some collector's private museum.'

'People actually do that?' said Penny.

I thought it kinder not to answer that one. 'I haven't survived this long by relying on the kindness of strange organizations.'

'Want me to look underneath the car?' said Penny.

'Too obvious,' I said.

I finally backed out of the Phantom and stood beside Penny, frowning thoughtfully. I hadn't found anything, and short of tearing the whole car to pieces I probably wasn't going to. But knowing in advance that I would search any car I was given helped keep the Colonel honest.

I opened the back door and took out the suitcase the Colonel had left for me. Inside was a smart black suit, white shirt and black tie, expensive black shoes, and a pair of very dark sunglasses.

The Colonel's idea of making a good first impression. I climbed into the back seat to get changed, while Penny stood guard to make sure I wouldn't be interrupted. Not that I gave a damn, but Penny can be surprisingly bashful over some of the more public forms of impropriety. There wasn't a lot of room to manoeuvre in the back seat, but I managed.

I finally got back out of the car, slipped on the sunglasses, and struck a pose. Penny clapped her hands delightedly.

'Oh, Ishmael, you're a Man In Black!'

She had a point. I looked just like one of those mysterious people who turn up to interview UFO contactees and lecture them on not talking to the media. Like that has ever worked. I wasn't sure Men In Black existed outside popular culture; but it was a really good look. I had to smile.

'Smell the irony . . .'

'You don't suppose the Colonel actually knows about you?' said Penny. 'And this is his idea of a joke?'

'No,' I said. 'No one knows, apart from you. I've gone to great pains to be sure of that.'

'Is there another suit in the car?' Penny said hopefully. 'I'd make a great Woman In Black . . .'

'Sorry,' I said. 'This is all the suitcase contained. Still, your black dress and hat should complement my look nicely.'

At which point the gusting wind snatched the hat right off Penny's head and sent it bowling across the car park. While Penny went racing off in hot pursuit, I retrieved my backpack and her suitcase from the hired car and transferred them to the Phantom. I travel light, so I can travel fast; while Penny likes to pack for every conceivable occasion. And then expects me to carry the suitcase. She came back with the broad-brimmed hat clapped firmly on her head, with one hand up to hold it there.

'Don't laugh,' she said. 'Don't even smile.'

'The thought never crossed my mind.'

'Are we going to just leave the hire car here?'

'The Colonel can send someone to pick it up,' I said. 'Should be safe enough. It's not like anyone's going to steal it.'

And so we set off for Coronach House, following the directions programmed into the Phantom's sat nav. The officious little box dispensed its instructions in languid, disdainful tones, as though the voice had been provided by some minor member of the aristocracy forced into gainful employment through savage death duties, intent on taking it out on someone. He always sounded just a moment away from criticizing my driving, my clothes and my attitude, but I'd never have found the House without him. I'd memorized all the relevant locations, but Coronach House wasn't on any map. It was a private place, and determined to stay that way.

The Phantom carried us swiftly along the narrow winding roads, the powerful engine barely murmuring. The car handled like a dream, and the ride was delightfully smooth. It only lacked front-mounted machine-guns and an ejector seat to make it the perfect secret agent's car. Penny practised waving at the passing countryside, like the Queen on a royal progress.

It didn't take long to get to Coronach House, for which I was quietly grateful. The light was going out of the day, the shadows were lengthening, and the first mists of the evening were gathering. They thickened and thinned as the road changed direction, so that the surrounding views came and went in a series of brief glimpses. Details became indistinct and directions uncertain, as though we were driving through a dream. I tried turning on the headlights, but the light just bounced back off the mists. My hands tightened on the steering wheel. I really don't like it when I can't be sure of what's going on around me. Dark shapes loomed up in the mists at the sides of the road, and then disappeared again. Penny sat up straight and stuck her face against the side window.

'What were those?' she demanded. 'Anything I should be worried about?'

'Not as long as they stay off the road,' I said. 'They were deer. We are in Scotland, remember?'

Penny glared suspiciously into the shifting mists. 'How can you be sure?'

'Because I recognized their scent.'

She turned her attention away from the window to give me a hard look. 'From inside a travelling car? I know you like to boast your senses are superior to anything we mere mortals might have been blessed with, but that is downright eerie.

Particularly since you still can't tell one of my perfumes from another.'

'Sorry,' I said. 'It's all just musk to me.'

Penny gave me a considering look, from under heavy eyelids. 'And does musk have the same effect on you as it does on mere mortals?'

I grinned at her. 'What do you think?'

'Drive on,' she said, satisfied. 'And keep your mind on the road. The last thing I want to see is the startled look on a deer's face as it bounces off our bonnet.'

Sometime later the mists began to lift, and the last of the sunlight bathed the road ahead in a golden glow. We left the woods behind and headed straight for the loch. The satnav instructed me to take a sudden sharp turning to the left that wasn't supposed to be there, and we shot past a large sign saying 'WARNING! TRESPASSERS WILL BE . . .'

'Will be?' said Penny. 'Will be what?'

'I think we're supposed to fill in the gap ourselves,' I said. 'With something suitably ominous and cautionary.'

'They don't know us,' Penny said happily. 'They're the ones who should be worried.'

We were driving down a long straight road now, heading into a characterless expanse of open ground with Loch Ness some distance beyond. At the very end of the road I could just make out a large old-fashioned house standing alone, perhaps just a little too close to the banks of the loch. The mists were forming again, adding a grey haze to the dimming sunlight.

Well short of the house the road was suddenly blocked by a heavy steel-barred gate. I brought the Phantom to a halt. There was no sign to confirm where we were, and the satnav had gone ominously quiet. I peered past the gate at what had to be Coronach House. A large three-storied structure of old grey stone, solid and stern, with an almost brutal sense of style. Built in the old days, when clan feuds and bands of marauding reavers were common dangers and a family dwelling had to be a man's castle as well as his home. Light blazed fiercely from all the windows, but that was the only sign of life. Coronach House looked like some last outpost of civilization, set in place ages ago to stand guard against a wild and threatening region.

I sounded the car's horn, to let everyone know two important guests had arrived. Somehow, what should have been an imperative blast sounded small and lost in the heavy quiet of the falling evening. Two dark figures came striding up the road to glare at us through the gate, both of them heavily armed and wearing flak jackets. They had the look of men just waiting for an excuse to use their automatic weapons, and kept their guns trained on the car as the gate slowly opened. Penny and I both decided we felt like sitting very still. One of the armed men came round to my side and frowned balefully at me as I lowered the window.

'You'd better have a really good reason for being here, sir,' he said. In the kind of voice that told me he was hoping I hadn't.

'Will this do?' I said, presenting him with the ID card the Colonel had given me. The guard reluctantly lowered his gun, and all but snatched the card out of my hand. He studied it for a long moment, his lips moving as he checked the number against the one he'd been made to memorize. He glared at the card and then at me, clearly hoping to find something he could argue about to make up for all the standing around in the cold with nothing to intimidate but the local wildlife. He returned my card but made a point of phoning ahead to the House, to make sure we were expected, while the other guard kept his gun trained unwaveringly on the car. The first guard then winced as someone on the other end shouted at him, and he put his phone away and quickly stepped back from the gate. The other guard lowered his gun and moved to the other side of the gate, and I smiled serenely at both of them as I sailed on by. The gate shut itself the moment the Phantom was through.

Important-looking limousines had been lined up in neat rows a polite distance away from Coronach House, so I made a point of bringing the Phantom to a smooth halt right outside the front door. The small crowd of impeccably uniformed chauffeurs standing by their cars watched silently as Penny and I got out of the Phantom. I ignored the chauffeurs and the House, and headed straight for the bank of Loch Ness. Penny scrambled quickly after me, one hand clapped to her big hat, just in case. The ground was bare earth and hardscrabble rock, with just the odd tuft of grass. I got as close to the edge as possible and looked out over the loch. Penny snuggled in beside me and we stood quietly together, taking in the view. We'd come a long way to be here.

Up close, the loch was huge and flat, and quietly enigmatic. It stretched away in both directions, between two lowering ranges of bare stone and scrub-covered hillside. The waters were disturbingly dark and opaque under an iron-grey sky, with not a trace of movement anywhere. No tourists on sightseeing trips, no scientific expeditions, and not even a solitary fisherman out trying his luck. No sign of any wildlife, or even a solitary bird in the darkening sky. Loch Ness had the cold, settled look of something that had been around for centuries which had every intention of still being there for centuries to come. As far as Loch Ness was concerned, people were irrelevant. The long stretch of dark waters seemed big enough and dark enough to hide any number of secrets.

Penny shuddered briefly, as much from the atmosphere as the chill evening air, and I didn't blame her. You can't work in the spying game for as long as I have without knowing when something is looking back at you. I left Penny standing on the bank to keep an eye on the loch, just in case it decided to spring a surprise or two, while I retrieved my backpack and her suitcase from the Phantom. And then I locked the car, because you can't be too careful. The uniformed chauffeurs were still watching silently. I turned my back on them with quiet dignity and went to stand before the front door, looking the House over. Penny came back to join me, and slipped a companionable arm through mine.

'You'd better carry the baggage,' I said. 'It wouldn't look right for a Man In Black, and an Organization agent at that, to act as a porter.'

'In your dreams, space boy!' said Penny. 'I'm sure they'll send someone out to take care of it if we glare at them hard enough.'

The front door opened suddenly. I quickly drew myself up to my full height, while Penny stepped a little away from me, the better to strike a glamorous pose; both of us ready for whatever the House might throw at us. Glowering from the doorway was a tall, heavily built middle-aged woman in a smart twinset and pearls. She looked less like a welcoming committee and more like a first line of defence. I gave her my best winning smile, while Penny positively dazzled. An effect somewhat ruined when the wind tried to take her hat again and she had to grab on to it with both hands. The woman in the doorway looked us over with a cold, unwavering stare. As though to make it exceedingly clear we weren't fooling her one bit. Her face was set in hard, uncompromising lines, under a heavy mane of dark hair thickly streaked with grey. She didn't move an inch, so after a moment I stepped forward, with Penny sticking close beside me. Though whether to back me up or so she could hide behind me, I wasn't entirely sure. The woman still didn't say anything, just glared at me challengingly, demanding I prove my right to be there wasting her time. My first instinct was to punch her out and walk into the House over her unconscious body, just to set the proper tone, but the Colonel had used the words 'tact' and 'diplomacy', so . . .

'Ishmael Jones and Penny Belcourt,' I said. 'We're expected.'

'You're late,' said the woman. Her voice had the sound of a steel trap closing. I just knew we weren't going to get on.

'Would you care to make a small wager as to whether or not I give a damn?' I said pleasantly. 'We're here now. Be grateful. Either all your troubles are over, or they're just beginning.'

'Ishmael . . .' Penny murmured.

'She started it,' I said.

Penny turned her dazzling smile on the woman again and turned up the wattage. 'What a lovely old house you have here.'

'It's not my house,' said the woman. 'I am the Major Domo.' She paused a moment, to see if I was going to be dumb enough to question a woman holding such a title; and when I didn't, she pressed on. 'I am Helen McGregor. I run the staff here and ensure that everything is as it should be.' She unbent a little, under the full force of Penny's unwavering smile. 'Coronach House is centuries old, but it has every modern facility. You will find it very comfortable here, and extremely secure.'

'I don't think the last operative we sent you would agree,' I said. 'I want to know everything about what happened to Jennifer Rifkin.'

'Of course,' said the Major Domo. 'House security is my responsibility.'

'Not any more,' I said. 'Now it's mine. Doesn't that give you a nice snug, safe feeling? Aren't you going to invite us in? Answer the second question first.'

The Major Domo looked down her nose at our paltry luggage. 'You'll have to carry that. All of my staff are busy, looking after the principals of the Baphomet Group.'

She turned her back on us and went back inside. Penny glared at me, and grabbed her suitcase. Because she knew I might need both hands free to protect us.

'You had to annoy her . . .'

'Start as you mean to go on,' I said, shouldering my backpack. 'I'm getting a strong feeling we should watch our backs at all times once we're in there.'

'You think we're in danger?'

'Always.'

She grinned suddenly. 'Danger is our business. Right, space boy?'

'Right on, spy girl.'

'Wipe your feet!' snarled the Major Domo, the moment we entered Coronach House. I ignored her, just on general principles, and strode on into the great open hall. Penny let go of her hat with a quiet sigh of relief and looked admiringly around, as the Major Domo slammed the front door with rather more force than was necessary. The reception area had been designed to be impressively large, with richly polished wood-panelled walls on all sides and a truly imposing parquet floor. Heavy antique furniture stood around, filling up space in a purposeful sort of way, like watchful guard dogs. Traditional hunting prints covered the walls, showing all kinds of local wildlife being pursued and torn apart by packs of hounds. The whole scene was so very traditionally Scottish it wouldn't have looked out of place on a tin of shortbread. Everything was very clean, every surface gleaming, as though a small army had passed through recently, polishing as it went. Penny dumped her suitcase on the floor beside me, with a meaningfully loud grunt. I pretended not to notice.

'I want it understood from the outset that I do not represent any of the principals,' the Major Domo said sternly. 'I come with the House and see to the needs of anyone it is rented out to. The Baphomet Group is currently in residence, and it is my responsibility to liaise between the House staff and those the principals have brought with them. Especially when, for any number of reasons, certain people have decided they're not talking to certain other people. The trouble with the principals is that they are often the inheritors of long-standing inter-family feuds. Still arguing over who said what to who, or which family cheated which over some long-forgotten business manoeuvre. I sometimes think the current incumbents inherited financial acumen and accumulated bitterness along with their mother's milk. Hard though it is to accept that these people could ever have been innocents. Their security guards squabble constantly, and sometimes violently, reflecting their principals' varying moods. The House security and staff answer only to me. They do not squabble. Because I do not permit such behaviour.'

'But do they perhaps sometimes squabble with the principals' security people?' said Penny, as always going straight to the heart of the matter.

The Major Domo inclined her head slightly, accepting the hit. 'There have been . . . incidents. Perhaps you can persuade them to act like grown-ups.'

'Love to,' I said.

She looked me over dubiously. 'You'll have a hard time getting any of the principals' people to listen to you. The principals are very important people, and the Organization is a long way away.'

'Not while I'm here, it isn't,' I said. 'Still, not to worry. I'm sure I'll find a way to win them over.'

'Oh, this is going to get unpleasant . . .' murmured Penny.

I fixed the Major Domo with a thoughtful look. 'What do you know about the Organization?'

She smiled, briefly. 'You'd be surprised.'

'I want to see Jennifer Rifkin's body,' I said. 'I've only been provided with limited information as to how she died. You do still have the body here?'

'Of course,' said the Major Domo. 'I knew you'd want to examine it. And anyway, we can't allow the local authorities in until the Group has finished its business.'

'When was she killed, exactly?' asked Penny.

'Late last evening,' said the Major Domo. Her face and voice were perfectly calm. She might have been discussing dinner arrangements. 'We have the body preserved in a temporary morgue. Follow me. You can leave your luggage here. No one will touch it.'

'I would advise against that,' I said. 'I haven't disarmed the booby traps yet.'

Penny nodded solemnly. The Major Domo's eyes flickered to the suitcase, and then she set off towards the rear of the House without looking back to see if we were following. I sauntered after her, as though I'd been meaning to go that way all along. Penny trotted along beside me, beaming happily at everything. Our footsteps sounded loud and carrying, as though warning we were coming.

A quick trip through some deserted back corridors brought us to a large kitchen, full of noise and bustle and escaping steam as the staff prepared the evening meal. Bare stone walls ran with perspiration, much like the staff, and the old-fashioned gas cookers were weighed down with all kinds of pots and pans. Someone was chopping up greens with grim determination, someone else was stirring sauce as though their life depended on it, and a third was doing something very unfortunate to a dead chicken. Two cooks in immaculate whites, one large and one small (it's always that way, I think it's some kind of rule), bullied their staff with harsh words and much waving of the hands, even though the staff seemed to be doing all the actual work. One of the cooks spun round to confront us, drawing himself up to his full height.

'No! You must not come in here! Not while we are working! How are we to work our culinary miracles without the correct atmosphere in which to collect our thoughts? The principals assured us we would be allowed our privacy!'

'You don't work for the principals,' said the Major Domo, entirely unmoved by such blatant theatrics. 'You work for me.'

'We are artists!' snapped the second cook, hovering agitatedly beside the first. 'You cannot expect us to provide our best work under constant interruptions!'

'Yes I can,' said the Major Domo. 'I pay your wages.'

The two cooks looked at each other, silently agreed that they weren't going to get anywhere with the Major Domo, and turned as one to glare at me. I glared right back at them, and they both decided their art required them to be very busy somewhere else. The kitchen staff didn't look up from what they were doing, but I got a definite sense they were enjoying the situation. The Major Domo strode on through the kitchen, ignoring one and all, and Penny and I drifted after her. An imposingly large steel door had been set flush into the rear wall, very firmly closed, with a heavy steel padlock to make sure it stayed that way. I could tell from recent tool marks that the padlock had only been added recently. The Major Domo produced a large key ring from about her person, selected one of the keys, unlocked the padlock, and pulled open the heavy door. She had to use both hands to do it. A blast of refrigerated air rushed out, shockingly cold in the overheated atmosphere. All the kitchen staff paused for a moment to savour the blessed relief. The Major Domo strode through the open door, not even gesturing for us to follow.

I looked at Penny. 'What say we slam the door on her and close the padlock? Just to encourage a change in attitude.'

'She'd probably gnaw her way out,' said Penny. 'I think she's in a bad mood about something.'

'I wonder what,' I said.

Beyond the open door lay a surprisingly large walk-in freezer. All kinds of food had been stacked up in tottering rows. Everything from canned preserves and boxes of cereal to plastic-wrapped haunches of meat; everything from the usual suspects to the most up-to-date delicacies. Some of it piled right up to the ceiling. There was only just room for me to ease my way through the piled-up boxes. Penny shuddered at the cold. I didn't. The Major Domo waited impatiently, apparently unaffected by her surroundings.

Jennifer Rifkin's body had been laid out on a bare table at the back. Food had been left stacked disrespectfully close, but to be fair there wasn't a lot of space. Penny and I ended up standing shoulder to shoulder with the Major Domo. Our breath mingled as it steamed on the bitter air. Penny hugged herself tightly. I eased past the Major Domo, to stand over the body. The dead woman stared impassively up at the ceiling, her face and open eyes covered with a layer of frost. A short sturdy woman in her late forties, she was wearing the same black suit as me, but no sunglasses. I took mine off and put them away. Jennifer's round face was pale and expressionless, as though she had no opinion as to who might have attacked her, or why. I thought about closing the staring eyes, then thought better of it. In this low temperature there was a real chance the eyelids might break off.

'I'm here, Jennifer,' I said. 'Sorry it took so long.'

'So you did know her,' said Penny.

'She investigated me, back when I was at Black Heir,' I said. 'She had no proof, no evidence, but she just knew there was something different about me. So we did the dance of question and answer, accusation and evasion, until we couldn't remember who was chasing who. It was a very close relationship.'

There was a dull heavy thud behind us. We looked quickly round, to find the Major Domo had returned to the freezer door and pulled it shut. Penny made an involuntary sound. The Major Domo looked at her condescendingly, as she came back to join us.

'I thought we could use some privacy. There is nothing to be concerned about, Miss Belcourt. The door can always be opened from the inside. It is a basic safety feature.'

'Is that why you put a padlock on the outside?' said Penny, quickly recovering her composure. 'Because you were concerned the corpse might get up and walk out?'

The Major Domo looked briefly shocked. The idea clearly hadn't occurred to her before; and now it had, she didn't like it one bit. She glanced uneasily at Jennifer, and then made a point of fixing her attention on me.

'The Organization gave orders that the body was to be kept secure,' she said. 'No one has even looked at it since my people put it here. I have the only key to the padlock.'

'Good to know,' I said.

I gave all my attention to the body on the table. No obvious wounds, and no obvious cause of death. No discoloration to the lips or the whites of the eyes to indicate poison. And no defence wounds to the hands to suggest she'd tried to protect herself. Her clothes looked neat and tidy, and undisturbed.

'She was a Woman In Black,' Penny said quietly. 'Good for her.'

I glanced at the Major Domo. 'Who found the body? And under what circumstances?'

'That evening there had been a question over which security people had precedence,' the Major Domo said steadily. 'Nothing new, the principals' staff are always butting heads. I was getting nowhere sorting it out, so I sent one of the maids up to Miss Rifkin's room to ask her to come down and shout at them. Sometimes the principal's people would stand down to her when they wouldn't to me. It was a way for them to save face; so they could explain to their principal that it wasn't their fault, they were just helpless in the face of Organization authority.

'Miss Rifkin was supposed to be resting in her room. No one had seen her for some time. When the maid got there the door was standing open; and when she looked inside, she saw the room had been wrecked. Apparently by some creature. You can see for yourself, when you're done here. We've kept the room locked and guarded, waiting for someone else from the Organization to arrive and take over the investigation.

'The maid didn't go in, just raised the alarm and waited till I got there. Every bit of furniture in the room had been over-turned or smashed. Miss Rifkin was lying still on the bed, apparently untouched in the midst of so much destruction. I examined her briefly, just enough to confirm she was dead. Then left the room and sealed it, and placed an emergency call to your people. The principals didn't like it, but even they didn't want to antagonize the Organization. I had the body brought down here and began a basic investigation. All of the principals' security people were quite firm: none of them had seen or heard anything while the room was being smashed and Miss Rifkin was being killed. I have no explanation as to how that could have been possible. You talk to them, perhaps they'll admit things to you that they wouldn't to me.'

'You don't want us here,' I said, meeting her gaze squarely. 'Do you?'

She didn't seem surprised or offended by my bluntness. 'There are enough conflicting interests in this house as it is. The last thing I need is more complications. I was hoping you would remove the body and leave any further investigations until the Group's business is over. But you're not going to do that, are you?'

'Jennifer was killed while the Group was here,' I said. 'That makes all of them potential suspects.'

'You can't be thinking of accusing any of the principals!' said the Major Domo. 'They're all . . .'

'Very important people,' I said. 'I know. Three guesses as to whether I give a damn, and you get the first two for free.'

'You can't upset the principals!'

'Oh, I think you'll find he can,' said Penny. 'He's really very good at it.'

The Major Domo shook her head. 'How long before you'll be finished?'

'It'll take as long as it takes,' I said. 'Until I find the murderer.'

'I'm not convinced there is one,' said the Major Domo. 'The state of the room suggested an attack by some kind of wild animal.'

'Then why doesn't Jennifer have a mark on her?' said Penny. 'Or are you saying she was frightened to death?'

'No,' said the Major Domo. 'I'm not saying that.'

'Has anyone with medical training had a look at the body?' I said. 'Do we know the exact cause of death?'

'There are no doctors here,' said the Major Domo. 'You'll understand I couldn't do anything that would attract the attention of the local authorities; the principals were very firm on that. Once it was down here, I examined the body as best I could. And I did find something unusual. Something . . . disturbing.'

'No teeth or claw marks, but you still favour an animal attack?' I said. 'All right, I'll bite. What did you find?'

'Two puncture wounds,' said the Major Domo. 'On the back of the neck, at the base of the skull.'

Penny and I looked at each other. Neither of us said the word 'vampire', but we were both thinking it very loudly. I took hold of Jennifer's shoulders and tried to sit her up, but she wouldn't bend at the middle. Rigor mortis had set in. I placed one hand on her thigh, took a firmer hold, and tried again. Loud cracking sounds filled the air as I sat Jennifer up in a series of jerks. A low moaning issued from her unmoving lips. Penny looked at me sharply.

'Just gas that's built up in the body,' I said. 'Nothing to worry about.'

'I'm not worried,' Penny said loudly.

The Major Domo said nothing. I bent Jennifer forward some more, and looked closely at the back of her neck.

No sign of the savage teeth marks I'd expected, nothing to indicate a vampire's attack. Instead there were two deep puncture wounds with a little dried blood crusted around the entrance holes, each wound big enough to stick a finger in. I gestured for Penny to move forward and take a look. She leaned in close while I held the body still, and then looked at me and shook her head briefly. Confirming what I already knew: this wasn't a vampire. I looked at the Major Domo.

'Any sign of heavy blood loss anywhere around the body?'

'No,' said the Major Domo. 'Just a little blood on her pillow. But . . . look for yourself.'

She produced a penlight from her pocket and carefully shone it into one of the wounds. I leaned in close, and saw something I really wasn't expecting.

'OK . . .' I said. 'This is weird. Her head is empty.'

'What?' said Penny. 'What do you mean by "empty"?' She tried to crowd in beside me, but I was still peering down the entrance wound.

'I mean, her brain is missing,' I said. 'All of it. As though it's been removed . . . sucked out through these holes.'

'You can see that?' said the Major Domo. 'I suspected, but . . .'

'I eat a lot of carrots,' I said.

'The ancient Egyptians used to remove the brain when they made a mummy,' said Penny, in a blatant attempt to distract the Major Domo. 'They hooked it out through the nose.'

'That was after death,' I said. 'I'm pretty sure this was done while Jennifer was still alive. This is what killed her.'

'What on earth could do that?' said the Major Domo.

She looked at me for an answer. So did Penny. And then both of them looked distinctly unsettled, as they realized I was considering the possibilities.

'Have you ever encountered something that could do this?' Penny said carefully. 'Have you seen wounds like this before?'

'No,' I said. 'But I have heard things. There is a Mexican legend of something called a Brainiac. A creature with a long fleshy proboscis that it sticks up people's noses to suck out their brains.'

'You made that up!' said Penny. She paused. 'You're not making that up? Really? Oh, ick . . .'

'We are not in Mexico,' said the Major Domo.

'I had noticed,' I said.

I stuck my index finger into one of the holes, just to see if it would fit. And then I froze, as I realized I couldn't pull it back out again. It was stuck. I tugged at it surreptitiously, but the finger wouldn't budge. I smiled meaninglessly at Penny and the Major Domo, put one hand on the back of Jennifer's head, and pulled hard. And my finger jumped out with a soft sucking sound. Penny shook her head slowly, and the Major Domo looked at me as though I'd just confirmed her worst suspicions. I wiped my hand on the back of my trousers. Not every idea I have is a winner.

'Is there anything else you want to know about the state of the body?' the Major Domo asked coldly.

'Not for the moment,' I said.

I tried to lay Jennifer down flat again, but she'd stuck in the upright position. I put one hand on her thigh and the other on her throat, and pushed hard. There was the sound of something important breaking inside her, and she lay down again. Penny gave me a long-suffering look. The Major Domo looked like she wanted to say a great many things, but didn't. I took a moment to get my breath back. Wrestling with corpses is hard work.

'What happened to Jennifer's notes?' I said. 'She might have been killed because of something she discovered, or because the killer thought she knew something.'

'You still think a person could have done this?' said the Major Domo.

'I'm not ruling out anything at this stage,' I said. 'Did you find her notes?'

'We have been unable to find Miss Rifkin's laptop,' said the Major Domo. 'It's always possible it was destroyed along with her room's furnishings and fittings.'

Or the room was wrecked to disguise the fact that the laptop had been taken, I thought, but didn't say.

'I need to see Jennifer's room,' I said to the Major Domo.

She nodded stiffly, strode over to the freezer door, pulled it open with both hands, and stepped quickly out into the kitchen. She was breathing a little more deeply, probably to settle her nerves, but on the whole I thought she'd coped very well under the circumstances. Most people get really spooked around bodies. Of course, her lack of reaction could be significant in itself. Some might even say suspicious. Something to think about, later.

Penny moved in close beside me, and lowered her voice. 'I have heard stories about aliens who take bits of people. Like in cattle mutilations.'

'Yes,' I said. 'I've heard those stories too.'

'Well? Is there any truth to them?'

'Not as far as I know,' I said. 'And anyway, what would aliens have to do with the Baphomet Group? No . . . this was a very loud kind of murder. Designed to draw attention to itself and distract us from something else.'

'Like what?' said Penny.

'I don't know,' I said. 'I'm distracted.'

Penny hugged herself tightly and shuddered. 'Can we please get the hell out of this icebox? I'm freezing my tits off. And I keep expecting Madame Major Domo to slam the door shut and padlock us in here.'

I had to smile. 'She does seem the type, doesn't she? All right, let's go.' I nodded to Jennifer Rifkin, lying on her table surrounded by piled-up provisions, with her brain stolen. Not much grace in death, and even less dignity. 'Rest easy, Jennifer. I will find out who did this to you.'

'Of course you will,' said Penny.

We walked out of the freezer, carefully not hurrying. The hot and heavy air of the kitchen was a relief after the bitter cold. The Major Domo went to slam the door shut, but Penny stopped her.

'Could we leave the light on? I don't like to think of her lying there alone in the dark.'

'She's dead, Penny,' I said. 'She doesn't care.'

Penny shot me one of her looks that meant I'd missed some human thing. The Major Domo cleared her throat.

'I'm sorry, Miss Belcourt. The light goes on and off automatically, as the door opens and closes. There's nothing I can do.'

She forced the heavy door shut, padlocked it, tugged at the lock a few times just to be sure, and then turned away. The two cooks and the kitchen staff watched all this carefully, but were quick to concentrate on their work the moment the Major Domo glared in their direction.

'I need to talk to the principals,' I said.

'But Miss Rifkin's room . . .'

'Can wait,' I said.

'The principals are in a meeting,' said the Major Domo, 'and not to be disturbed.'

'Tough,' I said. 'I want to see them. And disturb them, if necessary.'

The Major Domo looked like she wanted to argue. But didn't.

'Who are the principals, anyway?' said Penny.

The Major Domo gave me a reproachful look as she led the way out of the kitchen, and didn't start talking until we were well clear of the kitchen staff. 'Twelve in total, and all of them very important people. Don't expect them to tell you their real names. As long as they're here they'll only answer to their traditional cover identities – January to December.' She smiled, briefly. 'And good luck getting one word out of them that they don't want to part with.'

'Not to worry,' I said. 'I can be very persuasive.'

'It's true, he can,' said Penny. 'Really. Like you wouldn't believe.'

The Major Domo led us back through the House, resisting all attempts by Penny to open a conversation, until we finally ended up before a closed door guarded by a dozen armed men.

Hard-eyed types, with neat suits whose jackets had been
expertly tailored to allow extra room for shoulder holsters.
They all looked like they could take care of themselves, and
whoever paid their wages. The kind of men who were ready
to take a bullet, but would much rather someone else did it
first. Twelve guards, one for each of the principals. They were
all very professional: keeping their distance from each other
while still carefully maintaining clear lines of sight, so no one
could approach the principals without being seen and
challenged.

They nodded to the Major Domo as she approached, while
keeping their attention fixed firmly on me. I nodded briefly to
the guards, and headed for the closed door. They immediately
closed ranks, placing themselves bodily between me and the
door. Several of them drew their guns. The Major Domo fell
back a few steps, looking at me in a 'Told you so!' sort of way.
I considered the guards thoughtfully, and Penny looked at me
in a resigned sort of way.

'Try not to make too much of a mess, darling,' she said.

'Hello there!' I said to the guards. 'What nice guns you have,
and excellent reaction times. I'm impressed. Unfortunately for
you, I am Ishmael Jones and this is Penny Belcourt. We represent the Organization. So get out of the way like good little
soldier boys, before things get unfortunate.'

'Piss off and die!' said the nearest guard.

'Oh dear . . .' said Penny.

I stepped smartly forward and slapped the gun right out of
the guard's hand. And while he was standing there with his
mouth hanging open, wondering what the hell had just happened,
I kneed him briskly in the groin and elbowed him on the back
of his neck as he bent over. Before the other guards could react
I was in and among them, grabbing guns out of their hands and
throwing them away. Bouncing a few off the nearest wall, when
necessary. A few managed to point their guns at me, but none
of them got off a single shot.

It was all over in a matter of moments. I stepped back and
glanced around to make sure I hadn't missed anyone, while
Penny applauded loudly. The guards stared at me with shocked
eyes; bewildered at how easily I'd just disarmed them. The

guard on the floor was still curled around his pain, crying his eyes out. I looked down at him dispassionately.

'Shouldn't have been rude to me.' I smiled around at the other guards. 'You could of course try to defend the door with your bare hands. After all, there are eleven of you and only one of me. I suppose it is theoretically possible that one of you might get a lucky punch in . . . before I make a hole in the wall with him.'

The guards looked at each other, and then looked at the Major Domo.

'Don't look at me,' she said. 'He told you he was Organization.'

The guards moved away from the door. There was a certain amount of sulkiness on the air, along with a general sense of 'We're not being paid enough to deal with this shit!'.

I smiled at the Major Domo. 'Keep an eye on them. Because if I come back out and find one gun pointing in my general direction, you're going to have to redecorate this whole corridor.'

Some of the guards backed away even more. And while I was busy watching them do that, the guard I'd hit lurched back up on to his feet and directed a punch at my face with all his strength. But my hand came up at the last moment to intercept his. There was a loud meaty smack as his fist slammed into my open palm and stopped dead. My hand didn't budge an inch and the guard fell back, crying out, as the impact reverberated back through his arm until it hung limply at his side, paralysed. I shook my head at him reproachfully, and he sat down hard on the floor and started crying again. They don't make guards like they used to. I couldn't resist glancing at the Major Domo. To my surprise she was smiling, just a little. Penny was grinning broadly. I nodded to her.

'Ready to go see the principals?'

She laughed happily. 'Are they ready to see us?'

'Probably not,' I said. 'But then, who is?'

I put my sunglasses back on, kicked the door open, and marched into the Baphomet Group meeting with Penny striding grandly along beside me. The dozen men and women sitting around the large round table were waiting for us, with cold composed expressions. Presumably because they'd been listening to everything that had just happened. Between them they were all ages and races; and they had the air of aristocrats at Court, or even Knights of the Round Table. But that was only in their minds. My first thought was that they all looked like accountants: respectable people in respectable outfits, and the kind of faces you forget the moment they're not right in front of you. They looked coldly back at me, ignoring Penny; not even bothering to hide their annoyance that anyone would dare interrupt their very important meeting. I started to announce myself, but the oldest man at the table raised an imperative hand to cut me off. There was enough natural authority in him to silence anyone; apart from me. But I'd been told tact and diplomacy, so . . .

The man looked to be in his late seventies, with gaunt, harsh features and carefully arranged silver-grey hair. He was almost unhealthily slim, and his hands trembled on the table top before him. He cleared his throat carefully before he spoke, not because he was nervous but because he wanted to be sure he would be understood clearly. For a moment I wondered whether dust would come out of his mouth along with his words, like a mummy disturbed in its sarcophagus.

'I am December. As the oldest member of the present Group, I have seniority. I think I can speak on behalf of all of us . . .' He paused there, and actually looked round the table to make sure he had a consensus before continuing. '. . . when I say that you are not at all welcome. There is no need to introduce yourself, Mister Jones. We were told you were on your way. Probably before you were. Your presence here may be necessary, but your impertinence is not. You will show proper respect for this venerable Group, or we will have you replaced.'

I waited politely, to be sure he'd finished, and then gave him my best 'Screw you!' smile.

'Not going to happen,' I said calmly. 'I represent the Organization. Which is older and more venerable than all of you put together. If this entire Group dropped dead right now, the world would still keep turning until you could be replaced by your successors. The Organization would see to that.'

I was pretty sure I was bluffing; but they didn't know that. Because they had no more idea about who and what the Organization was than I did.

December cleared his throat again. He seemed a little thrown that his speech hadn't had the expected effect, and completely thrown as to what to do next.

'What do you want with us, Mister Jones?'

'To start with, indulge my curiosity. Why are you named after months of the year?'

December sniffed loudly, as though explaining such obvious matters was beneath him. 'In the past, principals of the Baphomet Group adopted identities from the signs of the zodiac. But that was in a more colourful era. In these more businesslike times, we prefer something a little less dramatic. We come and go, but the identities continue. It helps prevent personalities from getting in the way of doing business.'

'We don't need to explain ourselves to you,' snapped the elderly lady sitting on December's left. A tiny, delicate creature with a dark heavily wrinkled face, a tight bun of grey hair, and a glare that could punch through walls. 'I am November. And I say this interruption is a waste of our time.'

'Not necessarily,' said December, in his slow unhurried voice. 'Consider, if these people can get to us past all our guards . . . they are exactly the kind of people we need in charge of our security.'

There was a slow nodding of heads around the table. I half expected some of them to murmur 'Hear, hear!'. December raised his dry voice and called for the security guards in the corridor to come in. They filed into the room uncertainly, shuffling their feet and avoiding looking the principals in the eye. I counted only eleven; the one I'd had to discipline was probably still having a good cry somewhere. November scowled at the guards and shook her head disgustedly.

'Where are your guns?'

The guards looked at each other sullenly, like children hauled before a teacher. One of them gestured reluctantly at me.

'He took them away . . .'

'Then I suggest you go and find them,' December said sharply. 'And try to hang on to them. No, don't leave yet. The Group hereby confirms that Mister Jones is in complete charge of all security matters pertaining to Coronach House. With full responsibility for guaranteeing our safety. And I don't want to hear

any objections or excuses. You will cooperate with him on all
necessary matters. Is that understood?'

General mutterings and noddings took place among the
guards. For hard, experienced security men, there was a lot of
pouting going on.

'I think you passed the audition, Ishmael,' Penny said
solemnly.

'But,' said November, leaning forward to give me her best
hard stare across the table, 'from this moment on, you will not
speak to any of us directly. We have important matters to
discuss and we are not to be interrupted. If you feel the need
to communicate with us, you will do so through the Major
Domo. Is that understood?'

'Oh sure,' I said. That actually suited me. I'd made the necessary first impression, in order to establish my authority, but I
really didn't want to be remembered by such important people
once this mission was over.

'You can go now,' said December.

'I know that,' I said.

I turned my back on the Baphomet Group and marched out,
Penny striding proudly along beside me. The guards scattered
to get out of our way, almost falling over themselves to give
us plenty of room. The Major Domo bowed to the principals
at the table, and followed us out. As she closed the door behind
us, I could hear what sounded like the start of a lengthy
dressing-down for the guards. Penny and I shared a grin. The
Major Domo shook her head.

'It's all right for you, I have to work with these people. The
principals can say what they like to the guards, but after this
you won't get an ounce of cooperation out of them.'

'Never thought I would,' I said briskly. 'At least now they'll
stay out of our way.'

I looked around for the twelfth guard, but there was no sign
of him. The Major Domo's mouth twitched.

'He's gone for a little lie-down, and probably a good hard
think about whether to get into some other line of business.
You were a bit hard on him.'

I shrugged. 'Can't make an omelette without traumatizing
some eggs.'

'I would be grateful if you could avoid antagonizing the principals further,' said the Major Domo. 'The sooner they finish these talks, the sooner we can be rid of them and things can get back to normal around here.'

'What about Jennifer Rifkin's death?' Penny said bluntly.

'I have no doubt that whoever or whatever is responsible for her unusual demise is connected to the Baphomet Group's presence,' the Major Domo said carefully. 'And the killer will depart when they do.'

I looked thoughtfully at the closed door. 'What kind of discussions are they having in there?'

'Very private ones,' said the Major Domo.

'But what do they talk about?' said Penny.

The Major Domo stared impassively back at us. 'I don't know the specifics. No one outside that room does. It's none of our business anyway.'

'It is if I say it is,' I said.

'From what I can gather,' the Major Domo said reluctantly, 'they're here to talk about what they've achieved, or failed to achieve, in the previous year. How much money they've made or lost, problems arising, and what they intend to do next. The business of the Baphomet Group is business and nothing more. Whatever they eventually decide will remain strictly private, among them.'

'So,' I said, 'whatever happens at Coronach House stays at Coronach House?'

'Of course,' said the Major Domo.

I looked at Penny. 'Why am I not in the least surprised?'

'Experience, probably,' said Penny. 'Spy secrets are nothing compared to business secrets. Not because they're any more important, but because they're always so very transitory. Today's financial advantage is tomorrow's old news.'

'Speaking of secrets,' said the Major Domo, 'there is another complication to our already delicate situation. I have reason to believe an investigative reporter has found a way into the House, masquerading as one of the staff.'

I grinned at Penny. 'Told you!'

'Smugness is very unattractive in a man,' said Penny.

'He cannot be allowed to learn anything of the principals'

deliberations,' the Major Domo said loudly. 'The Baphomet Group can only continue to operate under conditions of absolute secrecy.'

'Are the principals really that important?' I said. 'A few people with months for names sitting around a table?'

'If the world knew the kind of things those people talk about and the kinds of decisions they make, the financial markets would wet themselves,' said the Major Domo. 'It's one thing to suspect someone is pulling strings behind the scenes, quite another to know it for sure.'

'How could an impostor take the place of one of your staff?' said Penny. 'Don't you know your own people?'

'Normally, yes,' said the Major Domo. 'But most of my regular staff couldn't meet the necessary security clearances, so I've had to bring in a lot of new people to deal with this many guests.'

'A reporter . . .' I said. 'Am I to take it we're not talking about the regular media?'

'Of course not,' said the Major Domo. 'Our impostor will be one of those wild-eyed fanatical types. The kind who live and breathe conspiracy theories.'

'Oh,' Penny said wisely. 'One of those . . .'

'What is the current situation with the staff here?' I asked.

'There are staff who come with the House,' said the Major Domo. 'They answer to me. Then there are the staff the principals brought with them to see to their personal needs, as well as their security guards.'

'How many does that make in total?'

'Two people for each principal and twenty under me,' said the Major Domo. 'Forty-four, in all. Not counting the chauffeurs, and the armed guards patrolling the grounds.'

I frowned. I didn't like the idea of so many potential suspects running around loose, complicating things.

'So many people . . .' said Penny. 'What do they all do?'

'The whole point of being exceedingly rich,' said the Major Domo, 'is never having to do anything for yourself. My staff are concerned with preparing meals, running errands, cleaning and general maintenance. It takes a lot of hard work to run a house this size.'

'So . . . we have a murderer, or possibly a creature, to catch,' I said. 'And a reporter hiding among the staff. We don't know how or why Jennifer was killed, or what the reporter is looking for. Or if these two problems are in any way connected. Tricky . . .'

The Major Domo sniffed loudly. 'If you've quite finished upsetting people for the moment, I can recommend a number of good hotels that can put you up for as long as you're working this case. Nothing too expensive, of course.'

I shook my head firmly. 'We're not leaving the House until the case is closed. So find us a room, or we'll take yours.'

The Major Domo looked like she'd just been waiting for me to say that. She also looked like she had an answer she knew I wasn't going to like. She led us back to the reception area to collect our luggage. Penny glared at me until I picked up her suitcase as well as my backpack, and then the Major Domo led us up to the top of the house and what looked very much like the attic. She unlocked a tucked-away door with a triumphant flourish, and ushered us into a small dusty room.

'This is all that's left,' she said flatly. 'All the other rooms are occupied. This used to be part of the servants' quarters. Make yourself comfortable. You'll find fresh sheets in the linen cupboard on the next floor down. Along with the nearest toilet. When you're ready, come back down to the reception area and I'll show you Miss Rifkin's room. Or what's left of it.'

She swept out with her nose so far in the air it was a wonder she could see where she was going, leaving Penny and me to look over our room. It was small and cramped. The single bed had nothing but a sagging mattress, the sink had two dripping taps, and there was no wardrobe, no chairs, and no window. I dropped Penny's suitcase on the bare wooden floor, and the boards creaked ominously.

'What is that smell?' said Penny.

'Best not to think about it,' I said. 'This is just the Major Domo trying to put us off, in the hope we'll give up and leave. But we are made of sterner stuff.'

'Speak for yourself,' said Penny, folding her arms firmly. 'I am not staying here.'

'Never intended we should,' I said. 'I thought we might kick

out one of the security guards and take his room. They're bound
to have nice ones.'

Penny smiled. 'Sounds like a plan to me.'

'We'll leave our luggage here for the time being,' I said.
'Once we've got the investigation under way, then we can go
room hunting.'

Penny nodded. 'Where do we start? This situation is a lot
more complicated than the Colonel led us to believe.'

'If it was simple, they wouldn't need us,' I said. 'But you're
right, this whole situation is a mess. There are far too many
people in the House. Too much security can be worse than too
little, if everyone keeps getting in each other's way. And too
many staff means too many unfamiliar faces. Who might or
might not be who they claim to be? I really don't like the fact
that everyone is claiming not to have seen or heard anything
while Jennifer's room was being trashed.'

'And of course there's one more complication, which you
carefully didn't mention to the Major Domo,' said Penny. 'The
possibility that one of the principals has been murdered and
replaced.'

'She has enough to worry about as it is,' I said. 'And besides,
there's always the chance she might be involved in the
substitution.'

'Let's go back down and annoy her some more,' said Penny.
'I feel on safer ground there.'

'Let's,' I said. I dropped my backpack on the bed, and the
mattress sagged a little more. 'Keep an eye out for a nice room,
on the way down.'

When we arrived back in the reception area, the Major Domo
was busy giving orders to a small but very attentive collection
of servants in smart old-fashioned uniforms. They wanted to
look at Penny and me as we came forward to join them, but
didn't dare take their eyes off the Major Domo. She finally ran
out of instructions, and dismissed her little army with a sharp
wave of the hand. They scattered immediately, disappearing
into the surrounding corridors before she could think of something else for them to do. I coughed meaningfully, and Penny
clapped me on the back. The Major Domo turned unhurriedly

to face us. She thought we'd come to complain about our room and make demands she could legitimately turn down, putting her back in control of the situation. So I just nodded briefly to her and didn't even mention the room.

'Hello again, Major Domo. Having a nice time drilling the troops? Nothing like a spot of shouting when you feel the need to exercise your authority. Now, take us to Jennifer Rifkin's room.'

'It's not convenient just at the moment,' said the Major Domo.

'It is for me,' I said.

'I'm busy,' said the Major Domo, drawing herself up to her full height, the better to glare down her nose at me.

I smiled calmly back at her. 'It's up to you, Major Domo. Either you cooperate or I will have the Organization send a small army of agents to occupy Coronach House and question absolutely everyone about absolutely everything. How do you think the principals will react to that, particularly when I explain to them that it's all your fault?'

The Major Domo looked like she wanted to throw her hands in the air and stalk off. But she didn't. She just inclined her head stiffly, and led the way up the main stairs to the middle floor. Penny leaned in close to murmur in my ear, as we followed after her.

'The Colonel said not to request reinforcements, because there wouldn't be any.'

'I know that,' I said, just as quietly, 'but she doesn't.'

The door to Jennifer's room was closed, but there was no one on duty. In fact, the entire corridor gave every appearance of being completely deserted. I gave the Major Domo a significant look.

'You said this room was secure, and under guard.'

'It was until you got here,' said the Major Domo. 'I didn't think our creature, or killer, would dare make a move while there was an Organization agent in the House. So I reassigned the guard to other duties. We're very short-staffed!'

'Tell me the room is still locked,' I said.

'Of course it's locked.' The Major Domo produced her key ring again and unlocked the door. 'There are no electronic locks in Coronach House, just old-fashioned locks and keys. That's part of the olde-worlde charm the clients are paying for. Besides, these days electronic locks are easier to pick than the old-fashioned kind.'

She threw the door open, and waved me into Jennifer's room with a sweep of the arm that challenged me to find something she'd missed. Some people have body language that shouts at you. I stood in the doorway looking around carefully, with Penny crowding in behind to peer over my shoulder. The room had been thoroughly trashed. The wardrobe, the chest of drawers, a bedside table and two chairs had all been thrown around or reduced to pieces. The killer couldn't have done more damage with a wrecking ball. A series of claw-marks had been gouged into the walls, deep and vicious. It looked like something had run amok in the room. But appearances can be deceiving . . .

I moved slowly forward, taking my time, inspecting everything while touching nothing. Penny stuck close, studying me as much as the room. The Major Domo stayed in the doorway.

'Well?' Penny asked finally. 'First impressions? I think I'm ready to go along with the Major Domo and call this an animal attack.'

'Of course,' I said. 'That's what we're supposed to think. But this is just like the way Jennifer was killed. A very loud kind of evidence designed to distract us. Don't look at what's here, Penny. Look at what isn't. All the signs suggest a frenzied attack, but there's no blood anywhere and the two puncture wounds were the only harm to Jennifer's body. The furniture has been smashed, but the carpet isn't rucked up. There was no frenzy in this, no hurry . . . This was all done very methodically. Our killer took his time, because he wanted to create a scene. One that would tell a misleading story.'

'Mislead us about what?' said Penny.

'I'm still working on that.' I turned to look back at the Major Domo. 'How could all this have taken place and no one heard anything? It looks like a rock group stayed here.'

'No one heard anything because no one was here,' the Major Domo said steadily. 'The principals were holding a meeting, so the security people were guarding them. And the staff were all busy in other parts of the House. No one had any reason to be on this floor at that time.'

I nodded slowly. I'd just realized something else. 'The bed is intact. The rest of the furniture was destroyed, but the bed was spared. The bedclothes are still mostly in place.' I moved in for a closer look. 'Just a few drops of dried blood on the pillow. From where Jennifer's head rested after she'd been killed. Why leave the body on the bed, in the middle of all this chaos?'

'I have no idea,' said the Major Domo. 'But I'm sure you're about to grace us with a theory.'

'Because the murderer wanted Jennifer's body to be seen,' Penny said patiently. 'Like Ishmael said, he was creating a scene.'

'Still think this was an animal attack?' I said to the Major Domo.

'I don't know what to think,' she said, not giving an inch.

'There is still the legend of the Coronach creature,' said Penny.

The Major Domo shook her head firmly. 'There hasn't been a sighting of the beast in centuries. The story's been largely forgotten outside the local area. I'm surprised you've heard of it.'

'You'd be surprised at the things I know,' I said.

'He's right,' said Penny, 'you would. How is it you know the story, Major Domo? Are you local?'

'This house used to be my family home, back when I was a child,' the Major Domo said steadily. 'Before my father suffered the financial reverses that made it necessary for him to sell it. I was only a young thing when we left, but I have always thought of Coronach House as my home. When the opportunity arose for me to take up the position of Major Domo here, I jumped at the chance. I should have known better. Acting as servant in a house that used to be my family's . . .'

'Do you believe in the Coronach creature?' asked Penny.

'I never did before,' said the Major Domo. 'Until I saw this. The destruction of a creature, guided by the malice of a man.'

She turned abruptly and left the room.

I got down on my hands and knees and crawled around on the carpet. Penny watched me, saying nothing very loudly.

'I'm looking for the tread of an animal,' I said, not raising my head. 'But all I'm seeing are shoe impressions, none of them distinctive. Any number of servants could have been in and out of this room, for any number of reasons.' I got to my feet again and peered around. 'No point in looking for finger-prints, for the same reason. Although . . . perhaps that was why the setting was destroyed so thoroughly – to disguise any evidence the killer might have left behind.' I sniffed at the air. 'I'm picking up human scents, but so faint they're little more than shadows. Nothing that smells the least bit beastly.'

'So what do you think happened here?' said Penny.

'I think we need to talk to people,' I said. 'Get a sense of what's going on in the House. I think the Baphomet Group is only part of it . . .'

All the way back down the stairs I was thinking about things hiding behind other things: the creature's attack that might have been a creation, a reporter disguised as a member of the House staff, and just possibly a killer masquerading as a prin-cipal. But I still couldn't see any obvious motive for Jennifer's murder. The Major Domo was waiting for us at the foot of the main stairs.

'The killer could have left the House,' she said brusquely. 'There's no telling how much time might have passed between Miss Rifkin's death and the discovery of the body.'

'No,' I said, 'he's still in the House.'

'Why?' said the Major Domo. 'What possible reason could he have to stay here and risk being caught?'

'Because his work isn't finished yet,' said Penny.

'How well do the people in the House know each other?' I said.

The Major Domo shrugged. 'All the principals' people are known to the principals. That includes both security and staff. Because they wouldn't trust their safety to anyone they didn't know already.'

'That leaves the House staff,' I said. 'You already said one of the new faces might not be what they seem.'

'I meant one of them might be a journalist, not a killer.'

'They're both very hard to spot,' I said. 'And then . . . there are the principals.'

'What about them?' said the Major Domo.

I wasn't ready to come right out and mention the possibility of a double, so I changed the subject. 'Tell me about the House's surveillance systems.'

'That's easy,' said the Major Domo. 'There aren't any. Normally we'd have the entire House under surveillance, but the principals insisted we remove every last bit of it before they would agree to use Coronach House for their meeting. And they sent their own security people ahead of them to check it had been done. The principals really don't want to be identified. Or risk having their very private discussions recorded and broadcast to the waiting world. They put their faith in manpower to keep them safe and secure.'

'What about outside the House?' I said.

'All the cameras were removed and the motion sensors disabled,' said the Major Domo. 'I've brought in extra guards to patrol the grounds.'

'More faces you don't know,' said Penny.

'Yes,' said the Major Domo.

'Are there any hidden doors or secret passageways in Coronach House?' Penny asked hopefully.

The Major Domo shook her head firmly. 'They were all sealed off long ago.'

'How long ago?' said Penny.

'Centuries,' said the Major Domo. 'That was one of the first things the principals' security people asked about. They even went around tapping on the walls to make sure the old entrances were still sealed.'

'Is there anyone else in the House you haven't told us about?' I asked.

The Major Domo looked like she wanted to pull a face, but didn't. 'So they wouldn't be distracted from their very important decision-making, none of the principals brought their husbands or wives with them. But . . . there are a large number of professional escorts present. Brought here to serve the principals' pleasure. All of them hired, and very thoroughly checked out in advance.'

'I'm going to want to talk to these people,' I said. 'Sex workers are like psychiatrists, people will say things to them that they wouldn't say to anyone else.'

The Major Domo nodded grimly. 'They're around. You can't miss them.' And then she stopped and gave me a hard look. 'I have to ask, why is the Organization taking such an interest in the Baphomet Group? They never have before.'

'We never lost an agent because of them before,' I said.

'But what was Miss Rifkin doing here in the first place?'

'You should have asked Jennifer,' I said.

'I did,' said the Major Domo. 'She told me it was none of my business.'

I smiled. 'Guess what I'm about to say . . .'

THREE
The Things People Tell You

There comes a time in every investigation when you just have to go and see things for yourself; when other people's help, opinions and well-meaning attempts at guidance merely distract you from what needs doing. I'd seen Jennifer Rifkin and her room, and now I needed to see Coronach House. To get a feel for the place and the measure of its people, and make up my own mind as to what was really going on.

'Penny,' I said, 'It is time for us to shake the dust of other people's preoccupations from our feet and undertake a grand tour of Coronach House.'

'Of course,' the Major Domo said immediately. 'Allow me a moment to make the proper arrangements and I'll give you the full guided tour.'

'That won't be necessary,' I said, just as immediately. 'This is something we need to do for ourselves. I'm sure you understand.'

It was clear from the look on her face that she didn't, but she knew better than to argue. Instead, the Major Domo gave me a long hard look, before addressing me with the kind of resigned contempt usually reserved for overindulged children who insist on doing something really dumb.

'Try not to get lost. You'll find certain areas have been designated out of bounds to ensure the principals' privacy and security. You'll know when you've wandered into one, because all the doors will be locked and men with really big guns will open fire if you annoy them.'

'That's all right,' I said cheerfully. 'If I decide there's something I really need to see, I'll just kick the doors in. And if any of the guards shoot at me and I notice, I will make such an example of them that people just hearing about it will dry-heave with horror. Spread the word for me, there's a dear.'

Realizing that I wasn't in any way joking, the Major Domo turned her back and walked stiffly off, projecting a definite air of 'On your own head be it! I wash my hands of whatever appalling things are about to happen!'. Penny watched her go and then turned to me.

'It's not like you to be so openly physical,' she said. 'Showing off what you can do, in front of strangers.'

'I really don't like being told what I can and can't do during an investigation,' I said. 'And something about the set-up in this house is definitely bringing out the worst in me.'

'Do I really need to remind you that if the principals feel sufficiently aggrieved or threatened they won't hesitate to order their people to open fire on you?' said Penny. 'And the guards will be ready for you this time. Just looking for an excuse to overreact. You may be more than humanly fast and strong, my dearest, but you're not bulletproof. And neither am I.'

'I would never do anything to put you in danger, Penny.'

'Not deliberately,' she said steadily. 'But you don't always stop to think about what you're getting into.'

'I thought that was part of my charm.'

'Ishmael . . .'

'Have faith in me,' I said, 'to know what I'm doing.'

She smiled suddenly. 'You do make it difficult sometimes.'

I smiled back at her. 'I do, don't I?'

I extended an arm to her and she slipped her arm through it, then we set off down the corridor.

'Why is it so important we do this on our own?' she said. 'Why not let the Major Domo give us the full tour? She must know all kinds of useful things about the House and its history and legends . . . And who better to tell us everything that's been happening here recently?'

'She could tell us all sorts of things,' I said. 'But I don't trust her to tell us what we want to know. She looks the type to hold things back until she decides we need to know them. I think it's important we develop our own impression of this place without being guided or deliberately misled. So far this case has been all questions and no answers, and that's no way to run an investigation.'

*   *   *

And so we went walking through Coronach House. A marvellous old building with all the latest modern touches, but still rich with carefully cultivated olde-worlde charm. Thick carpets, sturdy heavy furniture; and lots of paintings on the walls, some of which I recognised as major works by minor masters. Stags' heads mounted on wall plaques, with great sweeping antlers and cold resentful eyes. And one complete set of medieval armour, still standing guard; brightly polished and burnished within an inch of its life. It stood barely five feet tall: men were tougher in those days, but not as well nourished. I lifted the helmet's visor and took a quick look inside, just to make sure it was empty. Because you never know. I kept a watchful eye out for hidden doors or sliding panels built into the old walls, and even tapped speculatively in a few likely spots. But I didn't find anything. Maybe the Major Domo was telling the truth, and all the old secret entrances had been sealed off. I hoped so. There's nothing like a secret passage or two to really complicate a case.

Coronach House felt . . . comfortable, lived in; more like a home than a hotel. Servants bustled back and forth in their old-fashioned formal uniforms, doing their best to look busy, while security personnel stood guard at regular intervals, trying hard to look dangerous . . . but the House still felt like somewhere you wanted to be. As though you could be sure everything and everyone in the House were there to look after and protect you. It had been built to be a fortress against the dangers of the world, to be strong and solid and safe.

But then Jennifer Rifkin had no doubt felt the same way. Right up to the point where she didn't.

It seemed like security guards were everywhere, all of them carefully polite as Penny and I approached but more than ready to give us the evil eye from a safe distance. A lot of them looked like they would have preferred to turn us back but couldn't figure out a way to do so that wouldn't result in sudden violence, extreme loss of face on their part, and quite probably tears before bedtime. I was careful to be studiously polite to everyone, and in no way threatening. And that seemed to upset the guards even more. They were convinced I was planning something really unpleasant; and I was happy for them to think that.

I escorted Penny through wide corridors and open hallways, pausing here and there to admire a particular painting or antique, or an especially pleasant view from a window. Whilst all the time aware of being watched, even when I couldn't see anyone. Coronach House was remarkably free of shadows, but I still had no doubt it was keeping things from me. That there were things I wasn't supposed to know about hidden away. I led Penny up the stairs to the middle floor and we wandered back and forth, taking our time. No one got in our way, but no one wanted to speak to us either. Up the stairs again, to the top floor, and almost immediately we came to a series of closed doors guarded by some familiar faces. The principals' guards took one look at us approaching and quickly stepped away from their doors to stand together, shoulder to shoulder. They weren't dumb enough to draw their guns: just blocked the way with their bodies. I stopped and regarded them thoughtfully. Penny stopped with me, looking anxiously at me to see what I would do.

I took my time, carefully considering the situation. The guards had chosen a defiant but determinedly passive form of obstruction, thus putting the ball firmly in my court. I could always force my way through, but not without causing a major disturbance. Which was, of course, what they were counting on. So that whatever happened, they could tell their principals it was all my fault. I kept up my watchful gaze just long enough for some of the guards to start sweating, and for Penny to stir uneasily at my side. Then I turned around and walked back the way I'd come. Penny hurried along beside me, and I could feel her relaxing, just a little.

'For a moment there I thought you were going to be stubborn,' she said, 'and really ruin their day.'

'Wasn't necessary,' I said. 'They won't always be there. If I decide I need to see what's in the principals' rooms, I can always come back later and break in. After you've arranged something big and noisy to distract them. I've always found you capable of being very distracting.'

'You say the nicest things, sweetie. When you remember.'

At the top of the stairs we had to stop and step back to let a small crowd of servants rush past. All of them wearing

old-fashioned outfits in stark black-and-white. A pretty young
thing in a maid's costume, complete with lace trimmings and
sensible heavy shoes, paused to smile at me.

'Mister Jones!' she said. 'You're looking a bit lost. Can I
help you at all?'

'You know who I am?' I said.

'Of course,' she said brightly. 'Mister Jones and Miss
Belcourt, representing the Organization. We've all been briefed
and ordered to cooperate.' She gave me a big smile, and a
knowing look. 'And I can be very cooperative . . . I'm Emily,
sir. At your service. Would you like to interrogate me?'

'I don't mind,' I said. 'To start with, why the outfits?'

She shrugged prettily. 'All part of Coronach House's famous
and very expensive olde-worlde charm. I'm just playing a part
to keep the guests happy. Half the time it feels like I'm in a
television show or a fetish magazine. But for the kind of money
the principals are paying, it doesn't bother me. I'd dress up in a
clown's outfit and juggle the breakfast if that's what they wanted.'

'Have you worked here long?' asked Penny, just to make it
clear she wasn't being left out of the conversation.

'Not long,' said Emily, still concentrating her smile and her
heavy-lidded eyes on me. 'Most of us were brought in specially,
to look after the House while the Baphomet Group are in session.
Through a London agency that specializes in providing experienced staff with proper security clearances.'

'So you've worked in high-security situations before?' I said.

'That's right,' Emily said brightly. 'It's what I do. What we
all do. But don't you worry, sir. We never talk about anything
we see or hear. Being silent and reliable is part of the job
description. Among other things . . . I'm ready to do anything
you might need, sir. Anything at all.'

'How did you know who I work for?'

'Oh, we've all heard of the Organization! In fact, your arrival
here caused quite a flutter downstairs. We never thought to meet
an actual Organization agent in the flesh. Never mind three in
a row! Not that any of us ever got to know Miss Rifkin. She
kept herself to herself, only talked to us when she had questions
about something.'

'Questions?' said Penny. 'What kind of questions?'

Emily shrugged. 'None that ever made any sense. Do you know why she was here, Mister Jones?'

'Sorry,' I said. 'Penny and I are just here to find out who killed her.'

Emily didn't look like she believed me. I gave her my best meaningless smile. For someone who was supposed to be security cleared and security conscious, she was far too ready to talk. And to ask questions about things she should have known were none of her business. But then, there's nothing like a murder to tear down the social conventions. Because knowledge of what's really going on can help keep you alive.

'Is this a good job?' Penny asked Emily.

The young maid shrugged again. I was getting the feeling that was her default response. 'The job's OK, it's the people you have to deal with . . . The principals look right through you, even when they're giving orders or making complaints. We're always having to chase up and down stairs, delivering this or picking up that. And all we get in return is moaning; about how there's not enough hot water, or enough choices on the menu, or how long the laundry takes. The usual. And of course the principals' own servants are far too busy to bother themselves with things like that.

'The Major Domo keeps the principals off our back, as much as she can. She's all right. I've worked for worse. A bit strict and distant, but she always knows where everything is and what needs to be done. I've worked for all sorts and I'll take dependable any time.'

I raised a hand, to shut down the torrent of information. 'Were you anywhere near Jennifer Rifkin's room when she was murdered?'

'Oh it's murder now, is it?' said Emily, seizing on the word. 'We were told it was some kind of animal attack.'

'And you believed that?' said Penny.

Emily didn't quite laugh in her face. She shrugged again, and threw in a sniff for good measure.

'Not our business to say anything, miss. But none of us could see how an animal could get into the House, do what it did and get out again, all without being noticed by someone. Of course, there are the old stories about the Coronach creature . . . I'd never even heard of it until I came here. I was just hoping for a glimpse of the Loch Ness monster. Still, it makes you think, doesn't it?'

'Have you ever seen this creature?' I said. 'Have any of the staff?'

'No . . .' said Emily. She frowned, concentrating so hard she actually forgot to flirt for a moment. 'Not inside the House. But apparently people have seen things out in the grounds. Down by the loch. We're not supposed to go out there, but people can't help seeing things through the windows. Just a dark shape, they say; moving in the mists.'

'Have you told anyone about this?' I said.

'I know a few people spoke to the Major Domo, but they just got told to mind their own business.' Emily's eyes brightened. 'But there's more to it than just a few sightings! We've all of us heard things, in the night. When no one is supposed to be out and about. There's a strict curfew after ten o'clock, enforced by the principals' security people. Even the House guards have to obey it. But Ruby – she's one of the downstairs maids – told me she heard footsteps outside her door. And Laura, she says something tried to turn her door handle. Trying to get in. She'd locked her door, of course.'

'Animals don't normally turn door handles,' I said.

'But the Coronach creature is supposed to be part human,' said Penny.

'So there is something to the creature?' said Emily, looking quickly back and forth between us.

'I doubt it,' I said.

Emily pouted unhappily. 'But you do think Miss Rifkin was murdered?'

'Yes,' I said.

Emily nodded, satisfied. 'No one's actually seen anything inside the House. But I'll tell you this for free, we'll all be glad when this job is over and we can get the hell out of here.'

'You haven't answered my question yet,' I said.

'What question was that, sir?'

'Where were you when . . .'

'Oh, yes! No one was on the middle floor when Miss Rifkin was killed. All the staff were working on the ground floor,

following their regular schedule. And all the security people
were busy guarding the principals, as they were holed up for
one of their special meetings. We only found out what had
happened when the Major Domo sent Laura up to Miss Rifkin's
room. Poor girl lost it big time! We could hear her screaming
all over the House. She's still not right, but they won't let her
leave . . . Anyway, we were all told to stay put while security
went haring off up the stairs to investigate. Next thing we knew
they were carrying Miss Rifkin down on a stretcher, with a
blanket over her. Do you know how she died? Only we've got
a pool going . . .'

'It's not clear yet,' I said.

Emily leaned in close and lowered her voice. There was no
one else about, but I appreciated the effort.

'Have you seen the state of her room? I had a quick look
before it was locked up. How could anything human do that
much damage?'

'Good question,' I said.

Emily waited hopefully, until she realized I wasn't going to
say any more. She straightened up and smiled brightly.

'If you're quite finished with me, can I go now, sir? Only
the Major Domo can get really testy if we're not where we're
supposed to be when she wants us to do something.'

'Of course,' I said. 'You run along, Emily. I wouldn't want
to get you into trouble.'

She winked at me. 'Chance would be a fine thing.'

And off she hurried, wiggling her bottom perhaps a little
more than was called for in a Victorian maid's outfit. I looked
at Penny.

'I have no idea what just happened there.'

'You're not fooling anyone, space boy,' said Penny.

Eventually, we reached the point where we'd been everywhere
and seen everything, though not always as close up as I would
have liked. And I wasn't any the wiser. I hadn't uncovered
anything strange or disturbing, nothing that even looked like a
clue; and absolutely no sign that any creature had ever entered
the House. Not a paw print, or some shed hair, or even a scent
on the air. I started back down the stairs to the entrance hall,

thinking hard, while Penny tripped lightly along at my side, looking at me expectantly.

'So where do we go now?' asked Penny. 'Outside, to investigate the grounds?'

'No,' I said. 'There's one group of people we haven't talked to yet. The escorts the principals brought here to entertain them. Sex workers often know a surprising amount about the people they work for.'

Penny looked at me. 'And you know that, how?'

'People who live on the borders of society often have links to the hidden world,' I said. 'You'd be surprised.'

'I doubt it!' said Penny. 'But where are these escorts? We've been all over the House and I haven't seen one anywhere.'

'Then I'll just have to follow my nose,' I said.

I put back my head and breathed deeply, and all the scents in the House came to me. The air only looks empty; to senses like mine, there's always a lot going on. I was getting dust from the carpets and dry rot from the walls, individual human scents from all the people who'd passed this way . . . and something else. I fixed on one particular scent and followed it down the stairs, all the way to the ground floor. It was like trying to pick out one musical instrument while an orchestra is playing, but it was a very distinctive scent. I stopped at the foot of the stairs and breathed deeply again. Underneath the polish and wax and cleaning agents, the scent I'd locked on to was still there.

'You ain't nothing but a hound dog, space boy!' said Penny. 'What exactly are you picking up?'

'I'm getting artificial musk in almost industrial strengths, sweat ancient and modern, and a dozen chemicals normally associated with theatrical make-up,' I said.

'I never know when you're joking,' said Penny. 'Really?'

'Yes,' I said.

'Alien!' said Penny.

I pressed on through the ground floor, striding confidently along deserted back corridors, until I ended up outside what looked like the door to a storeroom. But the scent was sharp and clear now, and beyond the closed door I could hear conversation and occasional laughter. I straightened up and knocked politely. It all went very quiet. I tried the door and it wasn't locked, so I just threw it open and strode in, with Penny right there at my side.

It turned out to be a private bar, with a surprisingly good stock behind the polished counter. The cosy little room was packed with glamorous creatures, staring silently back at me like so many wild things disturbed at a communal watering hole. All colours of the rainbow proudly on display, with heavily made-up faces and cool watchful eyes. The sex professionals brought in to keep the principals happy. Mostly women, with a handful of men; all of them attractive in an obvious sort of way. Even the well-dressed man serving behind the counter could have been a male stripper on his break. I looked from face to painted face, taking my time, refusing to be intimidated or hurried.

The escorts were dressed in silks and leathers, high couture and downtown sleaze, strings of pearls and studded dog collars. Everything from innocently pretty to dangerous predator; dark-eyed sirens and cute little sex kittens just waiting to be played with. So many exotic birds of paradise, with their meters turned off. Working people in their work clothes, just killing time until they were summoned again. They sat at tables or leaned on the bar, drinks in their hands, waiting for me to state my business so they could tell me to go to hell.

There was nothing particularly sexual about any of them, because they weren't trying. It was like being backstage at the theatre; with actors in their dressing rooms, still in costume but no longer playing their roles. In between engagements, but ready to take on their character again at a moment's notice. I nodded politely to the room.

'I'm Ishmael Jones . . .'

'Oh, we all know who you are, darling.'

A tall redhead stood up from her barstool to face me. Wearing a smart business suit, all pinstripes and shot cuffs, and smoking a cigar. Good-looking in a hard, collected way, with striking make-up and a great mane of hair in a shade of red never known in nature. She nodded to me calmly; one professional to another.

'I'm Scarlett. We all know who you are, and who you work

for and what you're doing here. Don't look so surprised, darling, you'd be amazed what some people consider pillow talk. We've all got the proper security clearances or we wouldn't be here. We specialize in soothing the troubled brows of the rich and influential, and then keeping quiet about it afterwards. Ask me your questions, and I'll tell you what you need to know.'

'You can speak for everyone here?' I said.

'Hardly, darling. I'm just the only one who's prepared to talk to you.'

'And why is that?' said Penny.

Scarlett's knowing crimson smile widened. 'Because I used to be a field agent. Before I discovered this job paid better and troubled me less at nights.'

She took us over to a side table, a little away from everyone else, so we had at least the illusion of privacy. Conversations started up again among the other escorts, who all made a point of not even glancing in our direction. I thought I detected a certain amount of relief, that the investigation had passed them by. I sat down opposite Scarlett, with Penny pressed in protectively close beside me.

Scarlett was a good head taller than me, well-built, calm and composed, and not even a little intimidated by me or who I worked for. Just looking at her, you knew immediately she could look after herself. She might have been in her thirties, or she might not; the mask she showed the world was entirely of her own creation. I would have loved to ask who she'd been a field agent for, but I knew she wouldn't tell me.

'Are you here because of the dead agent? Or to protect the Baphomet Group?' Scarlett asked sweetly.

'Both,' I said. 'What can you tell me about either of them?'

'Well, darling, since you ask so nicely . . .' Scarlett puffed lightly on her cigar, as she thought about her answer. 'None of us had anything to do with little Miss Rifkin. Not the kind to lower herself to mix with the likes of us. She was only interested in the principals; and once she found she couldn't pressure any information out of us, she wasn't interested. The first any of us knew about her death was when one of the servants found the body and screamed the place down. Several of us offered to examine the body, given that our job often involves medical knowledge, but the Major Domo had it locked away in the freezer with almost indecent haste. Anyone would think she had something to hide . . . The principals were all really rattled. We had to earn our money that night, calming the nerves of our respective clients.'

'And if I were to ask if any of them seemed particularly worried or knowledgeable about Jennifer's death . . . you wouldn't tell me, would you?' I said.

'Got it in one, darling. Though I can tell you some of the principals didn't want anyone with them that night. Just barricaded themselves in their rooms, behind armed guards. Which might or might not mean anything. But I have to say, they were all back at work the next day as if nothing had happened. Business as usual.'

I glanced around the room. The other escorts were going out of their way to seem not at all interested in our conversation.

'Do you know all of your fellow escorts personally?' I asked quietly. 'Is there perhaps anyone here you've not met or worked with before?'

'Darling, the number of boys and girls with our level of security clearance is not large in our line of work. We all bump into each other regularly, at this gathering or that.' Scarlett ground out the last of her cigar in the ashtray. 'It's a small world, after all. Everyone here receives assignments from the same highly exclusive London agency, and we're all used to working with very important people. If you're asking if anyone here could be a ringer or an undercover agent, the answer is no.'

'Were you really a field agent?' said Penny.

'It's all about keeping secrets,' said Scarlett. 'And code names. You didn't think I was christened Scarlett, did you? Over there at the bar we have Lovely Lola, Range Rider and Wanda Whiplash.' She smiled as she caught Penny's expression at the last name. 'Don't judge, sweetie. Everyone here has their own speciality, and between us we cover all the angles. So whatever the client is in the mood for, there's someone here to help them out. It's all about getting them off; the only difference lies in how you get there.'

'And your particular area of expertise?' I said.

Scarlett grinned. 'I make them grovel. And they love me for it.'

Other escorts drifted over from the bar to join us, once they saw how easy Scarlett was in our company. They pulled up chairs and sat down, happy to gossip in a general way about various celebrities they'd known. No names, just stories. Penny was fascinated.

'Sex professionals are like doctors,' said Scarlett. 'We have to provide complete confidentially or no one could relax with us. But apart from that, it's just a job. Like a physiotherapist. Manipulating body parts, for fun and profit.'

'Have any of the principals been behaving oddly?' I said, doing my best to sound casual as I glanced around the group. 'Has anyone been acting . . . out of character?'

There was a general shaking of heads and shrugging of shoulders.

'We only met these people when we got here, darling,' said Scarlett. 'We don't know any of them well enough to know what is or isn't in character. And besides, away from home all clients are different people. It's only when they're on their own that their secret selves can come out to play.'

'What about the Coronach creature?' said Penny. 'Have any of you seen or heard anything?'

'Not a thing,' said Scarlett.

'You don't believe in it?' I said.

'Of course not.'

'You haven't heard any strange noises at night?' said Penny.

'Darling,' said Scarlett, not even trying to hide her amusement. 'That's when we're working hardest. None of us had even heard about this creature until we got here. The servants were full of it. A few of us have taken walks along the loch, hoping for a glimpse of the monster, but no one's seen anything. The creature is just some old fantasy; and we know all about fantasies.'

'All right,' I said. 'Who do you think killed Jennifer Rifkin?'

'Yes . . .' said Scarlett. 'It's definitely a who, not a what. No one here believed that animal attack nonsense for a moment. Your agent was murdered by someone in the House. We were all ready to pack up our things and run, but the principals wouldn't hear of it.' She smiled sourly. 'Not that they could have stopped us if we'd really wanted out. But for the bonuses they were offering . . .'

I was reminded of what the maid Emily said. The power
of money.

'When we're not working we lock ourselves in our rooms
or stick together,' said Scarlett. 'Like here. Free drink, good
company, and a stout door. That the Major Domo let us have
this place surprised me, because I didn't think she approved
of us. The only thing I can tell you for sure is that the killer
is definitely not one of us. Because we know better than to
shit where we eat.'

I could happily have spent more time there, drinking and talking,
but I had work to do. I made my goodbyes, courteously, and
left. I almost had to drag Penny along with me, she was enjoying
the conversation so much. We headed back to the reception
area, and that was when someone with a very familiar face
came striding down the corridor towards me. I stopped dead,
and so did he. Penny looked back and forth between us, alert
to the sudden tension on the air.

'Ishmael? Who is that?'

'Someone I know,' I said. 'And someone who knows me. We
have a lot in common; including the fact that both of us still
have the exact same face as when we first met. Back in 1964.'

'Are you . . . friends?' said Penny.

'Depends,' I said.

'On what?'

'On which side we're working for.'

I started forward slowly, and he advanced just as cautiously
to meet me. A sturdily built medium-height man, wearing a
distinctive red-leather jacket and moving with the easy grace
of a natural predator. His face was nicely anonymous, the usual
field agent's practised mask. He could walk past you in the
street and you'd never notice him – until he slipped a package
into your hand or a knife between your ribs. He had the look
of a man in his twenties, just like me, even though he had to
be in his seventies now. We finally came to a halt again, standing
face to face. His gaze was cool and thoughtful, and I had no
doubt mine was too. Penny stood close beside me, being
supportive.

'So,' I said finally, 'what name do you prefer these days?'

'Christopher Baron,' he said, in a light easy voice. 'Call me Chris. And you're Ishmael Jones. These days your reputation precedes you. Which can be dangerous in our line of work.'

'You should know,' I said.

'They told me you were coming,' said Baron. 'And I wondered if you'd still look the same. Of course you do, you always do. But I keep hoping that one day time will catch up with you.'

He let the quiet accusation just lie there on the air. I ignored it.

'You know who I'm working for these days?' I asked.

'Of course,' said Baron. 'I like to keep track of the people who matter.'

'I wasn't told about you,' I said. 'But then I wouldn't have recognized the name. You do like to hide your light behind all kinds of bushels. What are you doing here, Chris?'

'I was brought in to be Head of House Security,' said Baron. 'No kind words, Ishmael? No welcome for an old friend?'

'We were never really friends,' I said. 'Just colleagues, on occasion.'

Baron glanced briefly at Penny. 'I know your name too, my dear. Delighted to meet you.' He didn't offer to shake hands, and his smile didn't reach his eyes. Penny smiled dazzlingly back at him, pretending she hadn't noticed. Baron looked at me thoughtfully. 'A partner . . . That's something new for you, Ishmael. You were always the proverbial lone wolf. Apart from the old Colonel, on occasion. But then he was your boss. What happened? Started feeling lonely in your old age, did you?'

'Sorry,' I said. 'That's classified. I could tell you, but then I'd have to rip out your windpipe.'

'You two worked together in the past?' asked Penny. I could feel her trying to make sense of the undercurrents running between Baron and me.

'We bump into each other from time to time,' I said. 'Sometimes as allies, sometimes as enemies. Hardly surprising, given the number of subterranean groups we've worked for in our time. Who are you working for these days, Chris?'

'Strictly freelance now,' he said easily. 'It's the only way to be in these complicated times. I'm here because the Baphomet Group refused to accept the House's previous Head of Security.

Apparently he didn't have a high enough security clearance. Fortunately for them I was available. Frankly, they're lucky to have me.'

'Have you ever been here before?' I said.

'In this desolate back of beyond? I wouldn't be here now if the money hadn't been so tempting.'

'And yet the Group is only here for a few days, and already someone is dead,' I said. 'On your watch.'

Baron raised an eyebrow. 'If I hadn't been brought in at the last moment, I would have insisted on setting up some proper defences. I've ordered more armed guards, and they're on their way. Are you accusing me of something, Ishmael?'

'Not yet,' I said. 'But I'm working on it. Why did they pick you, in particular, to run security here?'

'Because of my illustrious reputation,' said Baron. 'My current identity is spotless, and they don't need to know about all the other people I've been. You should appreciate that, Ishmael. Still, I suppose I'm glad you're here. This hasn't been the easiest of positions, with so many vested interests all pulling in different directions. Hopefully, we can use your Organization authority to make some of these idiots play nicely together. I seem to spend most of my time breaking up arguments before they can turn into fights. Just pissing contests, really; my principal is bigger than yours, so my needs must be more important than yours. The usual.'

He stopped, and looked at me thoughtfully. 'So . . . you're with the Organization these days. How long do you think that will last?'

'Until we're no longer of use to each other,' I said.

'What other groups did the two of you work for?' said Penny. 'I know about Black Heir . . .'

'Oh, we got around,' said Baron, flashing her another of his meaningless smiles. 'Ishmael and I have worked for all kinds of agencies, for all kinds of reasons.'

'Such as?' said Penny, determined not to be fobbed off.

'The past should stay in the past,' I said. 'It can do less damage there.'

But I could see from Penny's face that she wasn't about to let the question go. I've always avoided discussing my life before I met her. Because I wasn't always in a position to be the kind of person she could be proud of. Baron's smile widened as he saw me hesitate.

'If you don't tell her, I will.'

'All right!' I said. 'My first job was with MI13, back in the sixties. That's where I first met . . . Chris.'

'And we had a fine old time together,' Baron said happily. 'Hunting down monsters in the pay of foreign powers. Kicking the hell out of myths and legends that weren't content to remain myths and legends. And just generally taking care of business, with cases of the weird and uncanny. The Intelligence game got more than a little weird in the late sixties. Something in the air perhaps . . . Anyway, it was all going splendidly, adventuring by day and roistering by night . . . until suddenly our careers went into something of a nose dive after the Case of the Positive/Negative Double Agent. Both of us found it necessary to disappear in something of a hurry after that debacle.'

'And who's fault was that?' I said.

'Blame is for other people,' Baron said loftily. 'Anyway, I went to work for the Science Pirates, and Ishmael joined the Demon Runners.'

'I didn't stay with them long,' I said. 'They were too weird, even for me. Chris and I met up again in the seventies, when we both worked for the Beachcombers – the group that was eventually replaced by Black Heir.'

'Happy times,' said Baron. 'Clearing up after close encounters, and collecting all the alien flotsam and jetsam that got left behind. Then we both got involved in running security for the Beachcombers' attempt to produce a superagent – a human chameleon who could change shape to impersonate anyone.'

'Did it work?' asked Penny, fascinated. She loved to hear stories from behind the scenes of the world.

'Unfortunately, no,' said Baron. 'The process killed every subject they tried it on. Often in distressingly messy ways. The scientists didn't properly understand what they were working with. Ishmael walked out on them.'

Penny turned to me. 'Why did you leave?'

'Because I was lied to,' I said. 'I was told all the test subjects were volunteers.'

'They were very well paid,' said Baron.

'But they weren't properly informed about the dangers!'

Baron shrugged. 'For the kind of money they were getting, they should have known . . .'

'I left,' I said, 'but you stayed.'

'In my defence, I was being extremely well paid,' said Baron. 'And there was always the chance the scientists might pull it off.'

'Down the years we've both worked for any number of subterranean groups,' I said. 'But even after all the things I've done, I like to believe there's no innocent blood on my hands. Can you say the same, Chris?'

'Probably not,' said Baron. 'You always were more fastidious than me. I always thought the most important thing was to be good at my job.' He smiled engagingly at Penny. 'And I have worked for some quite remarkable people. I was with the Carnacki Institute for a while – the Ghost Finders.'

Penny shot me a mischievous glance. 'Ishmael says he doesn't believe in ghosts.'

'That's all right,' said Baron. 'They believe in him.'

'Change the subject,' I said.

Something in my voice must have got through to Baron. He stood up a little straighter and cleared his throat.

'I have to say, I wasn't that surprised to hear you'd joined the Organization, Ishmael. The two of you were made for each other. Equally mysterious and hard to understand.' He nodded at me, in a thoughtful sort of way. 'You know, you really haven't changed a bit. You look exactly the way you did when we first met, back in '64.'

'So do you,' I said.

'Ah yes,' said Baron. 'But I've had a lot of help. I've never denied it. Plastic surgery is the secret agent's best friend.'

'Why did you leave the Beachcombers, Chris?' I said. 'You seemed so suited to each other. Equally ruthless and hard to live with.'

He shrugged easily. 'With no surviving subjects, the shape-changing experiment was deemed a failure. No project, no need for security. So I just quietly disappeared, while everyone else was busy pinning the blame on each other. Didn't take me long to find another berth. There's always a need for someone with my experience.'

'And yet Jennifer Rifkin was killed on your watch,' I said. 'Do you have any idea as to who might be responsible?'

'Haven't a clue,' said Baron. 'Quite literally, I'm afraid. Or at least none that make any sense.'

'Did you come up with the idea of an animal attack?' I said.

'You've seen the state of her room, and the odd nature of her death,' said Baron. 'Neither suggests a human killer. And there is the legend of the Coronach creature . . .'

I thought about it. 'Did you have much contact with Jennifer?'

'She had her own business here,' Baron said stiffly. 'Which she preferred not to share with the likes of me. I did get the impression she was concentrating on the members of the Baphomet Group, rather than their work. But whatever she was looking for, she wanted the glory of discovery all for herself.'

And because she didn't know who was really who, I thought, *she couldn't know who to trust.*

'Do you think the Coronach creature is the killer?' Penny asked Baron.

'It's a possibility,' he said carefully.

'Have you seen any sign of the creature?' I said.

'Not in the House,' said Baron. 'No one has. The servants have been gossiping about hearing things, but nothing I could confirm. If it is some kind of unnatural thing . . .'

'Have you personally seen or heard anything to suggest an unnatural presence?' I asked pointedly.

'Not in the House,' said Baron.

'If only we had proper surveillance measures in place, things would be so much simpler,' I said.

'First thing I complained about, when I got here,' said Baron. 'The principals had even had the exterior cameras ripped out, and they rarely go outside! I tried to convince them that rein-stalling the cameras was in their best interests after a murder; but they didn't want to know. They trust their guards to keep them safe. But of course . . . they can't be everywhere.'

'As Jennifer found out,' I said.

'Exactly!' said Baron. 'Something got to her past all the security and all the staff and got out again, without being noticed. You have to admit that does sound . . . unnatural.'

'What kind of an investigation have you pursued into Jennifer's death?' I said.

For the first time, Baron looked uncomfortable. 'I haven't been allowed to do much. The room was immediately sealed off, and the body locked up in the freezer. I've questioned all the staff, and as many of the security people as I could persuade to talk to me. But no one will admit to knowing anything.'

'You haven't questioned any of the principals?' I said.

'What do you think?' said Baron.

'If the killer is one of the Baphomet Group,' I said, 'we can't let any of them leave Coronach House.'

'How do you plan to stop them?' said Baron. 'Does even the Organization have any real power over people like these?'

'Jennifer was on to something,' I said. 'And I will find out what it was.'

'She was killed for whatever she found out,' said Baron.

I smiled at him. 'Any creature comes after me, I'll turn it inside out and stamp on its lungs.'

'He would, too,' Penny said sweetly.

'Wouldn't surprise me in the least,' said Baron. 'I have searched the House thoroughly, from top to bottom. Including all the principals' rooms, while they were busy at their meetings. No evidence, no clues, and no sign of a killer hiding anywhere. Human or inhuman.'

'What about the undercover reporter?' said Penny.

Baron pulled a face. 'Like I don't have enough to worry about . . . Short of firing all the House staff and replacing them, I don't see what I can do. And anyway, the reporter would probably just sneak back in with whatever new staff I hired. All we can do is keep our eyes open and hope they give themselves away.'

And then he stopped, and looked at me thoughtfully. 'This creature . . . I have seen something. Out in the grounds, down by the banks of the loch. Just a dark shape moving in the mists. I challenged it but there was no response; and by the time I got there, it was gone. I had the exterior guards search the whole area, but they couldn't turn up anything. When I talked to them afterwards a lot of them admitted they'd seen something, or thought they had, at one time or another. And they all agreed on one thing, a constant feeling of being watched by unseen eyes . . .'

'Could have been the reporter,' I said.

'It didn't move like anything human,' said Baron. 'Come on, Ishmael! We've both seen enough strange stuff in our time to know monsters happen.'

'Yes,' I said. 'But men who act like monsters are far more common.'

'We need to work together on this case,' Baron said persuasively. 'People will talk to an Organization agent, where they wouldn't talk to me. The principals' security people are already scared shitless of you, so let's use that. Come on! It'll be just like the old days. We always did good work together.'

'Clearly, you remember the old days very differently from me,' I said. 'Mostly I remember us trying to kill each other.'

'Only when we were on different sides!'

Penny was starting to look a little disturbed, so I changed the subject. 'What do you make of the Major Domo?'

He shrugged. 'Strict, stern, very proper . . . Runs a tight enough ship. But she does tend to swan around the place like she owns it. And she strikes me as someone who likes to keep things to herself.'

'You should know,' I said.

'Hark who's talking,' said Baron.

'Put your claws away, boys,' said Penny. 'Concentrate on the case. What do you make of the principals, Chris?'

'Bit of a disappointment, really,' said Baron. 'They're not the cat-stroking Bond villains I was expecting. Just . . . business people.'

'Accountants,' I said.

'Exactly!'

'They must be incredibly wealthy already,' said Penny, frowning, 'so why bother with the Group?'

'Because they were born into it,' I said. 'It's all they know.'

'At least it's just people, these days,' said Baron. 'Remember when the Immortals got involved with the Baphomet Group?'

Penny's ears pricked up. 'The Immortals? Ishmael told me about them! Were they really immortal?'

'Someone once said to me "You're only immortal until someone kills you",' I said. 'After that, you are just long-lived. The Immortals were wiped out sometime back. Just as well. They really were complete bastards.'

'One big extended family of shape-changers,' said Baron. 'The Beachcombers supposedly acquired their shape-changing tech from the Immortals. Though that could have been just gossip.'

'This gets better and better,' said Penny. 'The Immortals really could change their shape?'

'They could make themselves look like anybody,' I said. 'Infiltrate any group, steal any secret.'

Or replace a member of the Baphomet Group, I thought, *without anyone noticing. The family may have been wiped out, but there have been rumours of a few surviving Immortals . . .*

'Wouldn't surprise me if they sabotaged the tech they sold the Beachcombers,' said Baron. 'They never did like competition.'

'What about the Illuminati?' Penny asked excitedly. 'Were they part of the Baphomet Group too?'

She stopped, as she realized Baron and I were trying hard not to laugh.

'The Illuminati were just an early form of urban legend,' I said, trying hard not to sound condescending. 'A joke that got out of hand. Later groups encouraged gossip about the Illuminati as a distraction, to steer people's attention away from what the real subterranean groups were getting up to.'

'But . . . wouldn't that be just what a real Illuminati conspiracy would want you to believe?' said Penny.

'Oh, she's good,' said Baron. 'Also just a bit unnerving.'

'I think there are enough real secret groups out there without worrying about fictional ones,' I said judiciously. 'The Baphomet Group is all about business. They're not interested in ruling the world, because that would be too much like real work. They just set policy and let other people get their hands dirty.'

'Precisely,' said Baron. 'Now, if you'll excuse me, I was on my way to sort out a problem with the chauffeurs. They're all demanding separate rooms, but there aren't enough to go round.'

'Why is that a security problem?' I said.

'Because all the chauffeurs go armed,' said Baron. 'The principals' last line of defence against terrorists and kidnappers. They take their personal security very seriously.'

'Then why are they staying on in a House where someone has been murdered?' said Penny. 'Where it has been demonstrated that someone or something can get in and out without being noticed?'

'Good point,' said Baron. 'The Group meeting must be really important . . . Or maybe they just trust their security guards to keep them safe.'

'I wouldn't,' I said. 'But then I've met them.'

'Don't be snotty, Ishmael,' said Penny. 'They don't normally come up against people like you.'

'There are no people like him,' said Baron. 'Now, if you'll excuse me, I have work to be getting on with.'

He strode straight past us and off down the corridor. I watched him go until he was out of sight.

'You don't like him, do you?' said Penny.

'He's very smooth,' I said. 'Very plausible, whoever he's pretending to be. I've always envied the way he can make himself at home in any company. But I've never known him to be loyal to anyone or anything apart from himself.'

'What kind of cases did you work on together?' said Penny.

'The difficult, dangerous ones. Baron is good at his job . . . as long as you can keep him pointed in the right direction. But no matter what kind of case we worked on, he was never really happy until he'd spilled somebody's blood.'

'Is he . . . special? Like you?' Penny said carefully.

'Not like me,' I said. 'But his background is almost as mysterious as mine.'

'Why was there so much tension in the air just now? Is there bad blood between you? Did you really try to kill each other?'

'Now and again,' I said. 'When we both wanted the same thing, but for different reasons. Don't misunderstand me. We couldn't hope for a better Head of House Security. As long as no one else makes him a better offer.'

'You don't trust anyone, do you?' said Penny.

'No,' I said. 'Apart from you, obviously.'

'Nice save, space boy.'

'You're welcome, spy girl.'

'Hold everything!' said Penny. 'If Baron is the same age as you . . .'

'He's older,' I said. 'When we first met, he was the same age I was supposed to be. At that time I was only a year old, newly made by my ship's transformation machine, but he was already in his twenties.'

'So how can he still look the same?' said Penny.

'He's had a lot of help, down the years,' I said. 'He's always been very open about it. But I didn't see any of the scars you'd expect in his face or neck from such extensive plastic surgeries. And I'm pretty good at spotting things like that. Still, when you work for groups like the Beachcombers and Black Heir, access to alien tech is one of the perks. He could be half cyborg by now, for all I know. Except I can usually hear their parts working . . .'

'How do you feel about him, really?' said Penny. 'It sounds like he's been a part of your life for a long time.'

'We've both been secret agents for the same kinds of groups,' I said. 'Shadows on the walls of the world. Always changing identities and allegiances . . . But despite all the things we've done together and done to each other . . . All the rooftop chases and vicious back-alley fights . . . He's as much a stranger to me now as the day I first met him.' I stopped looking back through decades of memories. 'I suppose he is what I've always wanted to be. Easy, charming, smooth, assured . . . He could afford to be liked and applauded, while I couldn't afford to stand out.'

'But you're real,' Penny said wisely. 'He's just a series of roles.'

Real? I thought but didn't say. *Because I play only one role – being human?*

'There are too many people in the House,' I said, deliberately changing the subject. 'So many I'm a bit lost as to where to start looking for suspects. Which could always be the point – the killer hiding himself in the crowd. Far too many people have guns: the House security, the principals' security, the chauffeurs . . . And on top of that, there's the undercover reporter to worry about and the possible double in the Baphomet Group.'

'Could they all be connected?' said Penny.

'Let's hope so,' I said. 'Or we're in real trouble.'

I broke off as the Major Domo came striding down the corridor, heading straight for us. From the look on her face, it was obvious she had something urgent and important to say to me. And I just knew it wasn't going to be anything I wanted to hear.

'What do you think?' said Penny. 'Is it too late to run?'

'She'd probably catch us,' I said. 'Stand your ground, they can smell fear.'

The Major Domo slammed to a halt in front of us, and started talking without bothering with any of the usual pleasantries.

'I've been talking to Baron. I didn't know you two knew each other. What do you know about him?'

'He's your Head of Security,' I said cheerfully. 'Didn't you read his references?'

'I didn't hire him,' said the Major Domo. 'The House's owners did that, when the principals rejected my usual Head of Security.'

'Why, specifically, did they pick Baron?'

'I wasn't told,' said the Major Domo. 'He came highly recommended by a London agency I've worked with before, so I didn't foresee any problems. But he'd barely taken up his post before Miss Rifkin was killed. I need to be sure he's up to the job.'

'He's very experienced,' I said. 'And anyway, I'm here now and I'm in charge. I want Coronach House sealed up tight, to make sure our killer can't get in. Or out. There's always the chance he's hiding somewhere here in the house.'

The Major Domo was already shaking her head. 'That was the first measure I suggested after Miss Rifkin's death, but the principals wouldn't hear of it. The very idea made them feel trapped. And what the principals want they get.'

'Then I can't guarantee their safety,' I said.

'You'd better,' said the Major Domo. 'Because now you're in charge, they are your responsibility. And they'll ruin you if you fail.'

'Better not fail then,' I said.

FOUR
Questionable Deaths

A noise loud enough to wake the dead, or at least make them clap their hands to their ears, erupted not far away. Penny and I immediately stood shoulder to shoulder, glaring around and ready for anything. The Major Domo bestowed a withering look on both of us.

'That is the dinner gong, summoning the House to evening meal. Will both of you please relax before you strain something? You'd better follow me . . . No, wait. I don't suppose either of you thought to bring formal wear, to dress for dinner?'

'I have my nice big hat,' said Penny.

'I have my sunglasses,' I said.

'Besides,' said Penny, 'I look fine.'

'It's true,' I said. 'She does.'

The Major Domo looked like she wanted to say a great many things, but didn't. She did allow herself a brief but clearly heartfelt sigh, before leading the way back to the reception area. Penny and I sauntered along behind, amusing ourselves by pulling faces at her back. I glanced out a window. Night had fallen, and darkness surrounded Coronach House like an advancing army. Exterior lights lit up the grounds here and there, a fierce illumination that left nowhere for anything to hide, but there were still large areas the lights couldn't reach. And beyond the glare of the lights lay nothing but the dark unmoving waters of the loch. I could just make out guards patrolling in pairs, wearing body armour and carrying automatic weapons. The grounds seemed quiet enough, but it still felt like the House was under siege.

I hadn't realized I'd stopped to stare until the Major Domo cleared her throat in a meaningful sort of way. I turned away from the window, to find Penny looking at me inquiringly. I smiled and shrugged, and she nodded understandingly. She trusted my instincts. The Major Domo looked at us like a school teacher forced to deal with delinquent children of rich parents, and we followed meekly after her. She led us all the way to the far side of the House, where a huge door covered in obscure Celtic carvings opened on to a massive dining hall.

The hall clearly dated back to when Coronach House had been home to a fair-sized family. It was big enough to hold an entire Highland Games, with great stone walls and a cavernous raftered ceiling. And not one but three hanging chandeliers, intricate constructions of brass and steel with any number of light bulbs, shedding a warm and cosy glow the whole length of the hall. A real fire blazed in an impressively large fireplace, crackling loudly as the heavy logs shifted. I nodded approvingly at the long dining tables covered with gleaming white table-cloths, carefully spaced silver candelabra, any amount of delicate china and antique cutlery, and freshly cut flowers in expensive-looking vases. This was what an old-style dining hall ought to look like. The people sitting at the tables didn't even glance up at us as we entered.

'This is the Great Hall of Coronach House,' said the Major Domo, making sure we heard the capital letters. 'The heart of the House, when it was still home to the old-established family who made it what it is. Generations drank and feasted here, plotting the destruction of their enemies and insurrections against kings and governments.'

She stood her ground just inside the doorway, not so much inviting as demanding Penny and I to take our time to look the hall over and give it its due. It was undeniably impressive, with its stained-glass windows, displays of ancient weapons mounted on wall plaques, and the traditional 'Stag at Bay' fire screens. But I was more interested in the people at the tables. They seemed such a small part of the scene, dwarfed by their magnificent surroundings and what seemed like acres of open space surrounding the tables. The hall had been designed for much larger gatherings than this. But the various diners didn't seem to care, concerned only with themselves and their own importance.

The principals sat on one side of a long table, with their backs to the wall, so they could look out at everyone else. For the moment, it appeared they were only interested in the contents of their plates. It took me a moment to realize there were only eleven of them, not twelve. One principal was missing. I turned to the Major Domo, who didn't wait for me to ask.

'October is late, as usual. I used to think he was deliberately hanging back so he could be sure of making an entrance. But having met the man, I am forced to the conclusion that he is simply appallingly absent-minded. To the point where it's a wonder he ever knows who he is without consulting the name tag sewn into the back of his shirt. You wouldn't believe how much running around his staff have to do just to make sure he's in the right place at the right time. I have been assured the man is in fact some kind of financial genius, and I can't see any other reason why the rest of the Group would put up with him. If he doesn't turn up soon, I'll send one of my staff up to his room to quietly remind him what the dinner gong means.'

'What about his staff?' said Penny.

'Oh, they're all here,' said the Major Domo. 'None of the principals' staff or security people are ever late for a meal. Never late in holding out their plates for a second helping, either.'

The security guards had their own table, a little to one side of the principals. They seemed to be spending as much time keeping an eye on each other as on the rest of the people in the hall. The only thing they could agree on was to glare suspiciously at Penny and me. So I waved cheerfully back at them, and Penny waggled the fingers of one hand in their general direction. The guards pretended not to notice.

The staff had their own table some distance away and were addressing themselves solely to their food. It was probably one of the few times in their day when the principals weren't ordering them about. The staff all had the look of people wondering quietly but firmly whether the pay was worth it.

The chauffeurs had their own table too. Still dressed in their formal uniforms, but without the peaked caps. They chatted cheerfully among themselves, and ignored everyone else. Given how tightly their expensively tailored uniforms fitted, I had to wonder where they kept their guns.

A thought struck me, and I turned to the Major Domo. 'Where are the escorts?'

'They are not invited,' she said coldly, with definite undertones of 'The very idea . . .!'

'They will dine separately. Like the House staff. The principals don't want to see the escorts until they want to see them.'

'I'm hungry,' said Penny. 'Where are we sitting?'

'There has been some discussion as to where the two of you should be seated,' said the Major Domo. 'On the one hand, you are here to serve the principals; but on the other, you represent the Organization. In the end, I decided you should sit with the principals' staff. I thought you'd be most comfortable there.' She smiled, briefly. 'I'm sure they'll make you very welcome.'

'You have got to be kidding!' Penny's voice was cold, but two hot spots on her cheeks showed how angry she was. 'We are nobody's servants! Ishmael has been placed in charge of this whole House!'

'It's all right, Penny,' I said. 'I don't mind. Really.'

'Of course you don't, you never do. You don't understand these things.'

'It's not important . . .'

'Yes it is! If you want these people to take you seriously and accept your authority, you can't let them get away with anything.'

I nodded. She had a point. I looked at the Major Domo. 'Where are you sitting?'

She indicated a small side table, where Baron was already attacking his food. Still wearing his distinctive red-leather jacket. The Major Domo looked as though she would have liked to say something about that, but didn't. 'I shall be dining with my Head of House Security.'

'Fine,' I said. 'We'll join you. That should make it clear to everyone where we stand. Or rather, sit.'

'Damn right!' said Penny.

We strode over to the side table, noses firmly in the air. The Major Domo stared after us speechlessly. I grabbed two unoccupied chairs from the chauffeurs' table, and they pretended not to notice. I slammed the chairs down opposite Baron, and he nodded briefly without looking up from his meal. I pulled one chair out for Penny and she seated herself grandly, with all the dignity of visiting royalty. I sat down beside her, took Baron's napkin out of its silver ring, because he wasn't using it, and spread it across my lap. I like to tackle my food with enthusiasm. In my experience, people who are inhibited about one appetite are often inhibited about others. The Major Domo sat down stiffly beside Baron, not even looking in my direction. Penny was right. In the Major Domo's world, things like this mattered.

Servants arrived, quietly and unobtrusively, to serve us food. It was like being waited on by robots in old-fashioned clothing. They never looked at any of us, intent only on carrying out their duties. The meal turned out to be surprisingly basic stuff. Cream of chicken soup, followed by roast beef with roast potatoes, and a selection of vegetables boiled almost colourless. I looked at it, and then at the Major Domo.

'All part of Coronach House's celebrated olde-worlde charm,' she said defiantly. 'Traditional food, to fill you up and stick to your ribs. The principals are probably used to more exotic fare, in which case this will no doubt come as a pleasant change.'

'I'm surprised their security people don't insist on food-tasters,' said Penny.

'That all takes place in the kitchens,' said the Major Domo. She didn't appear to be joking.

'Is there a wine list?' I said.

'You don't like wine,' said Penny.

'It's the principle of the thing,' I said loftily.

'You have principles now?' murmured Baron. 'My, you have changed.'

I fixed him with a thoughtful look. 'Don't push your luck, Christopher.'

Everyone talked quietly at their tables, but only ever among themselves, ignoring everyone else. From what I could over-hear, none of it was of any consequence. Interestingly, the principals showed no signs of being interested in each other. No small talk, no pleasantries; they just applied themselves to their food with barely a word passing between them. I supposed it made a kind of sense. They were business colleagues, not friends. Outside the Baphomet Group they probably had little in common.

The security guards ate in silence, giving all their attention to what was going on around them. They didn't even seem to notice what they were eating. They kept a watchful eye on their respective principals, in an overly protective and even possessive way; as though they didn't believe their charges could be trusted on their own. Some of them looked like they wanted to rush over and start cutting up the principals' meat for them.

The chauffeurs and the staff ate what was put in front of them, with the air of people determined to enjoy it because it was free.

At our table, the Major Domo ate mechanically, with no obvious signs of pleasure, as though this was just another task she had to get through. Baron cleared his plate with cheerful speed, shovelling it down. Penny looked quietly appalled at what had been placed in front of her, but said nothing, working her way through her food with quiet determination. I thought it was all fine.

Baron cleared his plate and then looked hopefully at me, in case I decided not to finish anything. Penny pushed what was left of her food around with a fork, searching for something worth finishing. I pushed my empty plate aside, and gave my full attention to the Major Domo.

'When can I send Jennifer Rifkin's body off for an autopsy, so a medical examiner can give us clear details on how she died?'

'Ishmael, please!' said Penny. 'Not a suitable subject for the dinner table!'

'Trust me,' I said. 'No one at this table has a weak stomach. Well, Major Domo?'

'I cannot release the body,' the Major Domo said flatly. 'None of the standard authorities can be allowed access to Coronach House while the Baphomet Group is still in residence. An autopsy will have to wait until the meeting is over and the principals have departed safely. We cannot risk anything that might draw public attention to the Group.'

'What do you think an autopsy could tell us?' said Baron, through a mouthful of Penny's leftovers. 'We know the brain is gone.'

'A proper examination might give us a better idea of how that was achieved,' I said.

'You still think the killer is human, don't you?' said Penny.

'What kind of man would kill like that?' said Baron, dabbing unselfconsciously at a stain on his shirt front. 'I mean, suck someone's brains out through holes in the back of their neck? And how would that even be possible? Some kind of vacuum machine with a long nozzle?'

'Oh, ick!' said Penny.

'Exactly!' said Baron. 'Even if they could smuggle such a machine into the House without anyone seeing, that would suggest the killing was planned in advance. Except no one knew Jennifer Rifkin was going to be here. From what little she said to me, I gather even she wasn't told till the last minute. And anyway, why kill her rather than one of the principals?'

'He may be obnoxious and he may eat with his mouth open, but he does have a point,' said Penny. 'Perhaps she was in the wrong place at the wrong time, and saw or heard something she wasn't supposed to. Something that meant she had to be silenced before the killer could start his real work . . .' She frowned. 'How she died still disturbs me. What possible purpose could it serve?'

'Perhaps the creature was hungry,' said the Major Domo.

We all looked at each other for a long moment, caught up in horrible visions, then I shook my head firmly.

'No. Forget the creature. This killing was designed to draw attention to the method and obscure the motive. Think about how carefully it must have been planned. The killer would have had to wait until everyone else was downstairs – giving him a clear run to Jennifer's room so he could take his time with her, free from witnesses or interruptions. That suggests knowledge of the House interior and the routines of all the people in it.'

'An inside job?' said the Major Domo. 'You mean one of my people? No. Impossible.'

'You said yourself Coronach House is full of new faces,' I said. 'You can't even be sure a journalist isn't masquerading as one of your staff.'

'So someone here in the House is the killer?' said Baron. 'Maybe someone in this room?'

We all looked around the hall. No one looked particularly guilty; or innocent, for that matter.

'Not everyone here is necessarily who they appear to be,' I said.

'You should know,' Baron murmured.

'But what about the state of Miss Rifkin's room?' said the Major Domo. 'All that destruction . . .'

'More misdirection,' I said.

'That's a lot of effort to go to,' said Baron, 'just to mess with people's minds. Isn't it?'

'Yes,' I said. 'It is. Which makes me think there has to be something the killer needs to draw our attention away from. And let's face it, if human, he'd have to be a real professional to take down a trained Organization field agent.'

'You think he could be an agent from another group?' said Baron.

'It would explain a lot,' I said. 'I don't see how any creature could hope to catch Jennifer by surprise. She might have been working or resting, but she would still have noticed someone entering her room. At the very least I would have expected her to fight back. But there were no defence wounds, not even scrapes or bruises on her hands. I think . . . she knew her attacker. And either trusted her attacker, or didn't see her attacker as a threat until it was too late.'

'The puncture wounds were on the back of her neck,' said Penny. 'Maybe she was attacked from behind?'

'That would explain why she didn't put up a fight,' I said. 'If she never saw the attack coming. But who in the House would she trust enough to turn her back on?'

'You honestly believe a man could do everything that was done to Miss Rifkin's room?' said the Major Domo.

'It seems the most plausible explanation,' I said. 'Until we find some evidence that couldn't be the work of a man.'

'You mean like puncture wounds or missing brains?' said Baron.

'I'm working on that,' I said.

The Major Domo looked to Baron. 'Tell him. Tell him what you told me earlier.'

'Oh by all means,' I said. 'Do tell me whatever it is you've been holding back, Christopher.'

'Well,' Baron said reluctantly, 'I've been talking to the guards patrolling the grounds. It turns out all of them have seen a wild beast of some kind down by the banks of the loch. Some of them more than once. And no, before you ask, not the monster. Something human-sized, or just a bit bigger. Fast-moving, seriously strange; and downright scary. And this is from trained, experienced men.

'All they ever see is a dark shape emerging into the moonlight or out of the mists. Only at night, never during the day. Something that doesn't move like anything human. The guards seem convinced there was something wrong about its shape or dimensions. Like something out of a nightmare . . . And these are men who don't spook easily. Most of them challenged whatever it was, even fired warning shots, but when they went in for a closer look there was never anything there. I'm not saying whatever they're seeing is the actual Coronach creature. But I'm increasingly convinced there is something out there.'

Penny and the Major Domo looked at each other. They didn't like the way he said 'something'.

'I can't help finding it very convenient that this creature should choose to emerge from the loch just as the Baphomet Group takes up residence here,' I said.

'Maybe somebody called it up,' said Penny. 'Maybe they're controlling it, using it to kill people.'

I looked at the Major Domo. 'Is there anything like that in the legends? Has it ever happened before?'

'Not that I know of,' said the Major Domo.

'When was the last verified sighting of the creature?' said Penny.

The Major Domo stirred uncomfortably in her chair. 'Over two centuries ago. There's a drawing, taken from a witness's description, in a book in the House library.'

'What does the creature look like?' Penny said eagerly.

'Hideous,' said the Major Domo. We waited, but she had nothing more to say on the subject.

'I think it would be pushing it to assume we're dealing with a creature and a human killer,' I said.

'We're missing something,' said Baron.

'I thought that,' I said. 'If it isn't a human killer, with human motivations, I don't see why Jennifer was targeted. This creature would have had to pass by all the people on the ground floor to reach the main staircase. Why go all the way up to the next floor to find a victim, when there were so many targets of opportunity close at hand?'

'Perhaps Miss Rifkin's room had some special significance for the creature?' said the Major Domo. She didn't sound too convinced.

'Maybe it saw Jennifer as a threat,' said Baron. 'She was the only person here with experience of the hidden world.'

'Apart from you,' I said.

'Yes, Ishmael, thank you for pointing that out,' said Baron. 'I was hoping to keep quiet about that part of my background. Maybe . . . the creature thought it had to get rid of Jennifer before it could safely pursue its real targets.'

'But it didn't,' I said. 'It killed Jennifer and then left the House. And besides, what you're suggesting sounds like pretty sophisticated thinking for something that is supposed to spend most of its time living in the murk at the bottom of Loch Ness. How would it even know about the Organization? Or the Baphomet Group?'

'It's a supernatural thing,' said Baron. 'Who knows what a creature like that knows or senses?'

'The stories say it was born of a human family,' said the Major Domo. 'Who knows how much of its humanity it might have retained? Or what it might have become after so many centuries of existence?'

'You really believe in this creature?' I said.

'Monsters are real,' said the Major Domo.

'Yes,' I said. 'They are. But people kill a lot more people than monsters ever do.'

And that was when the door crashed open, slamming back against the inner wall. A sudden hush fell over the dining hall as everyone looked up. A servant stood in the doorway, wide-eyed with shock, his uniform dishevelled. He didn't want to come into the dining hall. He looked at the principals and stayed where he was, beckoning urgently to the Major Domo. She stayed where she was, glaring coldly at the servant, refusing to be summoned by one of her own people. The servant almost stamped his foot in frustration, and edged into the dining hall in a series of short rushes, as though he had to keep summoning up extra nerve. Some of the security people started to rise to their feet, only to sit down immediately as the principals shook their heads. The servant finally stood trembling before the Major Domo, wringing his hands together in his agitation.

'What is it, Holroyd?' asked the Major Domo. 'Tell me what's happened, and stop making a spectacle of yourself!'

'You have to come with me!' said Holroyd, his voice low and urgent, with more than a hint of hysteria. 'You have to come with me, right now.'

'Calm down,' said the Major Domo, not moving. 'What could be so important that you have to interrupt me at my dinner?'

The servant just shook his head, refusing to say anything in front of the packed hall. He was breathing so deeply he was in danger of hyperventilating. He looked pleadingly at the Major Domo until she tutted loudly, threw aside her napkin and rose to her feet. Holroyd immediately backed away, forcing her to go after him. Everyone watched the two of them retreat to the open doorway, where the servant spoke rapidly, in hushed tones. Baron sat back in his chair, looking more amused than anything.

'You know, whatever this is, he should really be saying it to me. I am Head of House Security. But the staff all see the Major Domo as their mother. Or possibly one of those really strict nannies . . . What could be so bad that it couldn't be said in front of everyone?'

'I think we're about to find out,' I said.

The Major Domo listened, frowning, until Holroyd finally stopped talking; and then she gave him a quick series of orders, and he ran off. Looking glad to be gone, or at least to be doing something. The Major Domo returned to our table, carefully not hurrying, and leaned in close so only we could hear her.

'I've given orders for the House to be sealed,' she said. 'Something bad has happened. Mister Jones, Miss Belcourt, come with me. Mister Baron, you stay here.'

'Oh come on!' said Baron, not bothering to lower his voice. 'Something bad? Something bad would be the plumbing backing up again! I am Head of House Security, so I should be the one who decides whether or not the House needs to be sealed. That's my business.'

'The security of the principals is your business,' snapped the Major Domo. 'So stay here and watch them!'

Baron looked at her, and finally lowered his voice. 'Someone else has been killed, haven't they?'

'Apparently,' said the Major Domo.

'But all the security guards are here,' said Baron, 'and the chauffeurs. The principals are surrounded by people with guns.'

'Yes,' said the Major Domo. 'And how many of them do you trust? You stay right where you are and watch everyone until we get back.'

'Are you armed?' I asked Baron.

'What do you think?' he said.

The Major Domo went back to the door. I followed after her, with Penny bustling along at my side. The Major Domo paused in the doorway for one last look back at the silently watching principals.

'There's nothing to worry about!' she said loudly. 'Carry on with your meal. Desert will be served shortly. It's plum duff!'

And then she closed the door in their faces.

The Major Domo headed straight for the stairs, not quite running. The open reception area was completely deserted and ominously quiet. Off in the background, I could hear doors and windows slamming shut.

'It's the missing principal, isn't it?' I said. 'October. Someone has killed a principal, at last.'

'Holroyd found the door to October's room standing open,' said the Major Domo as she started up the stairs, not slowing her pace in the least. 'Just like Miss Rifkin's room. Apparently he dithered outside for some time, trying to work up his nerve before he finally pushed the door open and looked in. He said the smell . . . was pretty bad.'

'Was October's room wrecked?' said Penny.

'More than just wrecked,' said the Major Domo.

'Was October killed the same way as Jennifer?' I said.

'Holroyd couldn't tell,' said the Major Domo. 'This time the body wasn't left on display. It seems October has been . . . torn apart, and the pieces scattered round the room. Holroyd said . . . he couldn't see the head anywhere.'

We continued on up the stairs in silence for a while, thinking about that.

'Maybe the creature took it,' Penny said finally.

'Or maybe the killer wanted to make identification more difficult,' I said.

'It has to be October!' said the Major Domo. 'It's his room. Who else could it be?'

'Good question,' I said.

I was thinking about the possible double among the principals, and whether this could be connected. A quick glance from Penny told me she was thinking the same thing.

'The timing of this death seems very suspicious to me,' said Penny. 'This is the second time the killer has waited until everyone else was down on the ground floor, before attacking the one person left upstairs. So he wouldn't have to worry about witnesses, or anyone coming to help the victim.'

'And we can't be sure of the exact time of death,' I said. 'Making it hard for anyone to have an alibi.'

'You think the differences between the two murders mean something?' said the Major Domo. 'They're significant?'

She was starting to get out of breath, but refusing to let it slow her down.

'It means something,' I said.

I kept a watchful eye on the Major Domo as we reached the middle landing, and didn't even pause for breath before pounding on up the stairs to the top floor. She didn't seem particularly upset that October was dead. Just annoyed that someone else had been murdered in Coronach House while she was in charge. Meaning more work, and more trouble, for her. I had to wonder, why had she been so insistent that Baron stay behind? He was right: this was his business, as Head of House Security. Did the Major Domo really see a threat to the principals from among their own people? Did she know something I didn't? Of course, that wouldn't be difficult. I glanced at Penny. She was struggling to keep up with us, but was still hurrying gamely along. I slowed a little, to keep her company. This wasn't a good place for anyone to be left behind.

*   *   *

When we finally reached the top of the stairs, the Major Domo had to stop to catch her breath. The spirit was willing, but the lungs had gone on strike for better working conditions. She stood with her head bowed, breathing deeply and scowling fiercely at her body's treacherous weakness. Letting her down, when she had work to do. Penny was quietly grateful for the break. She put a hand on my shoulder to support herself, as she struggled to get her breath back. I stood between the two of them, not even breathing hard, and looked around. It all seemed very quiet on the top floor. The light was steady, the shadows few and far between, and all the doors I could see were firmly closed. Such a quiet respectable setting for sudden death and the return of a legendary creature. The Major Domo took one last extra-deep breath and strode determinedly down the corridor, heading for October's room. I offered Penny my arm to lean on, and we went after her.

The smell hit me first. The hot coppery scent of blood, with worse things underneath; all the associated aromas of violent death. The top floor of Coronach House smelled like an open grave. But it wasn't until we were close enough to see the door to October's room standing open that Penny and the Major Domo finally began to react to the smell. Penny wrinkled her nose, and pulled a face. The Major Domo frowned and shook her head. Neither of them slowed their pace.

I took hold of both women by the arm and brought them to a halt. The Major Domo scowled at me and started to say something, but reluctantly subsided when she saw the look on my face. I peered carefully up and down the long corridor, checking for any signs the killer might have left behind. They had to have come a lot further this time, without being seen. Which meant they had to hurry to make their escape and this time might have left some trace of their passing behind.

I let go of Penny and the Major Domo and knelt down to study the thick carpet. Any number of shoe imprints, of varying depths. A lot of people had come and gone in this corridor, some of them quite recently. But they were all full impressions; none of them the heavy toe and heel marks you'd expect from someone running. And definitely no paw or claw marks to indicate a creature. No blood trail, not even a few spots; which meant it was unlikely the killer was carrying October's head. Unless they'd found the time to wrap it first. I sniffed at the carpet, surreptitiously; but the heavy smells on the air buried everything else.

I got to my feet again, shook my head brusquely before the Major Domo could ask anything, and started toward the open door. Penny stuck close beside me, looking at me inquiringly, but I wasn't ready to say anything yet. When we reached October's door the Major Domo tried to brush past me and go in first, but I was having none of that. I wasn't expecting anything dangerous to still be in the room, but I wasn't taking any chances. Besides, I didn't want the Major Domo trampling over the evidence. I stopped before the door, blocking the way. Penny and the Major Domo crowded in behind me, breathing heavily down my neck. The door to October's room stood half open, as though politely concealing the horror that lay beyond. I placed one hand on the door and pushed it all the way open. The full stench of what had happened rushed out, and the Major Domo coughed harshly and turned her head aside. Penny made a low distressed noise, and put a hand to her mouth.

I stepped inside. October's room looked like a threshing machine had run wild. Every piece of furniture had been smashed, reduced to little more than firewood and kindling. It was all splinters and cracked veneer, and jagged pieces of wood not much bigger than my hand. I couldn't even tell which pieces belonged to what. The sheer scale of so much destruction was impressive. It had to have taken a lot of time, and not a little commitment. Nothing had been left untouched, unbroken. It made what had happened in Jennifer's room look like a trial run. Unless the killer had got a taste for it . . . alone up here and in no danger of being interrupted.

It didn't appear to me that the killer had been searching for something. It looked more like destruction for its own sake. The sheer completeness of what had been done spoke of concentration, rather than rage or frenzy. The bed had been dismantled as well, this time; the mattress torn apart, the sheets ripped to shreds, the headboard cracked in two. Even the heavy springs had been torn out and cast aside. No attempt to put

the body on display, though. As though this time the body
wasn't what was important.

I made myself look at what had been done to October. He
wasn't there, in any meaningful sense. He'd been reduced to
bloody bits, ragged scraps and tatters, and then thrown all over
the room. I wouldn't have thought you could take a man apart
that completely without using bone saws and a surgical kit.
All that was left of the principal was splintered bones and
stinking offal. And blood, everywhere. Soaked into the carpet,
spattered on the wreckage, and splashed across the walls and
ceiling in great crimson arcs. It was still dripping, and the hot
rich scent of it filled my head. I studied the patterns dispassionately. The pressure behind the arterial sprays made it clear
October had still been alive when the dismantling began. But
I still couldn't see any evidence of fury or revenge. What had
been done to this man was a deliberate attempt to horrify.

I looked back at the doorway. All the colour was gone from
the Major Domo's face, but her mouth was firm and her gaze
steady. She didn't like what she saw, but she wouldn't let
herself look away. Penny looked angry. After the bloody
slaughter she'd been forced to witness at her old family home,
death would never upset her again. It just left her with a driving
need to see the guilty punished. I gestured for them to come
forward and join me in the room. Neither of them hesitated,
though they were very careful about where they put their feet.
I nodded to the Major Domo.

'Did you know October, personally?'

'I rarely speak to any of the principals directly,' she said,
her voice quiet but unwavering. Not flinching at the horror
show set out before her. 'I usually receive my instructions
through their people. That's the way the principals want it.'

Penny tapped on my arm, and quietly drew my attention to
long jagged claw marks dug into the walls, gouged deep into
the plaster. There were more claw marks on the larger pieces
of broken furniture. I had to admit I didn't see how anything
human could have made them.

'How heavy would claws have to be to dig in that deep?'
murmured Penny. 'And how much muscle would you need to
do so much damage? What kind of creature could do this?'

'Something big,' I said.

'Human-sized?'

'Bigger.'

'Do you have anything particular in mind?'

'Not yet.'

I couldn't make out any animal tracks in the gore-soaked carpet. Which would not have been the case if the killer had been just some creature. Cleaning up after a kill is the mark of a professional. Penny realized what I was looking for.

'Would a supernatural creature leave tracks?'

It was a reasonable enough question, so I did her the courtesy of considering it seriously before answering.

'If the creature was real and solid enough to do this much damage, I would expect it to leave some evidence of its passage through the world,' I said. 'Which brings me back to my belief that we're dealing with a human killer.'

'What kind of human could do this?' the Major Domo said angrily.

'Fair point,' I said.

'Can you tell anything from . . . what's been done to the body?' asked Penny.

'Yes,' I said. 'October never stood a chance. The sheer strength involved was far more than human.'

'But you just said . . .' said the Major Domo.

'It's complicated! I'm still working on it!'

'Ishmael . . .' said Penny.

I stopped, and took a deep breath. 'Why kill October, out of all the principals? Did our killer target him, or did he just happen to be the only one on his own?'

'This case keeps throwing up questions!' said Penny. 'Speaking of which . . . can we get out of here yet, Ishmael? The smell really is starting to get to me.'

'Almost done,' I said. 'I'm looking for October's head . . . Ah! Yes, there it is.'

'Where?' said the Major Domo.

She started forward and I stopped her with a look.

'I need you and Penny to step back out into the corridor. This is a crime scene, in its own horrible way. The least the evidence is disturbed, the better. I'll get the head.'

The Major Domo nodded stiffly and backed out of the room, followed quickly by Penny. I stepped carefully over and around the bloody body parts and broken pieces of furniture until I reached the far corner of the room. The head had been set down neatly, upright, suggesting it had been deliberately placed there, out of the way. I bent over the head for a while, studying it without touching it. The neck wound was ragged, indicating it had been torn right off the body. Something I would have said was impossible for anyone with merely human strength. There were no marks, no damage, to the head's features. October's face had been left intact, so whoever found it could see the sheer terror of his last moments.

When I was sure I'd seen everything useful, I grabbed a handful of the grey hair and picked up the head to check the back of the neck. No puncture marks. Then I took another look at the distorted face, stamped with the awful mark of the last thing it had seen.

'Are you going to spend all night staring into his eyes?' said the Major Domo, from the doorway.

'Just thinking,' I said. 'October's brain is still where it ought to be. Why didn't the killer take it? What's different about this kill?'

'This was a principal,' said the Major Domo. 'No one's going to miss a secret agent. October was somebody.'

I held the head out before me, facing the Major Domo. 'Can you confirm this is October?'

She didn't flinch. 'Yes. That's him.'

And then her mouth flattened into a thin line and she had to turn away. Her shoulders slumped, as though she'd been running on adrenalin for so long that her strength had run out. Penny put a comforting hand on the Major Domo's shoulder. She nodded her thanks, but said nothing. She looked like she was just so very tired of having to be in charge.

I carefully put October's head back where I'd found it, and retraced my path through the wreckage and carnage until I could step through the doorway and out into the fresher air of the corridor. I closed the door carefully. The Major Domo's head came up and her shoulders squared. And just like that, she was back.

'I'll have the door guarded,' she said.

'First, pick some of your people with strong stomachs,' I said. 'I want that room mapped, showing where all the body parts ended up. Then have your people collect the pieces and put them in plastic bags. Properly labelled. You can store them in the kitchen freezer. Hopefully when all this is over, October's family can locate an undertaker who likes jigsaw puzzles and is looking for a bit of a challenge.'

'Probably best to double-bag the pieces, before we put them in the freezer,' said the Major Domo. 'We don't want the food getting contaminated.'

'Oh, ick!' said Penny. 'In fact, I would have to say the "ick" factor in this case is going off the scale.'

'Better put guards on the freezer door too,' I said.

The Major Domo looked at me. 'You don't really think October might put himself back together and try to get out?'

'No,' I said steadily. 'But someone might try to get in, to destroy the evidence.'

'Ah,' said the Major Domo. 'Sorry. It's just that . . . I don't know what to believe any more.'

'You've had the House sealed,' I said. 'That's a good start. I want every door and window locked. No one is to leave, I don't care who they are. You should go and see to that, make sure your people do a good job.'

'I never really believed in the Coronach creature,' said the Major Domo, looking at me steadily. 'I just thought it made a good story. I never dreamed anything like this could happen here.'

She walked away, not hurrying in case it looked like running. I watched till she was out of sight, then I opened the door to October's room and stepped back inside. I gestured for Penny to join me. She did so gingerly, but everywhere she stepped the carpet squelched blood.

'Tell me there's a good reason why I'm ruining these very expensive shoes,' she said.

'The killer went out of his way to leave no trace of himself behind,' I said. 'But he never expected anyone like me.'

I took a deep breath, concentrating on the various elements of the room's saturated air. There was nothing in the scents to disturb me.

'It's hard to get anything past the blood and other body fluids,' I said finally. 'But I'm not picking up anything animal. Maybe that's the point of all this – to drown out everything else.'

'What about fingerprints?' said Penny. 'You can see those, can't you?'

'Sometimes,' I said. 'But there's just so much mess . . . I can tell you October had sex in here not long ago.'

Penny looked at me. 'Are you seeing or smelling that?'

'You really don't want to know.'

'Ick! Definitely ick! Can you tell who with?'

'It's just fluids,' I said. 'Could be anybody. Though my bet would be one of the escorts.'

'I feel in urgent need of a stronger word than "ick",' said Penny.

I picked up various pieces of wreckage and examined them carefully. I couldn't see any cutting marks; the jagged breaks and jutting splinters indicated all the damage had been done through simple brute strength. But not a single claw or bite mark. I was sure I was missing something, but I couldn't think what. I threw the broken pieces aside, with perhaps more strength than necessary. They made a hell of a racket as they landed, which Penny kindly pretended not to notice. She leaned in close to the nearest wall, studying the claw marks.

'These are really deep,' she said. 'Obviously made with an effort. But why? It couldn't be part of a fight, because October wouldn't have been able to put up much of a struggle against anything that could do this . . . Wait a minute, hit the pause button! Ishmael, I'd say these marks were made after October was killed. The blood splatter had started to run down the wall before it was interrupted. But if October was already dead, what was the point?'

'Some kind of message?' I said.

'Like what?' said Penny. 'Don't get in my way because I'm big and nasty? I think we already got that.'

'No,' I said. 'I think . . . this was all staged. Everything in this room was intended to horrify whoever saw it.'

'And that's a human thing, not an animal trait,' said Penny. She glowered around the room, and made a loud aggravated sound. 'Do you have any idea what's going on here, Ishmael?'

'Not yet,' I said. 'I'm still working on it.'

'We were sent here to protect the principals,' said Penny. 'And I don't think Coronach House is a safe place for them to be. We should just let them leave. The killer can't chase all of them once they've separated. It could be that having them all together is what drew the killer here in the first place.'

'But what if one of them is the killer?' I said.

Penny looked at me sharply. 'You mean the double?'

'Maybe,' I said. 'If so, this could be our only chance to catch him.'

'We were sent here to protect people, not catch a killer,' said Penny.

'What about Jennifer?'

'Now it's Jennifer and October,' said Penny, meeting my gaze squarely. 'Are you really prepared to risk the remaining principals' lives just to identify who did this? Do we have the right to use them as bait in a trap?'

'Let's ask them,' I said. 'See what they think we should do. Although I can probably guess their answer.'

'Can you blame them?' said Penny.

'They'd be better off staying,' I said. 'At least, here they've got us on their side.'

We closed up the room again and cleaned as much of the blood off our shoes as we could, then went back down to the reception area. Only to find word of October's death had preceded us, and the whole place had descended into chaos. Security guards were glaring around them, pointing their guns at everything that moved, while trying to persuade their various principals to retire to their rooms and lock themselves in, so they could be properly protected. The principals huddled together, talking quietly, ignoring everyone else and refusing to be hurried into anything. They weren't used to being in a situation they couldn't control, but surprisingly they weren't panicking. They seemed actually pleased to see Penny and me, and silenced the general uproar with a series of sharp orders. Everyone stopped what they were doing and looked at me.

'October is dead,' I said bluntly. 'Murdered. Like Miss Rifkin, only more so. Principals, you need to make a decision. Do you want to leave, or stay and help catch the killer?'

December didn't even look at the others before speaking for the Group. 'You want to use us as bait?'

'Yes,' I said.

To my surprise, all the principals nodded. None of them looked happy about it, but these were people used to making hard decisions under pressure and then living with the consequences.

'We'll stay,' said December. 'Until you find the killer.'

'October was one of us,' said November, her voice low but steady. 'No one can be allowed to strike at the Baphomet Group and get away with it.'

The other principals nodded quietly in agreement.

'We will retire to our rooms now,' said December. 'Lock ourselves in, and let our security staff do whatever they feel necessary to keep us safe. While you track down the killer, Mister Jones. But don't take too long. The moment it seems to us you can't do the job, we will replace you with someone who can.'

The principals gathered up their people with a series of looks, and headed for the stairs. The security guards moved quickly to surround them, sweeping their guns back and forth and trying to look in every direction at once. From the way some of them looked at me, I got the feeling they were happy enough to leave me in charge of finding the killer. They were used to protecting people, not solving mysteries. Baron came striding forward to join me, nodding briefly to Penny.

'We have another problem,' he said, without any preamble. 'The chauffeurs and all of the House staff have locked themselves in the dining hall. And made it very clear they're not coming out again until the killer has been caught. The Major Domo is currently shouting at them through the door, and getting nowhere.'

'They can stay there,' I said. 'Less people around means less to complicate the situation.'

'Less targets?' said Baron. 'Or less suspects?'

'If the killing stops, then we'll know where the killer is,' I said.

The escort Scarlett came hurrying over to join us. I took in the determined look on her face, and just knew she was there to complicate my life even more. She planted herself in front of me and fixed me with a cold stare.

'We've caught a journalist masquerading as one of the House staff,' she said. 'That may not be as important as finding a murderer, but I still think you need to talk to her. She gave herself away by asking too many questions, about things servants would know better than to discuss. We've got her trussed up in our private bar. Do you want to interrogate her?'

I needed another distraction like I needed two deep puncture wounds in the back of my head, but there was always the chance a reporter who'd spent the last few days asking everyone questions might know something I didn't. I nodded to Scarlett, and then turned to Baron.

'You're Head of House Security, let's see how secure you can make Coronach House. Check all the doors and windows are properly locked, and then tell your people out in the grounds to shoot anyone who tries to leave the House.'

Baron grinned. 'They'll like that.'

He hurried off to spread the good news, and I turned back to Scarlett. 'All right, show me what you've got.'

'You're not the first man to say that to me,' said Scarlett.

The first thing I noticed in the escorts' private bar was that the atmosphere had changed. The good cheer was gone, replaced by tension and resentment. Several escorts were shouting angry questions at a young woman in a maid's outfit as she sat perched uncomfortably on a bar stool, her wrists held together in her lap by a pair of fluffy pink handcuffs. It was Emily, the maid Penny and I had talked with earlier. She sat silently, sullen-faced and cold-eyed, stubbornly refusing to answer any questions. The escorts surged dangerously around her, like hounds who'd cornered a fox and were just waiting for the order to tear it apart. Emily glowered back at them defiantly.

The second thing I noticed was that half the escorts were missing. I looked at Scarlett.

'Summoned by the principals,' she said, without needing to be asked. 'Nothing like the threat of imminent death to make people feel like being comforted. Or at least like having their minds taken off it.'

She yelled at the other escorts to knock it off, and the shouting died away. The escorts reluctantly fell back to allow me access to Emily. The maid looked at me in a supercilious sort of way, and smiled coldly.

'Fooled you, didn't I?'

'I had a lot on my mind,' I said. 'So, you're an investigative journalist.'

'Of course!' she said. 'You think I'd miss a chance at the biggest story of the year? Maybe of the century? I thought it was all over when you started questioning me, but all I had to do was simper and bat my eyes and I could jerk you around by your dick just like any other man.'

Penny made a noise behind me, but I didn't look back.

Emily sneered at me triumphantly. 'You didn't have a clue, did you? Mister Big Bad Secret Agent. And yes, I have heard of the Organization!'

'Good for you,' I said. 'Can you tell me who they are?'

She looked at me. 'Don't you know?'

'How did you get in here?' I said.

'Easy,' said Emily. 'I bribed one of the new maids to let me take her place and brief me on what I needed to know. It didn't cost much. Far less than I was expecting. The House should pay its staff better. Since I've been here, I've seen and overheard all kinds of things. Fascinating things! Because those stuck up aristo-wannabes in the Baphomet Group never notice the servants who come and go around them making their pampered lives possible. We might as well be invisible, just part of the fittings and furnishings.' She glared at me challengingly. 'From the way the principals talk about you, I'd say they were scared of you. And I didn't think the Baphomet Group was scared of anyone. Who are you, really?'

'Pray you never find out,' I said. 'What did you hear about the Group's secret meetings?'

'I couldn't get into the room while they were there,' she said. 'But someone had to go in afterwards to clean up the mess they made. And then it was simple enough to plant a few bugs. Because the security people didn't see mere servants as any kind of threat. You wouldn't believe some of the things those bugs recorded . . .

'I was actually ready to leave. I had all I needed, and I was getting really fed up with being ordered around. But I couldn't resist having a go at the escorts. The only ones who knew the principals with their defences down . . . and a little bit of sex always helps to sell a story. I thought they'd be happy to talk, for a little cash in hand. That's what they're here for, after all. Just meat for hire.'

Scarlett slapped Emily round the back of the head, almost knocking the maid off her bar stool.

'Don't be rude, dear. Even Daniel in the lion's den had enough sense not to pick a fight.'

Emily glared at her. 'I'm a professional!'

'So are we, sweetie,' said Scarlett.

'Who do you work for?' I asked Emily.

'Strictly freelance,' she said haughtily. 'I go where the stories take me, in pursuit of the truth. Then if the story's good enough, the editors come to me and pay my price. I've been chasing this story for years.'

'But why choose this particular meeting of the Baphomet Group?' said Penny. 'Why here? And now?'

Emily shrugged. 'Because this was the first meeting of the Group on British soil in decades. I jumped at the chance.'

'And it's just a coincidence that people started dying immediately after you arrived?' I said.

'The murders are nothing to do with me,' said Emily, with a certain amount of dignity. 'That's not what I'm here for. Don't think you can blame all this on me! There are lots of people with perfectly good reasons for wanting the principals dead, given everything they've done. I didn't come here to kill anyone, I came here to expose the truth and save Humanity.'

There was a pause.

'From what?' said Penny.

'Look at you,' said Emily, her voice full of contempt. 'Pretending like you don't know. Paid lackeys of an Organization that doesn't officially exist! Chasing around after the secret masters of the Earth, and cleaning up their messes!'

'What is she talking about?' asked Scarlett. She looked round at the other escorts, who seemed just as mystified as her. 'The principals aren't anyone special. They're just businessmen and businesswomen.'

'They're not even men and women!' snapped Emily. 'Underneath their disguises, they're all lizards! Descendants of the old snake gods who crawled out of the German Black Forest in the fifteenth century, infiltrated all the major families of Europe, and set about dominating our civilization. The Baphomet Group are just one of the many secret institutions who really run things. Grinding Humanity into the dirt for their own purposes. They are just lizards in human skins!'

There was a somewhat longer pause.

'I think we'd have noticed that,' Scarlett said finally. 'I mean, I've seen three of the principals naked – two men and one woman – and none of them had a zip down their back.'

'I should have known,' I said. 'She's just another conspiracy nut. Looking for evidence of Greys and Lizardoids and Secret Ascended Masters.' I couldn't help smiling at Emily. 'If anything like that was going on here, I'd know. The Baphomet Group are just very important accountants.'

She sniffed derisively. 'Well of course you'd say that. You're here to protect them. To keep the truth from getting out.' She glared around the bar. 'You're all traitors to Humanity! Selling out your human birth right for a mess of cash!'

Scarlett looked at me. 'She's not right in the head, is she? Unless you know something we don't?'

'Lots,' I said. 'But nothing that applies to what's going on here. I don't think she's got anything to do with the murders, so she's nothing to do with me.'

'What do we do with her?' said Penny.

'Lock her up somewhere safe until it's all over,' I said.

'You can't silence me!' said Emily.

Scarlett smiled at me. 'We've got a nice selection of gags . . .'

'We don't need to silence her,' I said. 'Let her say what she likes. No one will listen, apart from the True Believers, who've already made up their minds.'

'I'll tell the world all about you!' said Emily.

'You don't know anything about me,' I said.

Something in my voice stopped her. She looked at me uncertainly. 'I can tell everyone your name. And that you work for the Organization.'

'What makes you think Ishmael Jones is my real name?' I said.

'Oh, shit!' said Emily.

And that was when the Major Domo came striding into the room. The escorts scattered to get out of her way as she headed straight for Emily.

'How could you?' she said loudly. 'You have betrayed our trust!'

Emily laughed in her face. 'Oh please! You don't pay enough to get away with that. You don't pay any of your staff enough. That's how I got in. You're the traitor, pandering to the enemies of Humanity. Lizard lover!'

Scarlett slapped Emily round the back of her head again.

'Ow!' said Emily. 'Stop doing that!'

The Major Domo blinked at her a few times, then looked at me. 'Enemies of Humanity? What is she talking about? Is she a Communist?'

'Worse,' I said. 'She's a conspiracy wonk. Thinks the principals are actually lizards wearing people suits.'

The Major Domo allowed herself one of her brief smiles. 'Has she seen them eating?' She turned her back on Emily and gave all her attention to me. 'My security people have swept the House from top to bottom, and found no trace of a creature anywhere.'

Emily's ears pricked up at that. She started to say something, and Scarlett slapped her round the back of the head again.

'I'm a reporter!' said Emily. 'I have a right to ask questions!'

'Somebody get me a ball gag,' said Scarlett. 'One of the big ones.'

'Lock her up somewhere safe,' I said to the Major Domo. 'You can let her out when this is all over. She can say what she likes then. The Organization will see to it there's no evidence left to back her up.'

'You can't silence me!' Emily said stubbornly. 'I'll tell the whole world what the Baphomet Group was up to here.'

'You don't know what they're up to,' I said.

She sneered at me. 'I bugged their conference room, remember? I have recordings of all their meetings. If you only knew what they've been talking about . . .'

The door banged open again as Christopher Baron strode

into the private bar. He walked right up to Emily, produced a gun and shot her in the head. Scarlett jumped back, as half of Emily's skull was blown away. Several of the escorts cried out, then the whole bar fell silent. The body slid sideways off its bar stool and slumped to the floor. Scarlett looked down at the blood and brains spattered across her smart city suit, and glared at Baron. He shrugged easily and raised an eyebrow at her, and she said nothing. The rest of the escorts stood very still, watching Baron with thoughtful eyes. They weren't shocked, nothing much could shock them any more, but they were angry at being made witnesses to something that was none of their business.

Baron looked around him, like a hunter facing down a pack of wild animals that might turn on him if he showed any sign of weakness.

'I trust I don't need to tell any of you not to talk about anything you might have seen at Coronach House?' he said. 'I thought not. Be good little boys and girls, and there will be a nice little cash bonus in your pocket when you leave.'

He waited a moment, and when no one challenged him made his gun disappear about his person. He looked at the Major Domo, and she looked away. He turned to me.

'You should have called me in earlier, Ishmael.'

'I was afraid something like this might happen,' I said.

He smiled. 'You always were too soft-hearted to make a good agent.'

He knelt down beside Emily's body and searched her pockets with practised thoroughness, moving the body this way and that with easy confidence. Not bothered in the least by the brains leaking out of the massive hole in her head. He didn't find anything. He got to his feet again, wiping blood off his hands with a handkerchief.

'No recordings on her. I suppose it's always possible she was bluffing. I'll turn her room over later, just to be on the safe side. Don't worry about disposing of the body. I'll have my men dump it in the loch. The waters are very deep, and very dark.' He grinned at the Major Domo. 'Give your creature something to play with.'

'You really are a shit!' said the Major Domo.

He shrugged easily. 'Comes with the job.'

'She was part of my staff,' said the Major Domo. 'It's my responsibility, my duty, to see she's properly put to rest.'

'She only pretended to be part of your staff,' Baron said patiently. 'And as Head of House Security, it's my responsibility to clean up the mess. That is what you hired me for. I don't know why you're making such a fuss. She had to die. She knew too much and she couldn't be allowed to talk.'

'No one would have listened,' I said.

'Not your decision to make,' said Baron.

'Not yours, either,' said Penny. 'One of the principals told you to do this, didn't they? Which one was it?'

He smiled at her. 'None of your business.'

'Time you were leaving, Christopher,' I said. 'You've done enough damage.'

He looked at me. 'I don't take orders from you, Ishmael.'

'The Organization put me in charge,' I said. 'You want to pick a fight with them?'

He was still smiling. 'You should be asking yourself who put me here.'

I took a step forward. And his gun was suddenly in his hand again, pointing directly at me.

'You might be fast enough to disarm a bunch of hired goons,' he said. 'But do you really think you're faster than me? You can't take me, Ishmael. You never could.'

I smiled back at him. 'I don't need to.'

Penny clubbed Baron over the back of the head with the base of a brandy bottle. He should never have taken his eyes off her. There was a heavy thud and Baron groaned, sinking to one knee. Penny went to hit him again, but I shook my head. Then took the gun away from him.

'You never did understand the value of a partner you can trust, Christopher.'

And then everyone's heads snapped round, as the sound of massed gunfire came from somewhere far off in the House. A whole lot of guns, firing again and again.

'Now what?' I said. I gave Baron's gun to the Major Domo. 'He's your Head of Security, make him secure!'

I raced out of the private bar, heading towards the sound of gunfire, with Penny pounding along at my side.

'I told you there were too many guns in this house!' I said.

'I'm more concerned about who they're shooting at,' said Penny.

'Or at what!' I said.

FIVE
Dangerous Situations

I charged through the empty reception area, ready to run right over anyone who got in my way. But the place was deserted. I slammed to a halt at the foot of the stairs and stood listening. Penny joined me some moments later, already out of breath, and glared at me; demanding to know why we'd stopped when it sounded like everything short of World War III was breaking out upstairs. I didn't mention her harsh breathing.

'Just getting my bearings,' I said.

'Can you tell where the gunfire is coming from?' she said.

'Somewhere on the top floor.'

'Where the principals are! Oh, that is not at all good!'

I started up the stairs, with Penny beside me. Running headlong into danger isn't what I normally recommend; I much prefer sneaking up on it from behind, so I can take it by surprise. But whatever was happening at the top of the House, the sheer amount of massed gunfire suggested death and destruction on an appalling scale. And when there isn't time to do the sane and sensible thing, all that's left is to go charging in and meet the danger head on. In the hope that whatever it is will be so surprised it forgets to shoot at you. Or at least hesitates long enough for you to think of something else to do.

It's planning like this that makes me wonder how I've lasted this long.

'It has to be the security guards,' I said, thinking out loud. 'They're the only ones with enough guns.'

'But what,' said Penny, breathing really hard now as she struggled to keep up with me, 'could be such a threat that they need that kind of firepower to deal with it?'

'We'll find out soon enough,' I said.

'Make yourself wide,' growled Penny. 'So I can use you as a shield.'

We pounded up the stairs and hit the middle-floor landing. Penny had to stop and lean heavily on the banisters, head hanging down as she gasped for breath. I looked at her, and she gestured angrily at the next set of stairs.

'Go! I'll catch up!'

I didn't waste time asking if she was sure. She wouldn't have said it, if she wasn't. I bounded up the stairs, two or three at a time, accelerating rapidly now I didn't have to hold myself back. I reached the top-floor landing and looked quickly around. The roar of massed gunfire was definitely coming from the principals' private rooms. But it couldn't be the creature, it just couldn't. There was no way it could have sneaked back into the House, with all the doors and windows locked and guarded. And yet what else could justify this kind of armed response? The thoughts flashed through my mind in a moment, then I was off and running again.

I rounded a corner at speed and came straight into the long corridor that held the principals' rooms. A group of security guards had their backs to me, firing furiously down the corridor at another group of security men, who were firing back just as furiously from the far end. The guards were sheltering in the open doorways of the principals' rooms, leaning out just long enough to aim and fire, then darting back in. Bullets tore up and down the corridor, creating a deadly no-man's land, punching holes in the corridor walls and chewing up the wood-work around the open doors. But for all the endless sound and fury, it didn't seem as though anyone had been killed yet or even seriously wounded.

I really wasn't impressed by the abilities of the security men at Coronach House.

I yelled for everyone to stop firing. The nearest guards imme-diately spun round and opened fire on me. I threw myself back round the corner, and bullets whined through the air where I'd been standing just a moment before. They slammed into the corner of the wall again and again, sending puffs of pulverized stone and splintered wood flying through the air. The guards kept on firing, even after I was out of sight.

'This is Ishmael Jones!' I shouted. 'The Organization put me in charge here! All of you, stop firing and lower your weapons!'

If anything, the shooting in my direction actually intensified. I crouched down as heavy gunfire whittled away at the corner, and gave the matter some careful thought. Something particularly dramatic must have happened up here to drive all reason and discipline out of the guards' minds, but I hadn't seen anything to suggest what. I was still considering my options when Penny came staggering down the corridor to join me. Her face was flushed and wet with sweat and her breathing ragged from her exertions, but she was still determined to see what was happening. She went to look round the corner, and I grabbed her by the arm and pulled her down beside me. Just a glimpse of her face at the corner was enough to attract even more gunfire. The corner of the wall was starting to look really damaged now and was shuddering under the repeated impacts. Penny and I huddled together, keeping our heads well down.

'What the hell is going on here?' said Penny, once she'd got some of her breath back. She sounded more outraged than anything else. 'Who's firing at us?'

I explained the situation as best I could, and Penny stared at me.

'That's it? No creature, no assassin! They're all just firing at each other? Dear Lord, spare me from the curse of testosterone. What started all this?'

'I doubt any of it was their idea,' I said. 'This whole situation smells of standard operating procedure for a lone agent in the field. When up against a much larger force, trick them into turning on each other. Of course, once you get them started it can be very difficult to make them stop.'

'We could just wait here until they run out of ammunition,' said Penny. 'At the rate they're using it up, that shouldn't be long.'

'But a lot of people could die before that happens,' I said. 'These guards out there might be bone-headed overreacting arseholes of the first order, but they are still some of the people we were sent here to protect.'

'You get attacks of conscience at the strangest times, Ishmael!' Penny said.

The bullets stopped slamming into the wall. The guards had decided we were no longer an imminent threat, and had gone back to trying to kill each other.

'I could just very briefly stick my head round the corner and check what's going on,' said Penny.

'No you couldn't,' I said. 'First, we already know what's happening. And secondly, someone might be waiting for you to do just that.'

'We have to do something!' said Penny.

'I have a plan,' I said. 'But you're really not going to like it.'

She looked at me narrowly. 'Try me.'

'The only way to stop this madness,' I said carefully, 'is to physically stop the guards from shooting.'

'And how do we do that?' said Penny.

'We don't,' I said. 'I do. I go out into the corridor and disarm the guards. Suddenly and violently, and with extreme dexterity.'

Penny grabbed my arm, hard. 'No, Ishmael! You'll be killed!'

'Not if I'm quick,' I said. 'Not if I'm really quick.'

I gave her my most reassuring and confident grin, until she reluctantly let go of my arm. I stood up and breathed deeply, saturating my system with oxygen. I backed away from the corner, and shot one last glance at Penny. She didn't look convinced, but she didn't say anything. She had faith in me.

I charged around the corner and hit the guards at a dead run. Some of them heard me coming and were already turning their guns. But I was in and among them before they knew what was happening. They held back briefly for fear of hitting each other. That moment's hesitation was all I needed.

I grabbed men out of doorways and threw them across the corridor, slamming them into the opposite wall hard enough to knock them silly. I was already moving on before the first few hit the floor, throwing armed guards around like they weighed nothing, slapping guns out of their grasp, clubbing men down with my bare hands. Being very careful only to use necessary levels of force. Mad as I was at the guards, I didn't want to kill any of them just because they'd been tricked into doing something stupid.

The guards at the far end of the corridor were still firing, concentrating their aim on the guards who were still firing at them.

But soon enough those at my end of the corridor were either

lying groaning on the floor or sitting propped against a wall, wondering what hit them. And the guards at the far end of the corridor started firing at me, as the only thing still moving. I ducked into the nearest open doorway, while bullets slammed into the doorframe all around me. For supposedly well-trained professional bodyguards, they really were rotten shots.

But of course it's not often they'd come up against someone like me. Because there is no one else like me, as far as I know.

I looked round the room. December was sitting on his bed, wearing nothing but an old-fashioned dressing gown and fluffy slippers. He stared at me coldly, seeming almost as annoyed as I was about what was going on. I nodded briskly to him and raised a hand to forestall any questions, then looked round sharply as the firing stopped. I waited a moment, before peering cautiously out the door. It was always possible that sanity had broken out, but I wasn't ready to risk my life on it.

No one shot at me. Somewhat heartened, I took a deep breath and stepped confidently out into the corridor; doing my best to look like it had never even occurred to me that I might be in danger, while still being ready at a moment's notice to duck and dodge like a man possessed. The guards at the far end of the corridor covered me with their guns. I struck a casual but commanding pose.

'I am Ishmael Jones!' I said loudly. 'First, take a look at what I've already done and consider what I might do next. Second, I represent the Organization, who will be very upset with anyone who tries to kill me.'

I stood my ground, glaring coldly down the corridor, and one by one the guards lowered their weapons. I deliberately turned my back on them, and glowered at the guards I'd disarmed. Most were coming to their senses, and not looking at all happy about it. None of them wanted to meet my gaze. I think they were embarrassed at being taken down so easily. I looked back down the corridor at the other set of guards.

'Put those guns away! Don't make me have to come down there!'

The guards quickly holstered their guns and stepped out of the doorways with their empty hands in clear view, trying hard not to look like any kind of threat. I raised my voice again.

'Principals! This is Ishmael Jones, Head of Security. I want to see all of you out in the corridor, right now!'

There was a long pause, and finally four of the principals stepped out of their rooms. I recognized January, March, August and December. January was a sharp-faced young woman, March and August middle-aged men, and December the elderly gentleman I'd talked with earlier. They all looked very unhappy at having their precious rest disturbed. I waited a moment, until it was clear no one else was going to show their face, and then I turned to December, as spokesman for the Baphomet Group.

'There is no enemy, and as far as I can tell there never was,' I said bluntly. 'Someone tricked your people into shooting at each other.'

The four principals snapped out a series of orders, and the guards either stood to attention or scrambled to their feet. Clearly wondering how things could have got so out of hand. Some of the guards I'd had to bounce around looked at me reproachfully, as though it was my fault I'd made them look bad.

'All right!' I said loudly. 'What happened here? Who started this?'

The guards looked at each other and then all started to talk, or rather mumble, at once. It quickly became clear none of them were sure about anything. I strode up and down the corridor, firing questions at one guard after another, but most weren't even clear about the sequence of events. Someone had started firing. Someone had fired back. Someone had shouted that one of the principals had been killed by his own guards. Someone had shouted that terrorists had infiltrated the guards. And after that, everything had gone to hell in a hurry. But no one would admit to having fired the first shot. They had all just . . . joined in, caught up in the madness of the moment.

I wondered if there was an agent provocateur among them . . . Or whether this might be down to the putative double among the principals. But why would anyone want to start a gunfight here? In this kind of shootout, there was no telling who would get hurt. Unless that was the point. Maybe someone wanted to wipe out as many of the guards as possible, to leave the principals more vulnerable. I turned to December.

'Why am I looking at only four principals? Was it not clear that I wanted to see absolutely everyone? Am I going to have to kick in doors and drag the rest of the Group out here?'

'I wouldn't,' said December. 'The others . . . have escorts with them.'

'Ah,' I said. 'So you four are . . . on your own?'

'I am very happily married,' said December, with great dignity. 'And my wife would kill me.'

I looked at August, a grey little man with no discernible personality. He was actually wearing a smoking jacket. I didn't know anyone still wore those. He shrugged briefly.

'I've never really gone in for that sort of thing,' he said quietly.

Looking at him, I could quite believe it. The young woman January and the middle-aged man March stood together, staring defiantly back at me. Refusing to say anything. They were both fully dressed, but looking a little flustered. Thinking back, I remembered both of them emerging from the same door. Which meant they'd been in the same room when war broke out. Which was . . . interesting. I turned back to December.

'Tell your security people to stick to guarding their own particular principals. And not to open fire again unless they're sure they've got a really good reason.'

The security guards didn't even wait for orders, just gathered up their guns where necessary and moved quickly to take up positions at the principals' doors. Trying hard to look trustworthy and professional. A few were still limping. August disappeared into his room, and January and March went back into their shared room. December looked thoughtfully after them, and then nodded briefly to me before returning to his room. I waited till all the guards were properly in place, then strolled unhurriedly back down the corridor and round the corner.

Penny grabbed hold of me and hugged me to her. I held on tightly, and could feel her heart hammering next to mine. After a while we let go, stepped back, and smiled at each other. And then Penny stabbed me really hard in the chest with her index finger.

'Don't you ever do that again! You could have been killed.'

'It was a calculated risk,' I said carefully. 'I'm really very fast, when I have to be.'

'But you're not bulletproof, Ishmael. It only needed one of them to get in a lucky shot . . .'

'But they didn't,' I said.

I honestly didn't see what she was so upset about, which just seemed to annoy her even more. After a moment she shook her head and deliberately changed the subject. Which was fine by me.

'So!' she said. 'No creature, and no killer. What was the point of all that?'

'Something important must have been happening somewhere else, while we were being kept occupied here,' I said. 'Whoever's behind all this is good. And I mean professionally good. He's always one step ahead.'

And then I broke off, as my phone rang. I took it out of my pocket and looked at it, letting it ring. Only the Organization had this number, and the Colonel was the only one who ever used it. And he wouldn't disturb me in the middle of a mission unless it was really important. I put the phone to my ear.

'Yes?'

'It's Baron,' said a confident, slightly amused voice.

'How did you get this number?' I said.

'You're not the only one who knows things,' Baron said smugly. 'I do get around, you know . . . Almost as much as you. I have contacts in places you wouldn't believe.'

'There's only one way you could have got my number,' I said. 'You worked for the Organization, didn't you?'

'They do make a good haven for when you absolutely have to hide from everyone else in the world.'

'But you're not with them any more,' I said. 'Or the Colonel would have told me about you. So what happened?'

'I found out who they really are,' said Baron.

I remembered the traitor Frank Parker saying the same thing to me in his cell at Ringstone Lodge. That if I knew the truth about what the Organization really was, I'd run from them just as he had. Of course, Parker was a traitor. And Baron a troublemaker . . .

'Who is it?' Penny asked urgently. 'Who are you talking to?'

'It's Baron,' I said.

'Why isn't he unconscious?' said Penny.

I conceded the point. It was a good question. 'Why aren't you unconscious, Baron?'

'Really hard head,' said Baron. 'Saved my life on more than one occasion. Look, I've been talking with the Major Domo and she says there's an old, almost forgotten, cellar under Coronach House. It hasn't been used in centuries, and the only entrance was sealed off so long ago her security people never even bothered investigating it. But now she thinks maybe someone should go down there and take a look.'

'Let me talk to the Major Domo,' I said.

'She's not here.'

'She let you go?'

'I was able to reassure her that everything I'd done had been for the good of the House and the Baphomet Group,' said Baron. 'She's not as sentimental as you are, Ishmael. She'll work with anyone when the job demands it.'

'Where is she right now?' I said.

'Still trying to talk the servants and chauffeurs into leaving the dining hall.'

'I thought we'd decided we were better off with all of them in one place, instead of running around complicating things?'

'It seems the Major Domo is taking their mutiny as a personal affront,' said Baron. 'With everything that's going on, she needs to prove she's still in charge. I think she has trust issues. Anyway, to find the entrance to the cellar you need to go right to the back of the ground floor, past the escorts' private bar, until you come to the furthest wall in the House. Then look for a stretch of wall that has no framed prints or weapon displays. Which should have been a clue in itself, in a place like this. The entrance to the cellar is concealed in the woodwork, but no doubt you'll be able to find it.'

'Why me?' I said. 'And not you?'

'Ah,' said Baron. 'Apparently, the Major Domo doesn't trust me out of her sight for the moment. She hasn't exactly put me on a leash, but only because she couldn't find one.'

'She should have asked the escorts,' I said.

'I'm just hanging around here until the Major Domo finishes shouting at her people through the closed door. So far it's all threats and accusations, from both sides. There'll be tears before bedtime . . .'

'Wouldn't surprise me in the least,' I said.

'Anyone, or anything, could be hiding out in the cellar,' Baron said steadily. 'According to the Major Domo, there are old family stories concerning a secret exit in the cellar that connects to a tunnel which emerges somewhere in the grounds.'

'And she's only telling us this now?' I said.

'To be fair, she has been rather preoccupied,' said Baron. 'She did want me to make it very clear, however, that these are all just stories. She's never been down to the cellar and doesn't know anyone who has. As far as she knows, no one has tried to unseal the entrance in centuries.'

'But this could explain how the creature, or someone pretending to be the creature, has been getting in and out of the House unobserved,' I said.

'That's what I thought,' said Baron. 'Look, I've got to go. I think the Major Domo is getting somewhere with her negotiations. Either that, or she's about to start kicking the door again.'

The phone went dead and I put it away. I brought Penny up to date, and she bounced up and down excitedly.

'That's how the creature gets in here from the loch! That's why the exterior guards keep seeing something that's always gone when they get there. It explains everything!'

'Possibly,' I said. 'I've had another thought, a rather disturbing one. We've talked before about how the Baphomet Group might have been named after the demon or powerful being worshipped by the old Knights Templar. And how this Baphomet might have made a deal with the founding members of the Group. Power and wealth in return for some kind of service. If this Baphomet is still alive and linked to the current members of the Group, what if they bring it with them to their annual meetings? Because the point of each meeting is for the principals to rededicate themselves to the deal their ancestors made?'

'OK,' said Penny. 'You're right, that is a disturbing thought. But then why would the Group go to so much trouble to hold their meetings in different parts of the world? Given all the complications involved in transferring Baphomet from country to country . . .'

'Money can solve most problems,' I said. 'And enough money can make problems disappear. I've been wondering if Baphomet itself decides where the meetings should take place, for reasons of its own.'

'You've clearly been thinking about this a lot,' said Penny. Her eyes widened suddenly. 'What if the price for its gifts or services . . . is human sacrifice? And that's why they have to keep changing the meeting place, so no one will make the connection about the deaths that always accompany it! Do you suppose the Organization knew all this? And that's why they wanted you here?'

'Who knows what the Organization knows?' I said. 'The Colonel only tells me what they tell him, and they only tell him what they think he needs to know. But if the Group have brought Baphomet here with them, what better hiding place than the cellar?'

'Hold it!' said Penny. 'We're missing something. October's death. Why would Baphomet kill one of its own?'

'Maybe October tried to get out of the deal,' I said. 'Of course, another way to look at this would be that everyone in Coronach House is a potential sacrificial victim . . .'

Penny gave me a hard look. 'None of this is convincing me that we should go down into the cellar to confront a very old, very powerful and possibly very pissed-off demon-god thing.'

'Who else could we trust to do this?' I said. 'Ready?'

'After you,' said Penny.

We went back down the stairs in a rather more stately fashion than we'd come up. Taking our time for the sake of our dignity, not because we might in any way be having second thoughts about the wisdom of confronting an angry god thing in its lair. Penny grumbled under her breath.

'Far too many stairs in this case . . .'

When we finally reached the reception area, it was utterly deserted. A thought struck me, and I went over to the front door and checked it was properly locked. Just because people say a thing is locked doesn't mean it necessarily is. But the door was secure. I rattled it a few times, just to be sure, and nodded

approvingly at its weight and sturdiness. A door as heavy as
that would take a lot of getting through.

'Could you smash through a door like that?' said Penny. 'I
mean, if you had to?'

'Probably,' I said. 'If I really had to. Let's hope there's nothing
in the House that's as strong as me.'

I followed Baron's directions to the rear of the House, and
Penny tripped along at my side, humming tunelessly under
her breath. A sure sign that she wasn't as calm and composed
as she appeared. When we reached the door to the escorts'
private bar, it was standing ajar. I looked inside, but the bar
was empty. Presumably they were all working. After the armed
commotion with the guards, the principals probably needed a
lot of comforting. A few more empty corridors brought us to
the furthest wall of the House, and it didn't take long to locate
the blank expanse of richly polished wood panelling. There
were lots of panels within panels and detailed carvings, any
of which could have concealed a secret entrance or a hidden
lock mechanism. Penny beamed happily.

'I always say it isn't a proper old-house mystery unless
there are hidden doors and secret passageways,' she proclaimed.
'I think it's a rule, or an old tradition or something. And if
it isn't, it ought to be.'

We walked up and down the long stretch of wall, leaning in
close to examine the wooden panels, tapping here and there
and testing for concealed entrance points. But there were no
hollow sounds, and not a single ornament or wooden carving
moved under our hands. In the end I spotted the cellar door
concealed in the lines of the panelling, simply because it wasn't
quite as well constructed as the rest. I pointed out the entrance
to Penny, but she still couldn't see it.

'I'll take your word for it,' she said finally. 'How do we open
the damn thing?'

'I don't know,' I said. 'But it's been opened recently.'

She looked at the wall, and then at me. 'You can see that?'

'Only just,' I said kindly.

We both spent some time searching for an opening mechanism, but couldn't find one anywhere. We stood back and looked
at the wall some more.

'Maybe it only opens from the inside,' I said.

'You're full of disturbing thoughts today, aren't you?' said Penny. 'Maybe we should go find the Major Domo and see if she knows any old stories about how you open the bloody thing?'

'Would take too long,' I said. 'I can open this.'

I punched the concealed door, and the heavy wood split from top to bottom. I hit it again and again, the wooden panel jumping and shuddering under the repeated impacts, until finally it just fell apart. I grabbed hold of the broken pieces and pulled them away, watching out carefully for splinters, until a large dark opening yawned in the wall. Just a bit ominously. I blew casually on my knuckles, to make it clear they weren't bruised or scraped, but Penny didn't even glance in my direction.

'Show off!' she said, studying the opening thoughtfully.

I huddled beside her and peered into the darkness. A set of very old, very rough stone steps fell away, descending into the dark further than even my eyes could follow. No railing, and no banisters. I put my hands on both sides of the opening to steady myself and leaned in as far as I could. Penny grabbed hold of the back of my belt, just to be on the safe side.

'Can you see anything, Ishmael?'

'No . . .' I sniffed cautiously. 'The air smells stale, dusty . . . And I'm getting traces of something else. Something I don't recognize.'

'Something alive?' Penny asked tentatively.

'Oh yes,' I said.

I stepped back from the opening. Penny let go of my belt and looked dubiously at the steps leading down into the dark.

'I am not going down there without a light of some kind,' she said, very firmly.

I produced a penlight from my inside jacket pocket. When I turned it on, the beam was surprisingly bright. It didn't travel far down the steps, but at least it was a light.

'This suit came with all kinds of useful items stored in the pockets,' I said. 'Let us praise the Organization and its generosity.'

'What else did they give you?' asked Penny, practical as always.

'Later,' I said.

'Before we start down those steps, descending blindly into

God knows what, shouldn't we contact the Major Domo?' said Penny. 'To tell her we've found the entrance and where we're going, so she can send in a search party or a heavily armed rescue force if we don't come back.'

'Baron knows,' I said. 'He'll tell her. You're just putting this off.'

'Well, yes!' said Penny. 'Come on, there could be anything down there!'

'I know,' I said. 'That's the point.'

We shared a quick grin, and Penny nodded.

'Go for it, space boy.'

'You got it, spy girl.'

I stepped over the rim and started down the stone steps, flashing the penlight's narrow beam ahead of me. There wasn't room for two of us on the stairs, so Penny followed behind me, sticking so close I could feel her breath on the back of my neck. The steps were roughly fashioned, with only an uneven stone wall on one side and an unknown drop on the other. I kept one shoulder pressed firmly against the wall as I descended. I could just make out signs of recent disturbance in the thick dust on the steps below. Someone, or something, had been this way before us. I couldn't make out any actual footprints or animal tracks, but that unfamiliar scent was still hanging on the air. Growing stronger, and more pungent, the deeper into the dark we went. It was unlike anything I'd ever encountered before. And I've come up against some pretty strange things in my time . . .

The stairs fell away into the darkness, going down long past the point where the House's foundations should have ended. We soon left the lights from the House behind, descending steadily in our own small pool of light. The air grew steadily colder, as though we were leaving the warmth of the living world behind.

The bottom of the stairs came as something of a surprise. I just suddenly ran out of steps and found myself walking forward across an uneven stone floor. I stopped, and Penny ran into me from behind. She said a few baby swear words, then broke off as the sound echoed on and on, suggesting we were in a much larger space than we'd anticipated. I swept the penlight's beam back and forth, until it illuminated part of the rough stone wall beside us, rising high above our heads. And on that wall was an antique iron bracket containing an old-fashioned torch; a mass of oil-impregnated wadding wrapped around the head of a wooden haft.

'This doesn't feel like a cellar,' Penny said quietly. 'It's bigger than any cellar has a right to be.'

'I don't think this was ever a cellar,' I said.

I moved over to the wall bracket, and produced a lighter from my pocket.

'You don't smoke!' said Penny.

'Another gift that came with the suit,' I said.

'You don't really think that old torch will light, do you?' said Penny. 'God alone knows how long it's been down here.'

'Someone soaked the wadding with oil recently,' I said. 'I can smell it.'

I pressed the lighter's flame against the head of the torch, and it burst into life. Yellow flames burned smokily, spreading a surprising amount of light. I turned off the penlight and put it away, before removing the torch from its bracket. The flickering glow revealed another wall torch, some distance away. I lit that one too, and the one after that. Warm yellow light spread out from the wall, revealing more of the great open space around us. I put the lighter away and held my torch higher, but I still couldn't see the ceiling. It was just too far above us.

'Someone else must have been down here before us,' said Penny. 'If only to prepare those torches.'

'I'm not getting any human scents,' I said.

'OK!' said Penny. 'Getting seriously spooked now . . .'

I moved slowly forward across the open space, holding the torch as high as I could. Penny stuck close beside me. The combined light from the three torches made it clear we were in a massive stone cavern deep under Coronach House. And from the rough nature of the walls and the uneven surface of the floor, it had not been made by human hands. This was just a hole in the ground, with a House built over it.

'If there's a secret exit with a tunnel leading out into the grounds,' I said, 'it could be that it was originally an emergency escape route for the family in case the House was ever invaded.'

'But who'd know about that now?' said Penny.

'The Major Domo,' I said. 'Maybe she mentioned it to someone else . . . Or maybe someone just found it.'

I kept moving forward, torch held high, and the cavern kept opening up around us. I got the feeling it was bigger than the ground floor of the House above. Shadows jumped menacingly every time I raised or lowered the torch. Damp ran down the dark stone walls, but there were no clumps of fungi or patches of moss. No trace of anything living, except that smell. We finally reached the opposite wall, and found an opening in the stone. Not a door; more like a wide crack, big enough for two people to pass through. I leaned in and extended my torch into the gap, revealing a rough tunnel stretching away. The light couldn't travel far enough to give any idea of how far the stone passage might go. I checked the tunnel floor for footprints or tracks, but there were just more scuff marks in the dust. I stepped back, turned away, and looked round the great open cavern again.

'There's no one else here,' said Penny, but something in her voice suggested she wasn't entirely convinced.

'Not now,' I said. 'But something was here before us. Can't you smell it?'

'No,' said Penny. 'Are we talking about the Coronach creature? Or Baphomet? Or what?'

'Beats the hell out of me,' I said. 'Whatever it is, it's left no tangible trace of itself behind. No droppings, no shed hair or scales, not even a claw mark on the stone floor . . . Which suggests to me that if some kind of beast has been kept down here, it has a human master to clean up after it.'

'Is there anything you can be sure of?' said Penny.

'I can feel fresh air gusting out of the tunnel mouth,' I said. 'And from the smell of it, I'd say it's coming from outside. That tunnel definitely leads out into the grounds.'

'So now we know how the creature gets in and out of the House!' said Penny.

'Not necessarily,' I said. 'Look at the size of that opening. Two men could pass through shoulder to shoulder, but that's about it. Whatever tore October to pieces has to be big, as well as powerful.'

'The Coronach creature is supposed to have been born of a

human family,' Penny said doubtfully. 'So it could be . . . roughly human in size.'

'I've been thinking about the creature,' I said. 'Or at least the one in the story. I wonder . . . Why did the family place their newborn child in the waters of the loch? To drown it? Or because that was the only place the child could survive? And if so, have we been misunderstanding the story all this time?'

Penny frowned. 'But if that's the case . . . why would it keep coming back for revenge?'

'Good question,' I said. 'I think there's a lot more to the original story than we've been told.'

Penny looked around the cavern. 'It's all very . . . clean, isn't it? As if it's been looked after. Maybe the family preserved this place so the creature could come here from the loch. To visit its family . . . A long-lost child coming home . . . Perhaps the entrance upstairs was only sealed off when the creature stopped coming, and they assumed it had died.'

'Hush!' I said, quickly looking round. 'Did you hear something? I heard something . . . Some living thing, coming our way.'

'Is it coming down the tunnel?' said Penny.

'No,' I said. 'It's coming down the steps, from the House. I think we've been led into a trap.'

'Baron!' said Penny. 'That bastard!'

'Could be,' I said. 'Or it could be the Major Domo. She knew about this place all along and never said anything about it till now.'

I moved back towards the stairs, holding my torch high. The yellow glare from the torches on the walls barely touched the bottom steps. Penny strode along beside me, scowling at the stairs.

'Whoever that is, I am going to give them a kicking you wouldn't believe,' she said quietly. 'I have had enough of being led around by the nose. I want some answers, and I'm way past the point of being fussy about how I get them.'

'You're assuming our steadily descending visitor is a man,' I said, just as quietly. 'But those footsteps sound . . . wrong. Too heavy and too widely spaced to be anything human.'

'Oh shit!' said Penny, succinctly. 'You know, this would be

a really good time for you to tell me you've changed your mind about weapons and that you have something really horribly destructive in one of your suit pockets.'

'Sorry,' I said. 'No weapons. Of course, I could always hit it really hard.'

'Sounds like a plan to me,' said Penny.

The footsteps were descending steadily now, a heavy deliberate tread that wanted us to know it was coming. From the sheer weight behind each impact, whatever made those echoing footsteps would have to be at least ten feet tall and maybe half as wide. And that weird scent was getting stronger, sharper. I strained my eyes against the gloom higher up the stairs, struggling for some glimpse of what we were up against. But it seemed to be deliberately holding back, just out of range. Playing with us. Taunting us.

Its scent made no sense at all. There were traces of creatures I recognized and something that was almost human, all of it wrapped up in something else. I laughed suddenly, letting the sound echo; because whatever it was wanted us to be scared, and I wasn't. I've gone head to head with all kinds of unnatural creatures from the darkest corners of the hidden world, some so unnatural they didn't even have heads. I'm still here, and mostly they aren't.

'Don't hold back!' I said loudly. 'I've come a long way to meet you, whatever you are. Come down into the light and let's get this show on the road!'

'You heard what he said!' Penny shouted defiantly. 'You have no idea who you're messing with!'

The footsteps stopped. It was suddenly very quiet in the cavern, apart from the faint crackling of the torches. Then I heard a great intake of breath, of massive lungs filling themselves; and a blast of stinking hot air rushed down the steps and blew out the nearest wall torch. It was suddenly that much darker in the cavern.

'Oh no!' said Penny. 'No, don't do that! Ishmael, don't let it do that!'

'Easy,' I murmured in her ear. 'Don't let it know it's getting to you.'

'But if it blows out the other torch . . .'

'I still have mine,' I said. 'And it'll have to come over here to get it.'

Penny laughed shakily. 'You say that like it's a good thing.'

'If it comes within reach,' I said. 'I will teach it the error of its ways.'

'What if it's bigger than us?' said Penny. 'What if it's as big as it sounds?'

'Then I shall just have to hit it really hard,' I said. 'I'll knock it down, you kick it in the head.'

'Good plan,' said Penny.

There was another great blast of breath, and the second torch on the wall went out. Darkness swept in, swallowing up all of the cavern outside the small pool of light Penny and I were standing in. I could hear her heavy breathing and the pounding of her heart; but she stood her ground because I did. I couldn't see past the bottom of the steps; everything else was lost in the dark. The footsteps started down the stairs again, solid and heavy and worryingly far apart. I concentrated, because suddenly I wasn't sure whether I was hearing something that went on two feet or four. It was coming down faster now, with an almost eager haste, its weight enough to crack some of the stone steps it landed on. I could hear the slow grating of claws on stone, the rasp of its hide scraping against the stone wall. And lungs that worked like massive bellows. How big was this thing? Its scent was strong now, wild and feral.

Another blast of its awful breath hit me in the face like a slap, and my torch went out. The creature sprang down the last few steps and landed with a crash at the bottom. I threw the useless torch away and scrabbled for the penlight in my pocket. The darkness was complete. I couldn't see a thing. The creature growled, like a long, slow roll of thunder. I felt the reverberations of its heavy tread through the floor as it started forward, along with the sound of claws gouging deep into the stone. I grabbed Penny by the arm, and turned her round to face the opening in the wall.

'Run!' I said.

'Run?' said Penny. 'What happened to hitting it really hard?'

'We don't know what we're facing, and I don't like the odds,' I said. 'Go!'

'I'm gone!' said Penny.

I flashed the penlight's beam on the gap in the wall, and she plunged into it. I was right behind her. Sometimes the better part of valour is running for your life and praying that you're faster than whatever's coming after you. The tunnel was just big enough to hold the two of us, its jagged stone walls full of nasty protrusions more than ready to bruise unwary arms. Penny stumbled over the uneven floor, but kept going. I yelled at her to run faster. Something was pounding across the stone floor of the cavern. Something so big I could feel the disturbance it made in the air behind me. I didn't look back.

The creature roared deafeningly, as though it sensed it was being cheated of its prey. It was almost at the tunnel opening. I was running beside Penny now, the penlight's narrow beam leaping ahead of us. I could have run faster; but I wouldn't leave Penny behind. I could smell fresh air up ahead, feel the night air gusting down the tunnel from the loch. And then the heavy footsteps behind us crashed to a halt, at the opening to the tunnel. It can't get in, I told myself. It can't come in after us, because it's too big to fit through the opening.

I braced myself for another of its deafening roars or the stench of its disgusting breath, but there was nothing. Not a sound. Penny kept running, and I ran with her. The tunnel stretched away before us, until suddenly it began to rise up and we were scrambling up a steep slope. We burst through a thick covering of bracken and out into the cool night air, right on the bank of Loch Ness.

Penny and I stood together, leaning on each other, looking out over the dark waters of the loch. We'd come out so close to them we could have jumped in if we hadn't stopped ourselves in time. Penny was shuddering, breathing raggedly as she struggled to get air back into her heaving lungs. I patted her shoulder absently, concentrating my gaze on the dark opening to the tunnel. I wasn't breathing hard, but I could feel my heart racing. I don't normally like to run from anything; but when you're caught in a trap with a creature you can't even see, only a fool hangs around to show how brave he is. There wasn't a sound from back in the tunnel, and the rank smell that had been filling my head was gone. Penny finally straightened up, took a deep breath, and pushed herself away from me.

'Look at you, you're not even sweating!' she said disgustedly. 'Don't you ever get out of breath?'

'Sometimes,' I said, diplomatically.

She shot me a suspicious glance. 'Did you run away to protect me? If I hadn't been there . . . If it had just been you, would you have stayed and fought that thing?'

'Hell, no!' I said. 'The best way to beat a trap is not to be in it.'

Penny didn't look like she was sure she believed me, but she nodded stiffly. The tunnel was still quiet, so I turned my back on it and looked around. The moon shone brightly, shimmering here and there on the thickening mists. Bright lights illuminated patches of the grounds around Coronach House, but most of the exterior was lost in the dark. There wasn't a breath of moving air anywhere, and the night was quiet. Not even a note of birdsong. The whole setting was oddly still, as though listening for something.

'Did you get even a glimpse of what that thing was?' said Penny. Most of her composure had returned.

'No,' I said. 'It kept to the dark, right to the end. But it sounded big and powerful, and very dangerous. I can't help feeling it was using the dark to hide from us. Why else would it deliberately blow out the lights? It went out of its way to make enough noise to let us know it was coming. As though it wanted to scare us . . .'

'Trust me,' said Penny, 'it succeeded!'

'But why would it need to?' I said. 'Something so big and powerful and dangerous?'

'Could it have been scared of us?' said Penny.

'Unlikely,' I said.

'Could it have known about you? What you are?'

'Even less likely.'

'At least now we know the creature is real,' said Penny.

'But was that the Coronach creature? Or Baphomet? Or something else entirely?' I said.

'And was that what killed Jennifer Rifkin and October?' said Penny.

'Seems likely,' I said. 'What are the chances of there being more than one horribly dangerous creature on the loose?'

'Don't even go there!' said Penny.

'But . . . was that thing the killer?' I said. 'Or just the killer's trained attack dog? The murderer or the murder weapon?'

'Baron sent us down into the cellar,' said Penny. 'Maybe it belongs to him.'

'Baron only knew about the cellar because the Major Domo told him about it,' I said. 'And I have to wonder . . . what made her suddenly think of it?'

Penny made a loud exasperated sound. 'Enough complications! My head hurts. Is there anything about this case we can be sure of?'

'Yes,' I said. 'That things are a lot more complicated than we thought.'

'I will slap you,' said Penny.

I flashed the penlight's beam down the tunnel mouth, but I couldn't see anything. Or hear or smell anything.

'It's not coming after us,' I said. 'Let's get back to the House. The mist's getting heavy, and it's cold out here.'

Lights burned fiercely from Coronach House, even through the thickening grey haze, but most of the building was lost in the gloom. I thought briefly of will-o'-the-wisps, that only exist to lure travellers to their doom, though it wasn't like we had anywhere else to go. We struck out across the open ground, leaning on each other for support. It was further than I thought; and the uneven earth was full of sudden potholes, and unexpected vegetation that snagged viciously at our clothes. With the loch quickly hidden in the mists behind us, and just vague lights ahead, I felt worryingly lost. I even began to wonder if we had emerged where I thought; if that really was Coronach House ahead of us. And then two armed guards suddenly appeared out of the mists, blocking our way. They took one look at us, screamed, spun round, and ran away; disappearing back into the mists and the dark. Leaving behind nothing but the wailing sounds of their retreat. I looked at Penny.

'You know, I am really not impressed by the quality of guards they have here.'

'Good to know we can still scare someone,' said Penny.

Somewhat heartened, we carried on towards the House. The night remained uncomfortably still and quiet. Thick mists surrounded us like a dull-grey ocean, and the lights from the House didn't seem to be getting any closer.

'Why didn't the creature follow us into the tunnel?' Penny said suddenly, in a way that suggested she'd been thinking about that a lot.

'It was too big to fit through the crack in the wall,' I said.

'Then how could it be using the tunnel to get in and out of the House?' said Penny. 'I thought the tunnel explained everything, but if the creature couldn't use it . . . we're back where we started.'

'And something that size would have had real problems trying to sneak around Coronach House,' I said. 'Someone would be bound to hear it, even if they didn't see it.'

'My head is really aching now!' said Penny. 'Nothing makes any sense. Ishmael, this case is getting seriously scary. And you know I don't scare easily. Whatever that thing was, it sounded big . . . I mean seriously big. I could feel the floor shaking under its weight . . . Could it be something supernatural?'

'Wouldn't surprise me in the least,' I said.

Coronach House suddenly loomed up before us, emerging reassuringly from the mists. I suppressed a sigh of relief, and soon we were threading our way through the rows of parked limousines, heading for the front door. Penny looked at the cars, and came to a sudden halt. I stopped with her.

'Ishmael, would you think me horribly weak if I suggested we just get in a car and leave? So we could put together an army of reinforcements, then come back and kill that thing?'

'That's just being sensible,' I said. 'But how many people here might die in the time it would take us to get back? You go if you want. I'll give you the car keys and some contact numbers. But I have to stay.'

'You know I wouldn't leave you,' said Penny. She shook herself briefly. 'Of course we can't leave. It's just . . . that thing shook me. And I'm not used to being shaken.'

'Neither am I,' I said. 'It's because it's unknown. That's what's getting to us. The thing in our heads, in our imagination, is far worse than anything real could ever be. Once we've had our first good look at it we'll feel a lot better.'

'Don't put money on it,' said Penny.

We reached the front door, and of course it was still locked. I pounded on the heavy wood with my fist, making enough noise to raise the recently deceased, but no one came to answer. I looked the door over carefully. It really was very heavy and very solid.

'Maybe we could go back and grab one of those guards?' said Penny. 'Have them contact someone inside the House.'

'I'm not in the mood to go running through the mists chasing after spooked security men,' I said. 'I am, however, very much in the mood to hit something.'

I punched the door with all my strength. The wood made a low disturbed sound, like a struck bell, but didn't crack or split. I hit the door with my shoulder, putting all my weight behind it. The wood did crack this time, but the door still wouldn't budge. I moved back several steps and hit the door at a run. The door shuddered in its frame, but held; and I was bounced back on my arse. Penny looked down at me, put a hand to her mouth, and tried not to laugh.

I got back up, dusted myself off with some dignity, and looked the door over carefully. When in doubt, cheat. I located the hinges and smashed the wood around them with my fists, hitting it again and again until splinters flew through the air. The door rocked in its frame. Once the hinges had been suffi- ciently loosened, all I had to do was hit the door again with my shoulder, and the sheer weight of the door ripped the hinges out of the frame. The door fell backwards into the entrance hall, measuring its length on the floor with a marvellous crashing sound.

'Nice one, sweetie,' said Penny. 'Very restrained.'

'I thought so,' I said.

I strode into the reception area like a conquering hero. Penny followed after me, shaking her head. I didn't look round to see, but I had no doubt that was what she was doing. The reception area was warm and bright, and completely deserted.

'Where is everyone?' said Penny. 'They must have heard the noise.'

'You would think so, wouldn't you?' I said.

I went back to the door, picked it up, and leaned it back into place. It filled the gap well enough, if a little crookedly.

'That isn't going to fool anyone,' said Penny.

'It's the thought that counts,' I said. 'Neatness is next to godliness. Provided you tear enough pages out of the dictionary.'

We both looked round sharply, as we heard footsteps approaching from a side corridor. Penny and I moved quickly to stand together, shoulder to shoulder.

'No running this time, right?' said Penny.

'Right,' I said.

'We stand our ground and fight.'

'Oh yes.'

'Those are human footsteps, aren't they?' said Penny.

'Absolutely,' I said. 'One man, by the sound of it.'

'Good.' Penny let her breath out and scowled fiercely. 'I swear I never used to be this jumpy.'

'Not to worry,' I said. 'I can always grab the door and hit him with it.'

'I can live with that,' said Penny. 'You flatten him, and I'll kick him till he dies.'

Baron came strolling out of the side corridor, and then stopped and looked at us. There was clearly something about our stance he found troubling. He blinked a few times, and then smiled uncertainly.

'Hello? Is something wrong? I heard this noise . . .'

'That was just me,' I said. 'Shutting the door.'

He looked at the front door, not quite in its proper place, and blinked a few more times.

'What are you doing here?' he said. 'I thought you were going to check out the cellar?'

'We did,' I said. 'And now we're back. We need to talk, Baron.'

'Yes,' he said. 'We do. But just you and me, Ishmael. Because I think we need to talk about our past. About the people we used to be. And that will almost certainly mean discussing some things you haven't got around to telling your new partner.'

I turned to Penny. 'He may be brusque, unpleasant and positively delighting in bad timing; but he's right. I need to do this. You'd better go and find the Major Domo, see what she's up to.'

'She still hasn't got her people out of the dining hall,' said Baron. 'They started making demands, and that was never going to go well.'

'There you are,' I said to Penny. 'You can help with that.'

'I don't want to leave you,' said Penny, glaring suspiciously at Baron.

'Don't worry,' I said. 'I can handle him. And I really don't want the Major Domo left to her own devices. You're not afraid to go on your own, are you?'

I knew that was the one thing I could say to make her go. Penny nodded stiffly, turned her back on me, and strode off. I gave Baron a cold, considering look.

'This had better be worth it.'

'It will be,' said Baron. 'We have decisions to make.'

'I've never needed your help to decide what to do.'

'You've never been in a position like this.'

I looked at him thoughtfully. 'What are we talking about exactly?'

'You and me,' said Baron. 'And what's really going on in the House.'

'Then lead on,' I said.

We walked through empty corridors, looking straight ahead and not talking to each other. There was no sign of anyone else; not even the guards who were supposed to be on duty. Baron took me all the way back to the escorts' private bar. When we got there, the door was standing wide open and there wasn't a sound from inside.

'They're all gone,' said Baron. 'We have the place to ourselves. Probably the only part of the House where no one will think to look for us.'

He had a point. I gestured for him to go in first. The bar was entirely deserted, though heavy scents from some of the escorts still lingered. Baron reached for a bottle left standing on the bar top as I closed the door carefully behind me.

'Most of the escorts are busy quieting the principals' nerves,' said Baron. 'In their various ways . . . Others have gone to ground, wherever they feel most safe. And I overheard a few talking about hot-wiring a limo and making a run for it. Can't say I blame them. Coronach House doesn't feel safe for anyone, right now. Would you care for a brandy? That always was your tipple of choice, whatever identity you were using.'

I was pretty sure the bottle he was holding was the same one Penny had used to hit him over the head, but I didn't say anything. Just nodded briefly. Baron grabbed a couple of glasses off the bar top and brought the bottle and glasses over to the nearest table. He sat down, and I sat down facing him. Both of us being very polite, like the practised colleagues and adversaries we were.

'How's your head?' I said.

'Better,' said Baron. 'You can tell your girl there are no hard feelings.'

'She's not my girl,' I said. 'She's my partner.'

'That is a change for you,' said Baron. 'You never trusted anyone to get that close when I knew you.'

'You never really knew me,' I said.

'We worked together.'

'Not the same thing.'

He nodded, conceding the point.

'So,' I said. 'What is it that you're so sure we need to talk about?'

Baron splashed decent amounts of brandy into the two glasses, and pushed one towards me. I accepted it casually, though long experience suggested he'd had more than enough time to poison the drink. And what were the odds of there being just one bottle left out on the bar top, and my favourite tipple at that? It would suit Baron's sense of humour, to make a weapon out of something that had been used to hurt him. Of course I was immune to most poisons, but Baron didn't know that. Or at least had no right to know it. That's the problem with being an agent: you see so many possibilities in everything that you can argue yourself into a position where you don't dare do anything. So I mentally crossed my fingers and took a good drink from my glass. Baron nodded approvingly at this apparent sign of trust, and had a good drink himself. Then we both sat back, smiled at each other, and waited to see if anything would happen.

'I did think about saying "To absent friends!",' I said, after a while. 'But that would have raised too many ghosts.'

Baron raised an eyebrow. 'I thought you didn't believe in ghosts?'

'Memories, then.'

'Ah yes . . . So many memories in our line of work. Sometimes we're the only ones left who still remember certain things ever happened.'

'Just as well,' I said. 'What did you expect me to find down in the cellar?'

'I don't know,' said Baron. 'Something useful, hopefully. What did you find?'

I was ready to tell him about the unnatural creature that had come after us in the dark, but at the last moment I changed my mind. It wasn't so much that I didn't trust Baron as I didn't trust some of the ways this conversation could go. There were times when we had achieved great things together, and other times when we were at each other's throats. Quite literally. People in our line of work don't usually carry grudges, because you never knew when you might find yourself in need of an ally. But something about this conversation felt off, felt wrong . . .

'The cellar turned out to be more like a cavern,' I said carefully. 'We did find a tunnel leading out into the grounds.'

Baron grinned, and toasted me with his glass. 'I knew it had to be there. It was the only way the creature could appear and disappear so easily.'

I just nodded. This didn't feel like the time to discuss my doubts on the matter.

Baron sat back in his chair and looked at me steadily. 'You know, I thought this job would be an easy number. Look after a few VIPs, take the money and run. But nothing's gone right since I got here. First Rifkin, then October, and all the time more mysteries piling up than I can shake a blunt instrument at. And you know the principals are going to find some way to stick the blame on us, whatever happens. Why do we do this, Ishmael? Why do we put our lives, and what's left of our sacred honour, on the line for people we know aren't worthy of us?'

It seemed like a serious question, so I did him the courtesy of considering my answer. 'Why do we do this? To protect the world, from people like us.'

Baron laughed briefly, bitterly. 'There are no people like us.'

I considered him thoughtfully. 'You haven't changed at all, from when we first met in '64. You're not telling me that's all down to plastic surgery?'

He smiled. 'No, that's just for public consumption. I've had more than a little help from some alien tech I was exposed to back when I was working for the Beachcombers. That was after you'd moved on . . . But what about you, Ishmael? Every time we bump into each other I look for some change, some small sign of aging, but you're always exactly the same. It's like time stands still for you. Either that, or you've got a really shocking portrait tucked away in an attic somewhere.'

'Clean living and a vegetable diet are two things I've always avoided,' I said. 'I can't help feeling there's a connection.'

'I thought for a while you might be an Immortal,' said Baron. 'Until I met one, and he was positive you were never one of the family.'

'Keep guessing,' I said. 'We all have our secrets.'

'Yes,' he said. 'We do.'

'Why did you leave the Organization?' I asked. 'What did you find out about them?'

'You have to discover that for yourself,' he said. 'Or you'll never believe it.'

We sat together, studying each other over our brandies, thinking our thoughts.

'We've both seen some strange places,' Baron said finally. 'Encountered all kinds of unnatural threats, and done harsh things necessary to keep the world safe. We've known all manner of wonders and horrors, and kept any number of secrets to ourselves. Have you ever wondered whether it was all worth it? The things we did and were forced to do?'

'The world is still here,' I said steadily. 'And so are we. That puts us ahead.'

'But we were always following someone else's orders,' Baron insisted. 'Someone else's agenda. Never captains of our own ships or masters of our souls.'

'Everyone has to serve someone,' I said. 'We all need to believe in some cause to give our lives purpose and direction. That's just how it is for most people.'

'But we're not most people,' said Baron. 'The things we do matter. Haven't you ever felt the urge to go out on your own, be your own man? To work one score big enough to give you serious "Fuck off!" money, so no one could ever pressure you again? Did you never want to see what you could really do, with the leash off and none of the restraints other people impose on you? Are we letting ourselves down . . . by not being everything we could be?'

He looked and sounded completely sincere. As though these were real questions about things that really mattered to him. He also looked like he really cared about what my answers would be. I had to wonder why. I gave the matter some thought, and chose my words carefully.

'Like I said, sometimes the world needs protecting from people like us. And all the things we might do.'

'Is ambition such a bad thing?'

'Depends where it leads you.' I looked at him steadily. 'What are we doing here, Baron? What is this all about? You were never the introspective type before.'

He looked into his glass, to avoid looking at me. 'It's all getting out of control. Something tells me we're only one step away from a bloodbath. This whole house is just a killing ground waiting to happen. And I've been wondering . . . whether it might not be better to just call it quits and get the hell out of here while we still can.'

'You mean, leave everyone here to die? Without our protection?'

'You think anyone in the House is worth risking our lives over?' said Baron.

'I think . . . it's not up to us to decide who is and who isn't worth saving,' I said.

'I don't know if you and I were ever really friends,' Baron said slowly. 'Colleagues, certainly. We've spent a lot of time in each other's company down the years. We've had some good times, done some good work.'

'When we weren't trying to kill each other,' I said. 'You've worked for some very dubious people in your time.'

He shrugged. 'If we'd really wanted each other dead, we would have done it long ago. I have more in common with you

than anyone else I know. Who else has seen the things we've
seen, done the things we've done? Who else knows what we
know, and the secrets we've kept? So if I tell you I don't want
to be here when everything goes to hell . . . If I asked you to
leave right now and come with me, so we could retire from the
insane world we live in, would you do it?'

'Why?' I said. 'Why would I do that?'

'To save both our souls, perhaps.'

I looked at him. Did he want to go but didn't have the
nerve to quit on his own? Or did he want me out of here
because I was getting too close to something he didn't want
me to know about? Or was I missing something? It didn't
matter. Whatever doubts I might have had about my job or
myself, I knew my duty.

'No,' I said. 'I wouldn't leave, not even if we really were
friends. I have a job to do.'

Baron pushed back his chair and got to his feet, his face
completely empty of emotion. 'All right then. That's it. Don't
say I never gave you the chance. Now we both have to play
this game out to the end, whatever it takes us. And let the blood
fall where it may.'

He left the bar, and I still wasn't sure what we'd really been
talking about.

SIX
Questions Without Answers

I went wandering through the deserted corridors of Coronach House. Going nowhere in particular, just thinking. I couldn't shake off the feeling that Baron had been trying to tell me something and I'd missed it. I couldn't believe he was so ready to run out on his job. For all his flexible morality and constant readiness to look out for his own best interests, he'd always been dependable when we worked together. Had he discovered something about the principals or the killer that made him believe he had no choice but to run for his life? Did he foresee some threat or danger coming that I'd missed?

Of course, it had been some time since I'd last seen him; but given some of the things he and I had faced together in the past, I wouldn't have thought there was anything that could break his nerve. Though anyone can break if they're hit hard enough.

Had Baron known about the creature in the cellar? Was that why he'd sent us down there? Did he expect it to kill me? Or was I supposed to kill the creature because he couldn't? Did he think it would scare me so much I'd agree to leave with him? He should have known better than that. I walked faster, as though I could leave behind all the questions that were worrying me. Would Baron run now, on his own? Or would he hang on until he could convince someone else to go with him and keep him company? Running might not seem so bad if he wasn't the only one doing it.

I was frowning so hard my forehead ached and my hands had clenched into fists. None of this made any sense. I'd known Baron under a dozen different names and identities, fought beside him and against him; and whether I was guarding his back or trying to stick a knife in it, I'd always known where I stood with him. We'd fought in underground wars and hunted with hell hounds, gone on pub crawls with gods and monsters, and brought the hammer down on alien incursions. And I never once saw him flinch. So why was he so determined to run? And why did he think I'd go with him?

All right, I'd run from the creature in the cavern. But that had been more in the nature of a tactical retreat. I'd always intended to go back and face it again, once I'd fixed the odds so they were more in my favour. It was Baron who taught me to never let your enemy set the terms of engagement. I couldn't believe he'd changed that much, so I must be missing something. What did he know about what was really going on in Coronach House that I didn't?

Angry voices caught my attention as I entered the reception area, and I sighed quietly because I recognized both of them. Penny and the Major Domo were standing at the foot of the stairs, deep in something that wasn't actually a conversation; more an armed stand-off. They were right in each other's faces, and the only reason they weren't shouting was because some things need to be said in a conversational tone in order to have the full and proper impact. The two women were so wrapped up in scoring points off each other they never even saw me coming. I looked around in case there was a bucket of cold water handy.

'You don't give me orders!' said the Major Domo.

'I'm trying to solve your problems,' said Penny. 'Since you don't seem able to.'

'You are the problem!' said the Major Domo.

'Ladies . . .?' I said tentatively, and then gave them my best innocent stare as they both turned to glare at me. 'So . . . what's up?'

'You went off without me!' said Penny. 'Leaving me to deal with this impossible woman!'

'This is my House!' said the Major Domo, glaring impartially at Penny and me. 'I will not have my orders defied by people under my authority!'

'We're not under your authority,' Penny said sweetly, moving to stand beside me. 'We speak for the Organization. Isn't that right, Ishmael darling?'

'We do,' I said cautiously. 'But preferably in a calm and supportive way. We're supposed to work with people on the ground, not antagonize them. Unless we feel we absolutely have to, of course. What's the current problem, Major Domo?'

'My staff are still refusing to come out of the dining hall!' said the Major Domo. 'Despite all my best efforts to persuade them.'

'Persuade?' said Penny. 'You mean threaten and intimidate. Honestly, Ishmael, I've never heard language like it. And I've worked in publishing.'

'I think the staff and chauffeurs are safe enough where they are,' I said judiciously. 'At least they aren't getting under anyone's feet or causing trouble. And as long as they're locked in, we always know where to find them. There! Problem solved! What's next? Ah . . . yes. Major Domo, I need to talk to the principals. All of them, right now. It's time I got some straight answers.'

The Major Domo looked like she wanted to laugh in my face, but didn't. 'You really think you can give orders to the Baphomet Group? You don't have anything like the authority.'

'The Organization does,' I said. 'Be so good as to inform the principals that if just one of them fails to cooperate, the Organization will send in a full security team to shut this meeting down, and drag them all off in chains to the nearest interrogation centre.'

My voice was cold, determined, and packed full of menace; and the Major Domo didn't so much as blink. She just nodded shortly, turned her back on Penny and me, and set off up the stairs. Penny waited till she was sure the Major Domo was out of earshot, then looked at me thoughtfully.

'Can you really do that? Can the Organization really do that?'

'I don't know,' I said cheerfully. 'Let's hope we don't have to find out.'

'You do like to push your luck, don't you?' said Penny.

'I do,' I said. 'I really do.'

'Where's Baron?' asked Penny, with the air of someone who'd only just happened to notice he wasn't with me.

'Sulking, somewhere. We had words.' I could feel my frown coming back. 'He wanted to cut and run, before things here get really bad. And he wanted me to go with him.'

'Cut and run?' said Penny. 'He doesn't know you very well, does he?'

'That's just it,' I said. 'He does.'

Penny didn't quite know what to make of that, so she just shrugged and slipped her arm through mine.

'He hasn't exactly contributed much to this case, has he?'

'No . . .' I said. 'And that's odd. He's easily as experienced as me when it comes to dealing with the more dangerous corners of the hidden world. I would have sworn he was one of the few people in the House I could depend on.'

'You make him sound someone special,' said Penny.

'He was,' I said. 'At one time all kinds of subterranean groups would line up for the chance to bid for his services. Just knowing he was on the case was often enough to make the other guys surrender or quietly disappear. He had a reputation, whereas I was just a rumour.'

'Then what's he doing here, slumming it as Head of House Security?' said Penny. 'A high-and-mighty title for someone who's basically just a glorified bouncer.'

'I don't know,' I said. 'He wouldn't tell me. Or perhaps he tried and I didn't listen.'

Penny waited until it was clear I had nothing more to say, and then squeezed my arm against her side comfortingly. The Major Domo came striding back down the stairs to join us. She addressed me directly, ignoring Penny.

'I've spoken to the security guards, and they are talking to their principals.'

'You've been all the way up to the top floor and back down again?' said Penny. 'And you're hardly sweating at all! You must be in really good shape, for a woman of your age and weight.'

The Major Domo allowed herself a brief condescending smile. 'I used my phone.'

'Then why go upstairs at all?' I said.

'Because I wanted to speak privately.' The Major Domo sniffed loudly. 'You seem to have made something of an impression on the security men, Mister Jones. They have promised to do their best to deliver their principals as soon as possible. I have suggested a suitable meeting place. This way.'

She strode off without looking back. I looked at Penny, she looked at me, and we both shrugged pretty much in unison before setting off after her. We deliberately didn't try to keep

up with the Major Domo, so she was forced to slow her pace
to accommodate ours. You can't let some people get away with
anything. We ended up at the room the Baphomet Group used
for their very private discussions. I supposed it made sense. It
had to be the most secure room in the House. The Major Domo
unlocked the door, stepped back, and invited us to enter with
a grand gesture. I strolled into the room as though it had been
my idea, with Penny sauntering grandly along at my side.

'I could make myself available to assist with the meeting,'
said the Major Domo.

'Most kind,' I said. 'But that won't be necessary. The principals will speak more freely on their own.'

The Major Domo looked like she was about to take umbrage,
but I forestalled her with a raised hand.

'Because they are almost certainly going to be talking about
things they won't want other people to know about. Things that
it wouldn't be safe for someone like you to know.'

The Major Domo nodded stiffly, conceding the point; and
left, shutting the door quietly but firmly behind her.

The moment she was gone, I set about searching the room.
Remembering what the undercover reporter Emily had said,
about secretly recording the Group's discussions. Penny quickly
caught on and helped me look, but there wasn't a single listening
device to be found anywhere. So either Emily had been bluffing,
to strengthen her position, or someone had removed them.
Someone professional. I abandoned the search, and Penny and
I pulled up chairs and made ourselves comfortable. Because
the one thing we could be sure of was that the principals wouldn't
hurry themselves to join us. Very important personages always
like to make the little people wait; to remind them of their
place.

In the end, only four of them turned up. January and March
came in together, looking like they owned the place and were
thinking of selling. January was a sharp-faced young woman
with a blonde buzz cut and an almost brutally cut business suit,
while March was a middle-aged man who dyed his remaining
hair and looked like he'd slept in his suit. I studied them thoughtfully, remembering how they'd both emerged from the same
room after the gunfire had stopped. They both glared at me,

because I hadn't stood up when they entered. I nodded cheerfully back at them. They tried glaring at Penny, but she just
waggled the fingers of one hand at them, entirely unconcerned,
and they gave up.

August walked through the door so quietly and unobtrusively
it took me a moment to realize he'd arrived. Another middle-
aged man, a grey little person with a grey personality and a
suit to match. He looked at me, and then at Penny, as though
we didn't matter. Then he looked at January and March in the
same way.

December was the last to arrive. The oldest member of the
Baphomet Group was smartly turned out in an old-fashioned
suit, as though his valet had only just finished dressing him. He
looked tired and drawn, but still carried himself with a certain
dignity. He nodded at the other principals, and looked coldly at
me. Saying nothing, leaving it to me to make the running.

'Where are the others?' I said.

'We are only responsible for ourselves,' December said
heavily. 'No one member of the Group has authority or influence over any other. That's the way it's always been.'

'Excuse me for just a moment,' I said.

I went back out into the corridor where, just as I expected,
the Major Domo was still hovering.

'I have only four principals,' I said. 'And I need the other seven
to complete my set. So be a dear and contact the other principals' security people. Tell them to get their principals down
here right now, by force if necessary, or I will come up there
and do it for them. In a way I guarantee the principals will not
thank them for.'

She must have heard something in my voice, because she
didn't argue. Just nodded quickly and got out her phone. I went
back into the meeting room, and closed the door.

The four principals sat together on the same side of the long
table, facing me and Penny. Trying to look like they were in
charge of the meeting. Though they might have to be here, their
expressions said, they had no intention of saying anything that
wasn't in their best interests. I decided to start with January
and March, because they looked the least interested in talking.

'Isn't this nice?' I said. 'All good chums together. Let's start with a simple one. Where were you two when October was killed?'

'Go to hell,' said January, her voice cold and clipped. 'We don't have to talk to you.'

'You have no authority over us,' said March, trying to sound confident and missing by a mile. 'You're just a jumped-up little functionary.'

I smiled, and they both stirred uncomfortably in their chairs.

'I speak for the Organization,' I said. 'You know what that means. So don't even think about mentioning lawyers or business privilege, or any of that happy crappy. Tell me what I need to know, right now, or I will make your lives a living hell.'

January and March looked at each other, and then January nodded stiffly, while March sulked.

'Well?' I said.

'All right!' said March. 'If you must know, we were together. In my room. The truth is . . . we've been having an affair.'

He put an arm round January's shoulders. I saw her stiffen, just for a moment, and then she smiled at me defiantly.

'Yes,' she said. 'That's right. We're having an affair. And it's none of your business.'

'Horse pucky!' Penny said loudly, and both principals jumped, just a little. Penny smiled nastily at January and March. 'They don't have the right body language for lovers. She's practically shrinking away from him, and he's sweating too much. I've never even seen them exchange glances, never mind hold hands. So try again, sweeties. You can't fool Auntie Penny.'

'No more lies,' I said to January and March, making my voice harsh and brutal. 'Either you talk to me or you talk to the Organization's interrogators at Ringstone Lodge.'

They both sat up straight, March's arm falling away from January's shoulders. It was obvious from their faces that they'd heard of the Lodge, and the kind of things that go on there. Even though, strictly speaking, they shouldn't have. Ringstone Lodge is where the Organization sends people to get the truth out of them. By any means necessary.

'Oh, all right,' March said crossly. 'No need to make such a fuss. The truth is . . . we've been holding secret meetings. Plotting together, combining our knowledge and resources so

we could seize the advantage at Group meetings. A purely
business relationship to give us a bit of an edge.'

December stared at them, aghast and outraged. 'That is
completely unacceptable! It goes against all the rules and
traditions of the Baphomet Group! Each member has always
been obliged to sink or swim through his or her own efforts;
it's the only way we can be sure of arriving at purely impartial
decisions. No previous generation of the Group has ever stooped
to such behaviour!'

January sneered at him, her mouth taking on an ugly
shape. 'And that's why you're on the way out, old man! You're
the past, and we are the future. You think business is a game,
while we know it's a war. Where everything is justified and
the sharks wait for those who sink.'

December was so shocked he had to fight to get his words
out, but he'd barely started before he had to break off again as
the door slammed open and the Major Domo came hurrying in.
She hesitated as she realized all the principals were glaring at
her, and then quickly turned away to look at me.

'I've contacted the security people on the top floor, and put
the fear of God into them. Or, to be more accurate, the fear
of the Organization. They've all sworn they'll get their principals
moving as soon as possible.'

'Hold everything!' said Penny. 'Now that is interesting . . .'

'What is?' I said.

'Something's going on between August and the Major Domo,'
said Penny. 'I don't know why I didn't see it before, but it's
obvious now we've got them both in the same room. It's all in
the body language. The way they move; the way their bodies
orient towards each other, almost unconsciously. The way they
look at each other and then quickly away, in case someone's
noticed. Take my word for it, Ishmael: if anyone in this room
is having an affair, it's August and the Major Domo. Who would
have thought?'

'I'll take your word for it,' I said. 'You always spot these
things before I do.'

December looked from August to the Major Domo, and then
back again. January and March looked intrigued, and grateful
that the spotlight had moved on to someone else. The Major

Domo was trying very hard not to look flustered. August just sat where he was, with no change of expression.

'Well?' December said harshly. 'Is this true, August?'

August looked at the Major Domo, and she moved quickly over to stand beside him, one hand resting possessively on his shoulder.

'Yes,' she said. 'It's true. We're together.'

'How did that happen?' said Penny.

The Major Domo looked at her defiantly. 'We met. There was a spark. Love isn't just for the young.'

'But it's not just sweet talk and larking around, is it?' I said. 'You're both too . . . businesslike for that. You're both getting something out of this relationship.'

'August has promised to buy Coronach House and give it to me,' said the Major Domo. 'So it can finally belong to my family again. In return . . . I encouraged my staff to keep their eyes and ears open around the principals and report to me everything they learned. So I could pass it on to August, and he could use the knowledge to his advantage. We're both of us alone in the world. We have to take our support where we can find it.'

December was shocked all over again. 'I am severely disappointed in you, Major Domo! We placed our trust in you, to preserve the security and integrity of our meetings while under your roof. You have let us down. You can be sure we will be making a formal complaint to your employers.'

'Complain and be damned!' said the Major Domo. 'I won't need employers once Coronach House is mine again.'

'And you, August,' said December, ignoring the Major Domo to turn his full scorn on his fellow principal. 'You should have known better. It's bad enough you've compromised this whole meeting's decisions for your own temporary advantage . . . But to lower yourself by entering into a relationship with a servant!'

'Oh shut up, December!' said August, only the slightest tinge of emotion entering his voice. 'January's right. You are old, and old-fashioned. You have no idea of what's really going on with the Group any more.'

'Well, really!' said December, and then seemed genuinely lost for anything more to say.

'Have you heard enough now, you grubby little man?' said January, scowling viciously at me. 'You've dug up all our sordid little secrets, and what good has it done you?'

'Right,' said March. 'Just a waste of everyone's time. And I've got a headache. I'm going back to my room.'

'None of you are going anywhere,' I said. 'This isn't about you, or the Group; it's about murder. First Jennifer Rifkin, and then October. January and March, you both have a motive for wanting the other principals dead . . . because if word of your agreement got out, your place in the Baphomet Group would be compromised. No one would trust you any longer, and you'd probably be dismissed from the Group. Right, December?'

'Of course,' said December, nodding firmly. 'They would be thrown out, and their positions taken over by the next most senior members of their families. They would both be financially and socially ruined.'

'Try it,' said January. 'See how far you get.'

'Oh, I will,' said December. And suddenly he was smiling like a shark.

'Of course, you have a motive too, December,' I said. 'You disapproved of the way the new generations were doing things. If you'd found out what January and March and August were up to, you might have thought making a hard example of a few bad apples would help discourage others.'

December snorted loudly. He seemed honestly amused. 'Then why would I start by killing October, who as far as I know was utterly blameless? And can you really see a man of my advanced years doing that kind of damage to October, or his room? Do I look like a killer?'

'Unfortunately, few killers do,' I said. 'And while you might not have been able to do the deed yourself, you could always have paid someone else to do it.'

'And then there's you, August,' said Penny. 'Why did you feel the need for a secret advantage at these meetings?'

'Because I'm not a real businessman, like the others,' said August. He sounded suddenly tired, and the Major Domo patted him comfortingly on the shoulder. He reached up to put his hand on hers, and then looked defiantly at me. 'I never wanted to be part of the Baphomet Group; never wanted to be head of

my family's business interests. I just inherited the whole mess.
But I couldn't give it up without sacrificing most of my wealth,
and endangering my family's security. I never wanted to be
here, never wanted to play the game . . . But if I had to, I didn't
want to disgrace myself or my family. So I turned to . . . Helen.'

He smiled at her, and she smiled at him.

'She has been my rock and my comfort,' said August. He
turned his attention back to me, his expression cold and
unmoved. 'I'm probably the only person in Coronach House
who doesn't have a motive for murder, because I never wanted
to come here in the first place.'

'But that is your motive, August,' I said patiently. 'If enough
of the Baphomet Group were killed, the Group would collapse
and then you'd be free of them forever.'

'I can alibi August,' the Major Domo said immediately. 'We
were together when Miss Rifkin was killed, and again when
October died. There's no way he could have done it. Or me,
for that matter. We can vouch for each other.'

'That just makes you sound like an accomplice,' said Penny.

The Major Domo looked at her sharply, and then looked
away. Some of the confidence seemed to go out of her. Clearly,
that thought hadn't occurred to her.

The door burst open, as several security men rushed in. They
all started to speak at once, shouting to be heard over each
other; until I stood up and glared them into silence. I pointed
to one guard.

'You. What's your name?'

'Irwin, sir.'

'What's happened?'

'They're all dead!' said Irwin. He had to force the words out,
his voice thick with hysteria. 'All the other principals have been
murdered!'

Everyone at the table was suddenly on their feet. Nothing
we'd been saying seemed to matter any more. The four surviving
principals moved to stand together, like frightened children.
Penny shook her head slowly, as though she didn't want to
believe it. I kept my composure, and nodded brusquely to the
security man before me.

'How?' I said.

'Just like October,' Irwin said sickly. 'They've all been torn to pieces and thrown around the room. It was horrible. Horrible . . .'

He broke off, looking tired and confused. The other guards milled around, not knowing what to do or say. And I had to wonder just how bad the murder scenes must have been to reduce experienced security men to such a state. I questioned them, and they hurried to add their confirmation, stumbling over each other to make clear what had happened. They seemed almost pathetically eager to talk; and desperate to make me understand they had no idea how it could have been done, because none of them had left their positions even for a moment. There was no way the murderer could have got past them, no way at all . . . I had to raise my voice again to get them to quiet down. They dropped into mumbles and frightened glances, huddling together like sheep in a storm.

I gave the matter some thought, while everyone looked expectantly at me.

'Did anyone leave the principals' rooms after the gunfight ended?' I said.

The security men looked at each other, consulted quietly for a while, and finally agreed that the only people to leave had been some of the escorts the principals summoned to serve them.

'How many escorts?' I said.

More consultation, and some arguing, before they finally agreed on a figure. Five escorts; four men and one woman. I pointed at two of the guards.

'Find them,' I said. 'Now.'

They left, in a hurry. I questioned the remaining guards carefully, working my way through the sequence of events until I had a fair outline of what had happened. They all insisted they hadn't seen or heard anything out of the ordinary after I'd brought the gunfight to an end. Everything had been perfectly calm and quiet until word came from the Major Domo that I wanted all the principals to come down for questioning. The guards had knocked on their principals' doors and politely explained the situation; and when they didn't get any answers, they assumed their principals didn't want to be bothered. Which was understandable, given that they had escorts with them.

When the guards were obliged to knock a second time, to make their case more firmly, and still couldn't get an answer, they braced themselves and unlocked the doors. They looked inside, ready to back straight out if they encountered anything embarrassing. And then . . .

'Hold it!' I said. 'You had keys?'

'We all do,' said Irwin. 'The principals trust us. Trusted us . . .'

'Not more locked room murder mysteries,' Penny murmured disgustedly. 'I hate those.'

'If only five of the escorts left,' I said to Irwin, 'what happened to the others?'

'We think they were murdered along with their principals,' he said quietly. 'It's hard to be sure, because the pieces were all over the place . . . And the heads were missing.'

'All of them?' I said.

The security guards nodded quickly. The consensus was that the killer must have taken them with him.

I thought about that. Practical considerations aside (like how anyone could carry off so many heads at once without being noticed), why take them at all? To disguise a growing appetite for human brains? Or to make identification of the victims that much harder, to slow down the investigation? Without the heads, how could I be sure all the principals and the unnamed escorts were dead? I realized everyone was waiting for me to say something, including Penny, so I did my best to look like I knew what I was doing. Details could wait. A massacre had taken place on my watch.

'I need to see this for myself,' I said.

'You'll have to do it on your own,' Irwin said immediately. 'None of us are going back to those rooms. Whatever happened up there . . . wasn't natural.'

'Wait a minute,' said the Major Domo. She seemed somehow smaller, her voice lacking its usual confidence. 'Where's Baron? Where's my Head of Security? Why isn't he here?'

'I saw Baron go into February's room, not long ago,' said August. 'I don't know what business Baron had with him.'

February's security guard reluctantly came forward, and the others stepped back to let him pass. He was carrying a bundle; something wrapped in a blanket. He unwrapped it to reveal a distinctive red-leather jacket, torn to ribbons and soaked in blood.

'I found this in February's room,' he said. 'Among the . . . pieces. This is Mister Baron's jacket, isn't it?'

I took the tattered thing from him. Beneath the stench of fresh blood, I could just make out Baron's familiar scent.

'Perhaps he had reason to believe February was a target,' Penny said quietly. 'Or maybe he had his own personal arrangement going . . . Either way, he must have been in the room when the killer came in. And was killed, trying to stop him. I'm sorry, Ishmael.'

'Did you find anything to confirm Baron was actually in the room?' I asked the security man.

'It was all just bits and pieces,' said the guard. 'And without the heads . . .'

'Of course,' I said. 'I understand.'

Penny moved in close beside me, trying to comfort me with her presence. 'Was Baron a friend of yours, Ishmael? I was never sure.'

'Neither was I,' I said. I dropped the blood-soaked jacket on to the table, and then took out a handkerchief to clean blood from my hands. It took a while. No one said anything. The four surviving principals stepped back from the table, but couldn't seem to take their eyes off the jacket.

'Baron was my colleague,' I said finally. 'And the last time we spoke, we parted on bad terms. He wanted to get the hell out of here, and he wanted me to go with him. If I'd agreed, he might still be alive. But I couldn't just go and leave the job unfinished.'

'Of course you couldn't,' said Penny. 'He should have known that.'

'Yes,' I said. 'He should.'

'If Baron had done his job, the principals might still be alive!' the Major Domo said loudly.

I looked at her, and she stopped talking. I turned back to February's security guard.

'Did Baron say what he was doing, visiting your principal? Had February sent for him?'

'February didn't explain his business to me,' said the guard.

'But then I wouldn't expect him to. I can say that Baron had never visited February's room before, and the principal let him in immediately.'

I turned my back on all of them, and moved off a way. Penny came after me.

'What is it, Ishmael?' she said quietly.

'One of the first rules in this line of work,' I said, just as quietly, 'is that if you don't have a body you can't be sure someone is really dead. It's always possible Baron took advantage of the situation to fake his own death; so he could leave the House and avoid taking the blame for what's happened. It wouldn't be the first time he's done that and then reappeared sometime later with a new identity.'

'Do we have to decide that now?' said Penny.

'No,' I said. 'For the moment, we assume he's dead. We have more important things to worry about.'

I turned back to the principals. 'It seems clear the other principals were killed because they had escorts with them. January and March were busy with each other, August had the Major Domo, and December . . . wasn't interested. That's what kept the four of you alive. I think the killer was one of the escorts. Or someone pretending to be an escort; like the maid Emily, who turned out to be an undercover reporter. The principal invited the escort in, and the escort killed him. Or if a creature was involved, the escort let it in.'

'How could a creature have been involved without any of the guards noticing?' said December.

'How does this creature do anything?' I said.

'Maybe it's invisible,' said Penny.

'Don't even go there!' I said. 'More likely, there are hidden doors and passages in the rooms, connected to the cellar under the House.'

'That's not possible,' the Major Domo said immediately. 'They were all sealed off long ago.'

'Yes, well,' said Penny, 'you would say that, wouldn't you?'

'The door to the cellar was unsealed,' I said. 'Who knows what else might have been done without your knowledge?'

'We're only alive because we had no interest in escorts?' said December.

'You had no reason to allow anyone into your rooms,' I said.

'Dear God!' said December.

The four surviving members of the Baphomet Group stood close together, trying to draw strength from each other. I expected them to announce they were leaving, immediately; but instead they all faced me with the same surprisingly stern resolve.

'None of us will leave Coronach House until you come up with some answers, Mister Jones,' said December. 'That is what you're here for.'

'Exactly!' said January.

'You must find the killer,' said March.

'Before he kills again,' said August.

Now they were back giving orders they all seemed on more comfortable ground.

'We need to know who wants us dead and why,' said December. 'Or we'll never feel safe again wherever we are.'

'We can't call in any of the usual authorities,' said August. 'The media would be all over a story like this. We'd never hear the end of it.'

'You are in charge here, Mister Jones, for the next twelve hours,' December said flatly. 'Because we know you, and you seem to know what you're doing. And you have the Organization's authority to help you find answers.'

'But once your time is up, we will have no choice but to demand the Organization remove you in favour of a full investigatory team,' said August. 'And risk the resultant publicity.'

'If we're forced to do that,' said January, 'We'll ruin you, for failing us.'

'Depend on it,' said March, smiling. 'We'll destroy you.'

'I don't respond well to threats,' I said.

'Then don't fail us,' said December.

Satisfied that they'd put me in my place, the principals came out from behind the long table and busied themselves giving orders to the security men. To guard them first and the House second, and shoot anyone who tried to leave before the killer was caught. The guards looked pleased to have someone taking charge, and to have useful work to do. The Major Domo quickly detailed people to cover all the exits and windows on the ground floor, and the guards left in a hurry. Grateful for a chance to show they were still worth something, after allowing their principals to be killed.

With the guards gone, the room seemed very quiet. The four principals looked steadily at me, but had nothing more to say. They seemed more astonished than horrified at what had happened. As if they couldn't believe people from their cosseted and heavily protected world could be murdered so suddenly and so easily.

'Has anything like this ever happened before?' I said.

'No,' said December. 'Not in our entire history. Personal security is one of the reasons we go to such lengths to preserve our anonymity.'

'Hold everything! Go previous!' said Penny. 'Your entire history? You mean all the way back to the Knights Templar?'

The principals shared a patronizing smile.

'That is just a story, my dear,' said December. 'The Group adopted the Baphomet name when it was first formed, some two hundred years ago. So people would go chasing after the myth, rather than try to uncover our true names and history.'

'We're just businessmen,' said March, smirking.

'So there never was a Baphomet?' said Penny.

'Originally?' said December. 'Who knows? But if there ever was such a thing, I can assure you it has nothing to do with us.'

Penny looked at me. We were both thinking the same thing. *Then what came after us, in the cellar?*

'Outside the Group, did any of you know the other principals?' I said. 'As friends or colleagues, business partners or rivals?'

'No,' said December. 'Contact between members of the Group outside annual meetings is strictly forbidden.' And then he glowered at January and March, who glared right back at him. December sighed heavily. 'But of course, I can't be sure of that any more.'

'Don't expect us to mourn the dead,' said August. 'We don't care, apart from how it might affect us financially. We don't care about anything unless it hits us in the pocket. That's how it is in the Baphomet Group.' He smiled, very briefly. 'And you wonder why I never wanted to be part of it?'

'What about the escorts who died along with the principals,

just for being in the wrong place at the wrong time?' said Penny. 'Do you care about them?'

'Of course not,' said January. 'What an odd question!'

'They were just people we hired,' said March. 'We can always hire more.'

Penny turned to me. 'You talk to them. Before I start throwing things.'

'I strongly advise all of you to stay in this room,' I said to the four principals. 'Lock yourselves in. You'll probably feel safer keeping an eye on each other, and I can station guards outside the only door. Admittedly that didn't help much the last time, but you'll know better than to open the door now, won't you?'

'And, of course, you'll always be sure where we are,' said August.

'That too,' I said.

'What will you be doing?' asked December.

'I need to examine the murder scenes,' I said. 'See if there's anything the guards might have overlooked.'

'While they were panicking and puking,' said Penny.

'Well, quite,' I said.

January and March looked like they might be about to object, but December glared them into silence. August looked at the Major Domo.

'I want to stay with you,' she said, 'but I can't. I have work to do. To keep you safe.'

'Then go,' said August. 'We'll be fine here.'

I thought for a moment they might kiss, but I don't think they liked to in front of so many people. The Major Domo left the room without looking back. And I looked after her and wondered how far she would go to help free August from the Group he hated.

As I climbed the stairs, heading yet again for the top floor, I realized I could smell blood on the air. I didn't hurry. It wasn't as if there was any point. And Penny was already growling under her breath as she grew short of breath. The smell became stronger once we reached the landing on the middle floor.

'You're smelling blood, aren't you?' said Penny. 'I know that look. Did you smell it before, when you were breaking up the gunfight?'

'No,' I said. 'With so much cordite on the air, it masked all other scents. I'm beginning to think that might have been the point.'

'You think our killer knows about you?' said Penny. 'I mean, what you are and what you can do?'

'I don't see how,' I said. 'But there's a lot about this case I don't understand.'

We finally reached the top floor, and I pretended to look around for a while as Penny got her breath back. She finally nodded curtly, and we headed for the principals' rooms. The corridor was almost unnaturally quiet. All the doors had been left standing ajar. Bloody footprints stood out clearly on the carpet outside some of the doors, from where guards had gone in and come out again. The stench of blood and death was now so heavy even Penny could smell it. She wrinkled her nose, but said nothing. I led the way slowly down the corridor, carefully pushing open one door after another so we could peer in. Every room was the same. Furniture wrecked, and deep claw marks gouged into the walls. Bones and body parts, organs and viscera, human insides reduced to a crimson and purple mess. And blood splashed over everything. This was more than murder, it was butchery.

The stench was almost overpowering. Penny had to put a hand over her mouth and nose again.

'All this destruction was deliberate,' I said finally. 'To conceal any evidence the killer might have left behind.'

'You really think a human being could do something like this?' said Penny. 'What about the creature that chased us out of the cellar?'

'I'm still thinking about that,' I said.

'Could the creature be some kind of . . . supernatural attack dog?' said Penny, just a bit desperately. 'Something that could appear out of nowhere, do its work, and then disappear again? That would explain how it could do all this and never be noticed. Are there such creatures; in your experience?'

'I've heard of such things,' I said carefully. 'But it seems to me . . . that what happened here is too deliberate to be the work of any animal. Someone, or something, went out of their way to tear these bodies apart beyond any hope of recognition. And then smashed up every bit of furniture in every room. They didn't miss a thing. The destruction speaks to a creature's strength and savagery; but an animal would get tired, or bored, long before it finished this many rooms. And it wouldn't do exactly the same thing, every time; that speaks to human planning, and forethought. Add to that the missing heads . . .'

'Which has to be connected to Jennifer's missing brains,' said Penny.

'No,' I said, 'That was only done to distract us. To make us think about what kind of creature would suck out someone's brain; so we wouldn't think about other things. Like why everyone here is dying. The missing heads don't necessarily mean anything.'

I chose one room at random and stepped carefully inside, bending right over to examine the wreckage and the scattered body parts up close. I tried to identify the various organs, so I could be sure exactly how many bodies I was dealing with, but most of them had been crushed to a bloody pulp. Presumably deliberately. Penny stayed in the doorway, doing her best to breathe through her mouth. No matter how carefully I examined the murder scene, I couldn't find a single piece of evidence to prove a creature had been present in the room. No tracks, no tufts of hair or shed scales . . . Even the claw marks in the walls weren't distinctive enough to point to a particular species.

'Could those marks have been made artificially?' said Penny, following my gaze. 'I saw a film once where they had this really big club with claws sticking out of it . . .'

'I don't know,' I said. 'There's no shortage of evidence in this room, but none of it adds up to anything. Are you sure you wouldn't care to join me?'

'No thank you,' Penny said firmly. 'These are new shoes.'

I understood. Penny had seen her share of blood and gore when her family and friends were murdered; but the brutal slaughterhouse atmosphere of this whole corridor was too much, even for her. There was a terrible casualness to all the death and destruction, as though whoever was responsible didn't actually care. There was no sense of delight in the slaughter, no personal satisfaction; just someone doing a thorough job. A professional. Like me. I went back out into the corridor, and Penny and I stood together for a while, thinking our separate thoughts.

'How could all this have happened without the security guards hearing something?' Penny said finally.

'Good question,' I said. 'With only one answer that makes sense. All these murders must have taken place during the gun battle. The sounds were drowned out by the constant massed gunfire.'

'Seven murders?' said Penny. 'And the wrecking of the rooms?'

'The gunfight went on for quite a while,' I said. 'Time enough for a professional killer who'd planned it all carefully in advance. I think the gunfight was deliberately started to provide a cover for the murders. The security guards were so taken up with shooting at each other and trying to stay alive, you could have rehearsed a brass band in these rooms and the guards wouldn't have noticed. It must have begun with the killer being invited into a principal's room, passing as one of the escorts. That principal would have been killed immediately. Then the killer tricked the guards into opening fire on each other and set to work. Slipping in and out of one open door after another, unnoticed in the general chaos.'

'I hate the thought of the first victim actually inviting his killer in,' said Penny, shuddering briefly. 'I mean, that's just creepy . . .'

'Yes,' I said. 'It is. The kind of cold-bloodedness you only get with a professional assassin.'

'You'd still expect experienced security guards to notice something,' said Penny.

'They were ducking in and out of doors up and down the length of the corridor,' I said. 'Firing at each other, dodging return fire . . . It would have been easy enough to miss one more figure, experienced in the ways of not drawing attention to himself.'

'He'd still have needed ice-cool nerves,' said Penny. 'And balls of solid brass.'

'Like I said, a professional.'

'But after everything that happened in these rooms, he would have been soaked in his victims' blood! Wouldn't he?'

'You'd think so, wouldn't you?' I said. 'I don't have an answer for that yet. But that's why only four principals appeared when I called for them to show themselves after the gunfight was over. The other seven were already dead. Along with their escorts.'

'And Baron?' said Penny.

'Almost certainly,' I said. 'I was really hoping he might have got away, but that's looking more and more like wishful thinking. You know . . . the killer was probably standing right here in the corridor when we arrived. Hiding in plain sight among the guards. I could have looked right at him and never known it.'

'So now we're assuming our killer is a man? And not a creature?' said Penny.

'I don't know,' I said. 'Given the state of the rooms and the bodies, and the strength and savagery involved . . .'

'Oh, come on!' said Penny. 'You can't have it both ways!'

'I think you'll find I can,' I said. 'Right up until some final piece of evidence decides it, one way or the other.'

'But your theory depends on the killer being human, disguised first as an escort, so no one would react to him entering the principals' rooms, and then as a security guard. Even though the creature we heard down in the cellar was big. Really big.'

I thought about that. 'The Major Domo was quite emphatic about there being no other usable hidden doors or secret passageways in Coronach House, but she took her own sweet time telling Baron about the door to the cellar and the tunnel connecting it to the grounds outside. She might be hoarding other secrets, for her own reasons.'

'Maybe she's doing it to protect August?' said Penny. 'You saw the way she was with him.'

'Yes,' I said. 'Well spotted there. What do they see in each other? She has all the warmth and emotional appeal of a dead fish, and he's such a grey little man. Clearly they're using each other to get what they want, but still . . .'

'It's probably just sex,' Penny said wisely. 'There's nothing like having one birthday too many, and noticing that the equipment's getting a bit old, to make you want to use it while it's still working. And anyway, even the shallowest personalities can find room for deep emotional waters.'

'It's possible, I suppose,' I said. I looked up and down the empty corridor, and nothing of any value looked back. 'We need to track down the missing heads. If only so I can count them and assure myself of the exact number of people who died here. I wouldn't put it past one of the principals to have staged all this, just so he could pull a disappearing act.'

'Like Baron?'

'Baron is dead,' I said. 'He loved that jacket.'

'All right,' Penny said steadily. 'What do we do now?'

'We locate the surviving escorts and question them. It's always possible they saw something . . .'

'You like that big Scarlett woman, don't you?' said Penny.

'Are you kidding? She scares the crap out of me.'

Penny grinned. 'I think that's part of her job description.'

We started back down the corridor, heading for the stairs. Penny stared straight ahead, so she wouldn't glance into any of the open doorways we passed. The stench of so much spilled blood filled the air, like so many silent screams.

'How could any man do this?' she said finally.

'You'd be surprised what some people are capable of,' I said.

'No,' said Penny. 'I meant how physically could any one man do all of this. The sheer strength and stamina involved in tearing so many people limb from limb, and then going on to totally destroy seven rooms . . .'

'You have a point,' I said. 'Even I'd be hard pressed to cover this much ground in the time available . . .'

'Are we back to thinking it must be a creature?' Penny said dangerously. 'Only I've had to change my mind so many times, my thoughts are getting whiplash.'

'I don't know what to think,' I said. 'There's still no clear motive for any of this. If someone hired a professional killer, how would they stand to profit? Could this be down to revenge? Someone who was ruined by the Group's business decisions? Or some conspiracy freak who thinks he, or she, is saving the world? Or . . . possibly some rival Group, running a power play

and hoping to take the Baphomet Group's place as secret masters
of the financial world? Have I missed anything?'

'What if the death and destruction is an end in itself?' said
Penny. 'Could the Coronach creature be trying to drive everyone
away from what it still thinks of as its home?'

'My head is going round and round in circles,' I said. 'And
I have a horrible suspicion it's about to disappear up its own
medulla oblongata.'

'Or . . .'

'Enough!' I said. 'One more theory and I will run screaming
from the House, plunge into the loch, and head-butt the monster
in the face!'

'I'd pay good money to see that,' said Penny. 'So what
approach are we going to take with the escorts?'

'I've changed my mind,' I said. 'I think before that we need
to talk to the servants holed up in the dining hall. The reporter
Emily said it first and the Major Domo confirmed it: servants
often overhear things they're not supposed to. It's always
possible the staff know something that they don't realize is
significant but we might.'

'Show me your hands,' Penny said sweetly. 'I want a good
look at these straws you're grasping at.'

When we got to the dining hall, the door was still firmly locked.
Beyond it I could hear a steady murmur of voices arguing
among themselves. I knocked politely. There was a sudden hush,
as all the voices broke off. A single set of footsteps approached
the door, cautiously.

'If that's the Major Domo again, you can piss right off!' said
a harsh voice. 'After what you said the last time, we're not
talking to you any more. Apart from this bit, obviously.'

'This is Ishmael Jones,' I said winningly. 'Representing the
Organization and investigating the murders. I need to talk to you.'

There was a pause, and some really agitated muttering,
before the voice spoke again.

'This is . . . John Smith. Chauffeur. Go ahead and talk. We're
listening.'

'Smith and Jones,' I said. 'What a coincidence! You know,
this would all go a lot easier if you'd just unlock the door . . .'

'Not a hope in hell,' said Smith. 'This door is staying locked until you've found the murderer and done something appalling to him. Don't even think of trying to force the door; we've barricaded it. All of us chauffeurs have guns, along with a complete willingness to use them on anyone who surprises us.'

'Please come out,' I said. 'Or I can't guarantee your safety.'

'You can't anyway,' said Smith. 'And anyway, we don't feel like answering questions. About anything. We don't want to be involved. We don't know what's happening, but whatever it is it's nothing to do with us. We're quite happy to just sit it out here until it's over. One way or the other.'

'Seven more principals have died,' I said.

'We know,' said Smith. 'The Major Domo told us. The general feeling in this room is better them than us. And we want to make it very clear that no one is going to pin the blame on us for anything that's happened here.'

'Why would anyone want to blame you?' I said.

'Because they always try to blame it on the little people! They think that's what we're for.'

'He has a point,' said Penny.

'Thank you!' said Smith. 'Whoever you are. Who is that?'

'I didn't hear anything,' I said. Just to mess with his head.

I looked the closed door over carefully. I was pretty sure I could smash it in, barricade or not, but I didn't see the point. And I really didn't like the idea of jumpy chauffeurs with guns. There was always the chance innocent bystanders might get hurt. I didn't need to question anyone in the dining hall that badly.

'All right,' I said. 'Stay put. I'll send someone to let you know when it's safe to reappear.'

'You couldn't send out for some pizza, could you?' said Smith. 'Only we're starting to get a bit peckish in here.'

'How would we deliver it to you?' said Penny.

'You could always shove it under the door.'

I was about to say something unfortunate when a familiar industrial-strength perfume came wafting my way. I looked round and there was the escort Scarlett, striding determinedly down the corridor. Still dressed up in her smart business suit, but looking tired and worn down and not especially glamorous any more. As I moved away from the door to greet her, Penny put a possessive arm through mine; I gave her an innocent smile, and she gave me a "You're not fooling anyone!" look.

Scarlett crashed to a halt in front of me. 'There are only a few escorts left,' she said flatly. 'We need to talk to you.'

'Suits me,' I said. 'Where are the others?'

'Holed up in our private bar again. Staying well out of everyone's way and hoping not to be noticed.'

'By the killer?' said Penny.

'By anyone,' said Scarlett. 'This has turned out to be one hell of a weekend.'

'Yes,' I said. 'So many dead.'

'And we probably won't get paid,' said Scarlett.

'I thought you people always got paid in advance,' Penny said sweetly.

'It's the extras,' said Scarlett. 'They mount up.'

We followed Scarlett back through the deserted corridors. Penny made a point of still hanging on to me firmly. Just in case Scarlett's perfume drove me mad with lust, instead of making my eyes water. The heavy quiet made the corridors seem disturbingly sinister. Scarlett was more than a little jumpy, though she was trying hard not to show it. She breathed a sigh of relief when we finally reached the door of the private bar, where she gestured for Penny and me to stand back while she performed a special knock and then announced herself loudly. Someone unlocked the door and opened it just the barest crack to look at Scarlett, before finally standing back and letting us in.

The four other surviving escorts had arranged themselves around a small table, looking tired and glum, like birds of paradise whose colours had run in the rain. Five opened bottles of spirits stood on the table. No one was bothering with glasses. Scarlett made a point of checking the door was properly locked before introducing her companions.

'That's Lola, cock in a frock. That's Georgina, professional tomboy. That's Maurice, muscle man. And that's Lady Paine, la Belle Dame sans Merci.'

The small quiet woman dressed mainly in black leather straps smiled tiredly. 'Only the one who hurts you can make the pain go away.'

'Rather more information than I needed,' said Penny.

Scarlett pulled some chairs forward, and the escorts made room for us at their table. No one offered us a drink.

'Is this really all of you that's left?' I asked.

'Just us,' said Scarlett.

'But if seven principals are dead,' said Penny, 'and there are five of you here, that means only two of you died up there . . .'

She broke off, as the escorts looked at her condescendingly.

'The principals often liked more than one of us at a time,' said Scarlett.

'Oh . . .' said Penny.

'I'm sorry about your friends,' I said. 'But there are questions I need to ask.'

'We don't talk about our clients,' Lola said firmly. A winsome presence in a pretty dress, with a deep contralto voice.

'Not those kind of questions,' I said. 'The five of you only survived the massacre on the top floor because you left before the gunfire started. Why did you do that?'

'Because our clients were sleeping,' said Scarlett. 'They'd had enough of us.'

'We'd worn them out,' said Maurice, a large muscle-man with an engaging smile and hardly any clothes.

'Part of our job is knowing when we're not wanted any more,' said Lady Paine.

'If we hadn't left when we did . . . we'd have died with the others, wouldn't we?' said Scarlett.

'Yes,' I said.

The escorts seemed shaken, but not particularly upset. Scarlett saw me looking round the table, studying faces and reactions.

'We're colleagues, not friends. Much the same as in your world.'

I thought about Baron. I'd last seen him right here, sitting at this table. I said nothing.

'You have to understand,' said Penny, 'leaving at such a propitious time does look just a teeny bit suspicious . . .'

'Cut it out!' said Georgina, a tall bulky woman in dungarees. 'It's not like any of us had a motive. We'd never even heard of the principals before we came here.'

'You had no idea who your clients were going to be?' I said. There was general shrugging around the table.

'It was an agency booking,' said Scarlett. 'And for the kind of money they were talking about, you don't ask questions.'

'Why would we want to kill any of them?' said Lola.

'Perhaps they wanted you to do something you weren't prepared to do?' Penny suggested.

The escorts all had the same smile.

'That can happen,' said Lola.

'And then we charge extra,' said Lady Paine.

I tried some more questions, but it was clear they had nothing useful to contribute. Scarlett only brought me here because she wanted to make it clear they were all just not-so-innocent bystanders, lucky to be alive. I looked at Penny, but she had no more questions, so we left the escorts to their drinking. They locked the door behind us the moment we were outside. I looked up and down the empty corridor.

'What now?' said Penny.

'Damned if I know,' I said. 'This whole case is a mess. No clear causes of death, no clear motives; and only a handful of suspects, none of whom stands out. Too many questions, and far too many dead bodies.'

'Typical case for us, then,' said Penny. She paused. 'That bar was where you had your last chat with Baron, wasn't it?'

'Yes.'

'If he wasn't your friend, what was he?'

'I don't know,' I said. 'It's just . . . there aren't many who've been in this business as long as me. Baron was one of the few people I could talk to about the places I've been and the things I've done.'

'You can always talk to me,' said Penny.

'But Baron wouldn't judge me.'

'You think I would?'

'I'd be disappointed if you didn't,' I said. 'I haven't always been a good man.'

'You're a good man now,' said Penny. 'Nothing else matters.'

'It matters to me,' I said.

* * *

We walked together for a while, not going anywhere in particular, just thinking our separate thoughts. I was trying to remember when sudden death and vicious murders had stopped bothering me and become the everyday business of my life. I've known a great many monsters in my time, and far too many of them were people.

'You've known Baron since the sixties,' Penny said finally. 'I sometimes forget how old you really are. You look like you're in your twenties, but you must be . . . what? In your seventies now?'

'I don't age like you,' I said. 'Sometimes I wonder if I'll ever age. But, as a wise man once said, it's not the years, it's the mileage.'

'All the changes you've seen,' said Penny. 'The world must seem very different now from when you first . . . arrived. Is there anyone else you can talk to? Anyone who knows you as well as Baron did?'

'A handful of old friends, some old enemies, and a few in between.' I smiled tiredly. 'If you last long enough in this game, the sides switch back and forth so often they can start to seem irrelevant. But there are some people I've got to know really well down the years.'

'People like you?' Penny asked tentatively.

'No,' I said, 'But . . . different people. Different from everyday Humanity, with their own need to stay hidden and make their lives in the shadows of the world.'

'Well?' said Penny, as I paused. 'Go on! You can't just stop there. What kind of people are we talking about?'

'Well,' I said. 'People like the Immortals. Or the Spawn of Frankenstein. Or the elves . . .'

'No . . .!' said Penny, her eyes wide. 'Elves? Really? Oh, I would love to meet an elf!'

'No you wouldn't,' I said. 'Trust me.'

'Have you ever found anyone who could understand what it's like to be like you?' said Penny. 'Human but not human?'

'I do get lonely,' I said. 'Sometimes.'

She slipped her arm through mine and snuggled up close to me. 'Come on, sweetie. Let us busy ourselves by being useful.'

'Yes,' I said. 'There's always that.'

SEVEN
Who's Really Who

A thought occurred to me, bubbling up to just below the point where it was any use. I wasn't sure what it was, but it felt important; so I allowed it to lead me back to the furthest rear wall in Coronach House. Penny strolled along beside me, looking at me curiously. She could tell I was concentrating on something. She didn't ask what, which was just as well, as I didn't have any answer for her. Just an increasing certainty that I'd missed something. I finally came to a halt before the ragged hole in the wall panelling; from when I'd got impatient with the door that wouldn't open and showed it the error of its ways. I looked at the dark opening for a while, and even leaned in to study the stone steps leading down to the cellar. Penny looked at me, trying to work out what I was thinking. Which made two of us.

'This means something,' I said, eventually. 'There's a clue here. An important clue.'

'Clues are good,' said Penny, encouragingly.

A breeze blew up the stairs and out of the hole; cool damp air from the depths of the House, carrying with it the distinctive smell of the cellar and just a trace of the creature we'd found there. Penny shuddered briefly, and I knew it wasn't from the cool air. She was remembering how the unseen beast stalked and terrorized us in the dark, until the only sensible thing to do was run for our lives.

'We did the right thing,' I said. 'We wouldn't have stood a chance against that creature in the dark.'

'That was the only reason I agreed to run,' said Penny. 'Because I couldn't see it. The dark made me feel . . . helpless.'

I nodded. 'Imagination can fill the dark with terrible things. Far worse than they could ever be in reality.'

'It was the sounds it made,' said Penny, hugging herself

tightly. 'The heavy tread, and the way its claws scraped on the stone floor. It sounded huge . . .'

'That's it!' I said. 'The size of the creature! That's what's been bothering me . . . I could feel the size and weight of it through the vibrations it made in the floor as it moved. It must have been huge!'

'It's nice when you agree with me so emphatically,' said Penny. 'But how is that helping?'

'The creature came down the steps to join us in the cellar,' I said. 'From up here, in the House. But how could a creature that big get through a hole that size?'

Penny looked at me, and then at the gap in the wall. 'We had to bend over to get through,' she said slowly. 'And the steps were so narrow we had to go down them in single file. There's no way a creature of the size we heard could get through that gap. Is there?'

'That's just part of it,' I said. 'We're still missing something. The details don't add up.'

I paced up and down, because that helps me think. Regular movement helps to dispel stubborn thoughts. Penny stood back and let me get on with it, knowing better than to try and prompt me in case it derailed a train of thought. I stopped suddenly as the pieces finally came together, in the only way they could.

'Sometimes the killer seems like a man,' I said. 'And some-times it seems like a creature. We've been assuming the creature is some kind of attack dog, following its master's orders . . .'

'That was my idea, actually,' said Penny.

'But I think it's simpler than that,' I said, pressing on. 'We're dealing with a man who can become a creature. Someone who can change their shape and size.'

'A werewolf!' said Penny. 'It's a werewolf!'

'Well,' I said, 'not necessarily. There are other kinds of shape-changers. But someone who can change their shape and size is the only answer that fits.'

'But . . . that means anyone in the House could be the killer,' said Penny. 'Changing into a beast to do the killing and then back again afterwards. Hiding from us behind a familiar face. Everyone's still a suspect! We're right back where we started.'

'At least now we can make sense of what's happened,' I said. 'We know how the murders were committed. The missing brains, the missing heads, the torn-apart bodies and the wrecked rooms . . . all just distractions. To keep us from thinking about the one thing that really mattered. How the killer was able to come and go so easily without being noticed.'

'I thought we decided he was using the hidden tunnel connecting the cellar to the grounds?' said Penny.

'Undoubtedly,' I said. 'But the tunnel was only big enough to hold the two of us. The creature couldn't follow us in.'

'Then why didn't he change to his human form and come after us?' said Penny.

'Because that would have meant emerging into the light,' I said. 'And we would have seen him. And the only reason he'd care about that is because we'd recognize him. The killer is someone we know.'

'A man with a monster inside him,' said Penny.

'Lots of men have monsters inside them,' I said.

'Not literally.'

'You'd be surprised.'

Then we both looked round sharply as the Major Domo came hurrying down the corridor towards us, with enough momentum to suggest she'd been building up a head of steam for some time. She was frowning heavily, her mouth set in a grim line.

'She doesn't look happy, does she?' said Penny.

'Maybe she's not regular,' I said. 'That can mess up your whole day.'

'I've been searching the whole House for you!' the Major Domo said harshly, as she crashed to a halt before us. And then she broke off, as she took in the jagged opening in the wall. 'What have you done to my wall! That panelling dates back to Jacobite times . . .'

'Well, next time it'll know to cooperate,' I said. 'Why have you been looking for us, Major Domo?'

'I'm going to have to contact the families of the dead principals soon,' said the Major Domo, reluctantly turning away from the damaged wall.

'Really?' I said. 'Why would you want to do that?'

'Because they deserve to know the truth about what's happened!'

'But not yet,' I said. 'The moment word gets out, we'll be at the mercy of the civil authorities and under siege from the world's media. All hope of finding the killer and keeping the situation contained will be gone. Is that what you want, Major Domo?'

'Of course not!' said the Major Domo. 'The scandal would ruin Coronach House. It was just something August said: about how relieved his family would be to learn he was safe, and not one of the dead principals. It started me thinking . . . But I suppose you're right.'

'I usually am,' I said. 'Consider the repercussions if word gets out before we're ready. The death of so many important financial figures will have a devastating effect on the world markets. Add to that the principals' families arguing over the wills and disputing who inherits what . . . We're talking about major economic chaos.'

'Could that be the motive for so many murders?' said Penny. 'Someone in the right place with the right advance information could make a killing in the markets . . .'

I nodded approvingly. 'Could be. We still don't know whether our monstrous killer is the mind behind everything or just a hired gun.'

'What monster?' said the Major Domo. 'What are you talking about?'

'It can wait,' I said. 'We're still throwing theories at the wall to see which of them sticks. For now, you need to concentrate on keeping a lid on the surviving principals. They're not to have any contact with the outside world. Take away their phones, if you have to. You can bet some of them will be getting restless, and want to go wandering. Don't let that happen. If you have any trouble keeping them in line, just refer them to me. And tell them I'm looking for someone to make an example of.'

The Major Domo sniffed loudly. 'The principals only allowed you twelve hours in charge, Mister Jones, and people like that can change their minds at a moment's notice. If you want them kept quiet, give me something I can use to distract them.'

'A thought occurs to me,' I said. 'Why was Jennifer Rifkin killed?'

They both looked at me.

'Well,' said Penny. 'We've been working on the assumption she saw or heard something she shouldn't have. Something that would interfere with the killer's plans.'

'Yes,' I said. 'But think about it. The murderer must have known killing Jennifer would be bound to attract the Organization's attention. That getting rid of one agent would only lead to the Organization sending another. So why would the killer do something that would be bound to increase the risk of his being found out?'

'Only one thing could justify that,' said Penny. 'Jennifer must have worked out who the killer was. Or at the very least, what he was planning to do. So the killer had to silence her before she could contact the Organization and give his game away.'

'She never said anything to me,' said the Major Domo, trying valiantly to keep up. 'Why didn't she say something? I could have helped her, protected her.'

'She probably wasn't sure who she could trust,' said Penny.

'What do you mean?' the Major Domo said sharply.

'We need to take another look at Jennifer's room,' I said. 'Major Domo, have your people cleared up in there?'

'Of course not,' said the Major Domo. 'It's still being preserved as a crime scene.'

'With a guard on the door, as I requested?'

'Well, for a while,' said the Major Domo. 'The security personnel are spread rather thin right now. They have to guard the whole House, to keep people in as well as out. I've had to position them where they can do the most good . . . I didn't have anyone I could spare to guard an empty room!'

'So no guard at Jennifer's door,' I said. 'Anyone could get in.'

'Why would they want to? And anyway, the door is still locked.'

'Locks don't seem to mean much in this house,' I said. 'Penny, we'd better go take a look.'

'Right now, if not sooner,' said Penny.

'Go back and sit on the principals, Major Domo,' I said. 'Keep them quiet, whatever it takes.'

The Major Domo nodded brusquely. She'd just started to turn away when Penny raised her voice.

'I was just wondering, Major Domo . . . you always refer to your personal principal as August. Has he got round to telling you what his real name is yet?'

'Of course,' said the Major Domo. And then she strode off down the corridor, with the air of someone who'd just snatched a point back from the jaws of defeat.

The door to Jennifer's room was closed, and the corridor was completely empty. I tried the door handle; it was still locked. Penny looked around her.

'The Major Domo said she had guards spread out all over the House, but I haven't seen any so far.'

'They're around,' I said. 'Guarding the main doors and windows, mostly. I can hear them moving around in the background.'

'You can?' said Penny. 'Of course you can. Mister Supersenses Space Boy! You can be really creepy sometimes, Ishmael. You know that?'

I didn't take offence. It was just her lack of wind from the stairs talking. I looked at Jennifer's door thoughtfully. Something about it bothered me.

'You've got that look again,' said Penny. 'What is it this time?'

'How did the killer get in?' I said. 'If Jennifer thought she knew who the killer was, or what he intended to do, that would explain why she retreated to her room. To work on her report before she sent it in. She'd want to be sure she had all her ducks in a row before she pointed a finger. Particularly if she suspected someone important.'

'But the principals wouldn't have sat still, if an Organization agent said they were in danger,' said Penny. 'She could have just given a general warning, and let security take care of it.'

'Perhaps she knew, but couldn't prove anything,' I said. 'Either way, she would still have locked her door. So how did he get in, to kill her?'

'Perhaps she knew who was behind the killer but not the killer himself,' said Penny. 'She might have opened the door to someone she thought she could trust.'

'Even so,' I said, 'the killer couldn't rely on being invited in.'

I hit the door a couple of times, just testing, and the sturdy wood rattled heavily in its frame. Not something that could easily be forced. I knelt down and studied the lock. Another old-fashioned keyhole, rather than a card slot. I leaned in as close as I could, pressing my face against the door.

'Ishmael,' said Penny, 'what are you doing?'

'Looking for signs the lock has been tampered with,' I said. 'Even the most experienced field agent will leave some marks when he picks a lock.'

'And you can see that without a magnifying glass?' said Penny. 'Of course you can. Alien . . .'

And that was when I smelled something. Just a trace, but definitely familiar. I breathed in deeply through my nose and realized the scent was coming from inside the keyhole. That strange scent, from the unseen creature in the cellar. I straightened up, and told Penny what I'd found.

'Inside the lock?' said Penny. 'How is that possible?'

'The creature we encountered in the cellar . . . is what our killer changes into to do his dirty work,' I said. 'But he's not just a shape-changer, he's a shape-dancer. Able to change any part of himself into whatever he needs it to be. He can be any animal or combination of animals, or any person he needs to impersonate. He changed his hand, transforming it into something that could enter the keyhole and operate the lock. That's why I'm getting the smell from inside the hole.'

'OK . . .' said Penny. 'That's several steps beyond a werewolf! That's inhuman! Have you actually met anything like that?'

'Yes,' I said. 'Quite often. You'd be surprised at the extremes life can take in the hidden world.'

'I don't think I want to know!' said Penny.

'That's a large part of how they stay hidden,' I said. 'But it is rare – and I mean really rare – for any of them to act so openly in the everyday world.' Then I stopped, as several things suddenly came together in my head. 'That's why our murderer becomes a creature to carry out his kills! He doesn't need a weapon, or anything else that could be used to identify him, when he can manufacture everything he needs out of his own body. Teeth, claws, massive muscles . . . Enough to tear his victims apart and wreck their rooms. I think he destroyed the principals' rooms so we wouldn't wonder why he wrecked

Jennifer's room. We were meant to think it was just part of his pattern, when really he only tore this room apart because he was searching for Jennifer's notes. To confirm what she knew about him. It's all been nothing but misdirection, right from the beginning. He's been using the legends of Baphomet and the Coronach creature to keep us from seeing what he really is and what he's been doing.'

'He must know the layout of the House from top to bottom,' Penny said slowly. 'Including the secret cellar and its tunnel. How would he know all that?'

'Someone must have told him,' I said. 'His unknown master . . . Maybe the Major Domo . . .'

'Really?' said Penny.

'How far would she go, I wonder, to get her old home back? What kind of deal with the devil might she be prepared to make to get what she's wanted for so long?'

'Hold it!' said Penny, holding up one hand in protest. 'All this jumping to conclusions is leaving me breathless. Are we saying she's the one behind the killer creature? Or just someone who's been supplying the killer's master with necessary information?'

'I don't know,' I said. 'I think we need to ask the Major Domo some very pointed questions.'

'You do that,' said Penny. 'I'll watch, from a distance. While hiding behind something substantial.'

'She's not that scary.'

'Oh, I think she could be if you annoyed her sufficiently.'

'Hasn't stopped you poking her with a verbal stick.'

'I can run faster than she can. She'd never catch me.'

I considered Jennifer's locked door again. 'First things first. We need to give this room a good going over. See what there is to see.'

I hit the door with my shoulder and it burst open, shattering the lock and sending pieces flying through the air like shrapnel.

'Doesn't that hurt?' said Penny, as she entered the room.

'Like you wouldn't believe,' I said, rubbing my shoulder as I followed her in.

'Well, be a brave little soldier and there will be treats later.'

The furniture still lay in pieces, surrounding the untouched bed. I moved around the room carefully, looking at everything and touching nothing. Penny stayed just inside the door, frowning thoughtfully.

'The damage here doesn't seem nearly as extensive as in the principals' rooms,' she said finally.

'He wasn't trying to make a mess here,' I said. 'Just trying to find Jennifer's report. He must have been desperate to know how much she knew.'

'If he found anything, he would have taken it with him,' said Penny.

'If he'd found it, yes,' I said. 'But field agents are trained to hide their reports in places no one else would think to look.'

Penny put her hands on her hips and glared around her. 'We're working on the scenario that the killer let himself in unannounced, taking Jennifer by surprise. She wouldn't have had time to hide anything.'

'Jennifer was a professional,' I said. 'She would have heard something, no matter how careful the killer was. No matter how fast he got to her, she still had somewhere she could hide her report in a hurry. If she was working on her laptop, all she had to do was swallow the memory stick and purge the information from her computer. The killer probably never even saw her do it.'

'But doing that gave the killer enough time to be able to jump her from behind,' said Penny. 'So she couldn't defend herself. Yes, that works!'

'There'll have to be an autopsy,' I said. 'To retrieve the memory stick and see what's on it.'

'We don't have time to wait for a pathologist,' said Penny. 'How badly do we need the information?'

'If it comes right down to it,' I said. 'I'll go down to the freezer with a really big knife and do the job myself. Wouldn't be the first time.'

'I could have lived without knowing that,' said Penny.

I closed the door carefully when we left Jennifer's room. But it didn't want to stay shut, sulking because I'd mistreated it. Penny smiled.

'I'm starting to see a trend here, with you and doors. So what do we do now?'

I wanted to say 'Why do you keep asking me that? I'm as much in the dark as you are.' But I didn't, because I knew why. I was the one with long experience of fieldwork, murder and bodies. I thought hard.

'Someone in this house must be pretending to be someone else,' I said finally. 'Our killer has changed his shape and is hiding behind a familiar face. That's why he took the heads – to help confuse the issue.'

'I thought we already had an impostor?' said Penny. 'The replaced principal? That is why we were brought in on this case in the first place.'

'Remember what I said about the killer being the murder weapon? I think our killer is taking his orders from whoever is impersonating a principal. But now he's hiding in plain sight, watching us from behind someone else's eyes. He could be anyone. Anyone at all.'

Penny looked at me, suddenly suspicious. 'OK . . . What present did I give you last Christmas?'

'*Fifty Shades of Grey*,' I said. 'And I couldn't get past Chapter three without wincing. Never having to say you're sorry shouldn't involve rope burns. What did I give you?'

'A whole tin of Quality Street, because they're my favourites. Though I made you eat all the toffees.'

We exchanged a quick smile and, having determined we were both who we seemed to be, continued with our theorizing.

'This is getting genuinely disturbing,' said Penny.

'Yes,' I said. 'It is. The killer could take on any friendly face in order to get close to someone. He became one of the escorts to get into the principal's room, and his victim never suspected a thing until the killer dropped his mask . . . and became something awful.'

'I'm going to have nightmares about this,' said Penny.

'After he was finished the killer changed again, to resemble one of the security guards. Which is why no one noticed anything out of the ordinary when he was slipping in and out of open doors during the gunfight. Who knows how many

different faces the killer used in all the confusion? That's how
he got to Baron. By appearing to him as someone he knew,
and telling him February wanted to see him. Maybe the face
he used was mine . . .'

'Don't!' said Penny.

We looked at each other for a long moment.

'How are we supposed to track down a killer who could be
anyone?' Penny said finally. 'Or . . . anything? For all we know,
he could be hiding as a piece of furniture and we wouldn't
know anything about it until we sat on him!'

I had to smile. 'No, there are limits, even for a shape-dancer.
He can change from one living thing to another, but that's it.'

'Are you sure about that?' said Penny.

'Want me to kick a few chairs around, just to be on the safe
side?'

A terrible howling burst out on the air, and we both looked
round sharply. It was the sound of some great beast, fierce and
feral. Some ancient thing, from the days when beasts were
predators and men were prey. Penny grabbed hold of my arm,
her fingers digging in painfully.

'What the hell was that?'

'It's the creature,' I said. 'While we've been looking for it,
it's found us.'

'Where did that awful sound come from?'

'Upstairs,' I said. 'The top floor.'

Penny made herself let go of my arm, and we headed for the
stairs.

'Remind me,' she said. 'Why exactly are we running towards
certain danger?'

'Because it's the job,' I said. 'And because this time we can
see what we're doing. I don't care what form the killer's taken
. . . If it's got an arse, I'm going to kick it. Didn't you say you
were determined never to run from it again?'

'Well, yes,' said Penny. 'But I meant, after we'd loaded
ourselves down with all kinds of weapons. Along with
body armour, explosives, and industrial-strength good-luck
charms.'

'You don't need any of that,' I said. 'You've got me.'

*   *   *

I stopped at the top floor landing, so Penny could get her breathing back under control, and looked around me. Nothing moved in the long open corridor, but I caught a trace of the creature's familiar scent. I could feel a tension in the air, as though something was watching. And then heavy vibrations echoed through the floorboards under my feet, growing steadily stronger. Something really big and really heavy was coming our way. I turned to face it, gesturing quickly for Penny to get behind me. There was a growing thunder of pounding feet, and then the creature burst round the far corner and came charging down the corridor towards us. Penny made a sound behind me, but I didn't dare turn my attention away from the creature. From my first look at the thing that had killed so many people. The thing in the dark that had made me run.

It wasn't hiding any more.

It wasn't a wolf, or even a wolfman. It wasn't any kind of creature from the natural world. The thing was huge, some eight feet long and five feet high at the shoulder; with a barrel chest and a sleek powerful body. It went on four legs, terrible muscles bunching and churning under thick silver-grey fur. Vicious claws on oversized paws tore chunks out of the thick carpeting. The creature had a wide feline head, and powerful jaws packed with teeth. It looked like every predator that ever was, concentrated into one deadly form. It looked like what it was: the killer instinct that lives in every man, given shape and form and malignant intent.

It slowed as it drew nearer, and its great head came up. I think it had expected us to run, like we had in the cellar. But Penny stuck close behind me as I stood my ground and grinned fiercely at the creature. I always feel better when I'm doing something, when I have a chance to get my hands on whatever it is that's been giving me grief. I leaned forward and braced myself. The creature snarled viciously and threw itself at me. I waited until it was almost upon me, and then lashed out with all my strength and punched it in the face.

I hit it right on its bristling nose, and my fist sank deep into the flesh and kept on going. The creature slammed to a halt, as though it had run into a brick wall. The neck compacted as its head was forced back into its body. The sounds of breaking bones filled the corridor.

The collision didn't force me back one inch. I was braced, keeping my arm extended, soaking up the impact through my shoulder. I knew I'd feel it the next day, but right then I didn't care, caught up in the savage satisfaction of the moment.

The creature collapsed in front of me, its head pushed right back between its shoulder blades. Its legs kicked helplessly as it thrashed and squalled on the floor. I jerked my fist back out of its shattered head, and my hand was soaked in black blood. It felt thick and cold.

Penny wanted to come forward for a better look at the creature. She thought the fight was over; but I knew better. I gestured sharply for her to stay back, and for once she didn't argue. The creature was already scrambling back on to its feet. It shook its broken head back and forth, and I could hear shattered bones reknitting themselves. The creature's head thrust forward, out of its body, and the face re-formed in a moment. The creature fixed me with horribly human eyes, and then smiled a calculating smile.

Up close, the thing's scent was almost overpowering. A mixture of all the beasts that have ever scared human kind. A scent designed to terrify, to reach the old atavistic parts of the human brain and reduce a man to a quivering helpless prey. But whatever my ancestors might have been, they weren't human. I took a deep breath, filling my head with the thick scent, and frowned. The human part was clearer than ever. And I recognized it. As though the creature knew what I was thinking, it reared up to its full height and the great head scraped against the ceiling. Its shape changed subtly to allow it to stand like a man. It towered over me, and I met its gaze unflinchingly.

'I know who you are,' I said. 'Who you really are. I always knew your scent contained a human component, but I had to get this close before I could recognize it. How long have you been a shape-changer, Christopher Baron?'

Penny made a shocked sound behind me. I didn't look back, keeping my eyes locked on the creature's burning gaze. And then, quite suddenly and simply, its shape melted away and Baron was standing before me in his distinctive red-leather jacket. Like a man who'd just slipped off one costume and put on another. He stood calmly before me and inclined his head briefly, like one player congratulating another on a good move. Penny moved forward to stand beside me.

'Hold everything!' she said. 'The last time we saw that jacket, it was ripped to shreds and soaked in blood. And where did the rest of those clothes come from? He wasn't wearing any a moment ago.'

'Really?' said Baron. 'That's your first question? That's what you want to go with? All right then, the jacket you were shown was my real jacket. A small sacrifice on my part, to help convince you I was dead. Because no one wastes time looking for a dead man. What I'm wearing now aren't clothes at all; they're just a part of me, like the fur I had before.'

'Oh, ick!' said Penny.

'You asked,' said Baron. He turned to me.

'That's why you weren't covered in blood between your kills,' I said. 'The blood disappeared along with your fur, when that became clothes again.'

'Well, obviously,' said Baron.

'What happened?' I said. 'How did you become . . . this?'

He smiled, in a self-satisfied sort of way. 'Remember the shape-changing experiments, back when we worked for the Beachcombers? After you left, I volunteered to serve as one of the test subjects. I was in a lot of trouble at the time, and I needed a way to disappear so completely not even my well-connected enemies would be able to find me. The process worked for me, even though it killed everyone else. Given that the scientists were basing their work on DNA material supplied by the Immortals, I suppose it's always possible an Immortal went skinny-dipping in my family's gene pool at some point and that saved me.

'I killed the scientists, so no one would ever know what I was capable of. Then I just put on one of their faces . . . and walked out into the world and disappeared. I could be anyone or anything I wanted, and you've no idea how liberating that can be. You wouldn't believe some of the things I've done . . . and been.'

'Then how did you end up here?' said Penny, cutting to the chase as always. 'Working as head stooge for the Major Domo?'

Baron looked at me. 'Is she always this irritating? Oh Ishmael, you're looking so disappointed in me.'

'You killed people you swore to protect,' I said.

'Not all of them,' said Baron. 'Not yet, anyway. And in my defence, the money is quite outstandingly good. Don't look at me like that, Ishmael! You have no more right to the moral high ground than I do. I remember some of the people you used to be, and the things they did. There's probably more blood on your hands than mine; it's just that mine's easier to see. Because I never tried to hide it.'

'The difference is that I give a damn,' I said steadily. 'You never did.'

'Don't get snotty, Ishmael. It's just business. Why am I doing this? Because even someone as versatile as me can still experience financial reverses. The money from this contract will allow me to retire, and disappear forever. You can't say I didn't give you a chance, Ishmael. I offered to just walk away from all this if only you'd go with me. With you at my side, I could have faced my enemies and dealt with them once and for all. But you wouldn't do it. So really, everything that's going to happen now . . . is all your fault.'

'You knew I wouldn't leave,' I said. 'You just wanted to see if I'd fallen as far as you.'

'Enough!' said Baron. 'Bored now. Let's do it, Ishmael. Let's dance.'

'Let's,' I said.

Baron's body rippled, like an image in a heat haze, and a massive grey-furred wolfman towered over me. Broad-shouldered, with clawed hands and a wide-stretched mouth packed full of teeth. The eyes were still human, still full of that terrible malevolent glee.

'For old times' sake!' he growled. 'You can't beat the classics.'

He lashed out with one long muscular arm, and the impact lifted me off my feet and sent me flying backwards. I slammed into the corridor wall, hitting it hard enough to crack the plaster from top to bottom. I slumped to the floor, my head dazed and muddled. The wolfman laughed soundlessly, and turned unhurriedly to face Penny.

'You can run, if you like,' he growled. 'I do so love the thrill of the chase. And I'll enjoy your heart so much more if it's still excited when I rip it out of your chest.'

'I wouldn't lower myself,' said Penny, 'to run from the likes of you.'

The wolfman shrugged, an eerily human gesture in such a large animal. 'Then Ishmael can watch as I kill you. I want him in the proper frame of mind for when I finally get to him.'

He advanced steadily, and the floor shook under his tread. Penny fell back, one step at a time. He reared over her, reaching out with both clawed hands. Penny stepped forward, inside his grasp, and booted him solidly in the nuts. The wolfman bent sharply forward, his eyes squeezed shut. A low agonized whining leaked out of his muzzle. And then he forced his pain back and straightened up again, raising one arm to club her down. And I jumped on his back from behind. He lurched forward, and almost fell. I slipped one arm round his throat, tightening my grip to cut off his air. For a moment he staggered back and forth, fighting for breath, and then thick bands of muscle formed inside his neck, forcing my arm away. He reached back with both arms. I held on tight, crouching down out of his reach, and his arms elongated unnaturally. I let go, and dropped off him.

'Penny!' I said. 'Get out of here!'

'No! I won't leave you!'

'I can't concentrate on him and you! Go!'

The wolfman swung round to face me, and I punched him in the head with all my strength. Bones shattered and teeth smashed, only to repair themselves in a moment. The wolfman moved remorselessly forward as I hit him again and again, but all I hurt was my hands. He roared deafeningly, and I laughed in his face. I grabbed hold of his lower jaw and ripped it away. A new jaw formed, even as I threw the first one aside. I grabbed hold of one long arm, broke it over my knee, and then ripped it right out of the shoulder socket. I went to use it as a club, but the flesh in my hand was already melting away to nothing. A new arm burst out of his shoulder. I moved in close and punched him under the sternum. My hand sank in deep, closed around his rapidly beating heart, and tore it out of his chest. He screamed horribly . . . but didn't die. I crushed the still beating heart in my hand. Bloody pulp

squeezed between my fingers. The wound in the wolfman's
chest had already closed over.

I caught a glimpse of Penny watching me. She looked horrified, at something alien and awful she could see in my face.
She started to back away.

The wolfman lashed out at me, but I was too quick for him.
I dodged and ducked, hitting him again and again, grabbing
handfuls of flesh and tearing them away. The wolfman fought
with savage fury, grunting and snarling, his vicious claws and
snapping jaws only missing me by inches. But he was no match
for me, for the dark part of me I usually only glimpse in dreams.
The wolfman screamed. Not from pain, but from the horror of
what he was facing. And I laughed.

It wasn't a human sound.

It had got out. The alien thing that hid in the depths of my
mind, behind the human mask, had finally got out. And even
as I used it to tear the wolfman to pieces, I wondered if I'd
ever be able to put it back inside again. Or if I'd ever want to.

I ripped out the wolfman's throat with hooked fingers, and
black blood spouted on the air. He bent forward, making almost
human sounds of distress. I raised my fist to smash in his skull
and rip out his brains, the only sure way to kill a shape-changer
. . . And then I looked past him, to see Penny still staring at
me. As though I was the monster, not Baron.

I slowly lowered my hand, and the wolfman collapsed to the
floor, panting and whimpering. I stepped past him to get to
Penny, and she turned and ran. Sprinting down the corridor, not
looking back, desperate to get away from what she'd seen in
my face. The wolfman scrambled to his feet and bolted off in
the opposite direction. I couldn't chase them both. So I went
after Penny.

I ran down the corridor, calling her name. She looked back
once, her face twisted with horror and revulsion. She must have
known she couldn't outrun me. She plunged round a corner,
and I heard a door open and slam shut. By the time I got there,
the corridor was empty and all the doors were closed. I stumbled
to a halt, and a cold affronted rage surged through me. Penny
was hiding from me. From me! After everything I'd done for

her! I stopped as I saw her big black hat lying on the floor, where she'd dropped it as she ran from me. I bent over slowly and picked it up, turning it over and over in my hands. And slowly I shook off the cold inhuman feelings, like the black blood I'd shaken off my fists. I shuddered, and started slowly forward.

I could hear Penny breathing harshly behind one of the closed doors. I could smell her; her scent was thick with sweat and panic. I moved towards the door she was hiding behind. And her breathing shut off as she clapped a hand over her mouth and nose, hoping that if I couldn't hear her I'd pass her by. I stood facing the closed door, my heart pounding in my chest. But I wouldn't let myself speak until I was sure I was back in control and my voice was mine again. Until I was sure there was no one left in my head but me.

'I know you're in there, Penny. Please come out. I won't hurt you. You're perfectly safe, it's only me.'

'But who's that?' said Penny. Her voice came clearly to me from the other side of the door. 'What was that I saw in your face? Was that the real you? Have I ever known the real you?'

'I never lied to you about what I was,' I said steadily. 'What I was before I was me. But all I've ever been to you is Ishmael Jones. The man I chose to be. Look, I'm not going to break down this door. Even though we both know I could if I wanted to. I only did what I did to protect you. I let out the part of me that scares me most because it was the only way to save you. I'd never hurt you, Penny. Never allow you to be hurt. You must know that.'

I waited. I could hear her breathing slowing. But she didn't answer me.

'Please!' I said. 'I need you to trust me.'

'Trust who?' said Penny. 'Trust what?'

'The man who loves you,' I said.

'Do you love me?' said Penny. 'As a man loves a woman? Is something like you capable of that kind of love?'

'I would die for you,' I said. 'Or if you want, I'll leave Coronach House. Just walk away and disappear, and you'll never have to see me again. I'll do that for you, if that's what you want. If that's what you need, to feel safe. Because I love you. It's up to you, Penny. You decide.'

She slowly opened the door and for a long moment we just stood there, facing each other. I showed her the black hat I'd picked up and offered it to her. After a moment, she took it from me.

'You were born into this world a man,' she said finally. 'But you were something else, before that. Do you know what?'

'No,' I said. 'All I know . . . is that I'm scared it might be realer than me.'

She reached out and took me in her arms, holding me close. And I held on to her like a drowning man thrown a lifeline at the very last moment. I could feel her heart slowing, next to mine. Two human hearts together. Eventually we let go, and looked at each other.

'So?' I said. 'What do we do now?'

Penny managed a small smile. '*You* are asking *me*? I suppose . . . we do our job. We still have a murderer to catch, and people to protect. We know Baron is the killer, but we don't know who's been giving him his orders. Or why any of this is happening. He can't get out of the House, no matter whose face he puts on, because the guards have orders to shoot anyone who tries to leave. And they're jumpy enough to shoot first and not bother with questions afterwards. So . . . let's go find Baron.'

'That's not going to be easy,' I said. 'He could be anyone by now.'

'But can he change his scent?' said Penny.

I smiled. 'Perhaps. If he thinks of it. He doesn't know me nearly as well as he thinks.'

'Well if he does, we'll just have to catch him the old-fashioned way,' said Penny. 'Through clever questioning and insightful deductions.'

'OK . . .' I said. 'You're pushing your luck now.'

'I know,' said Penny.

She clapped her big hat back on her head. We laughed quietly together, held hands, and went back down the corridor.

When we finally reached the bottom of the stairs, the Major Domo was already there, in the reception area, waiting for us. Looking strained and tense, and more than ready to take it out on someone else. She saw Penny and I were holding hands, but chose not to comment.

'Hello, Major Domo,' I said. 'You're looking very much yourself. What is it this time?'

'I've found the missing heads,' she said flatly. 'Those of the principals and escorts.'

'Where were they?' said Penny.

'In the one place no one would have been expected to look. Except I did.'

'Stop patting yourself on the back,' I said. 'You'll strain something. Where were they?'

'It was just common sense, really,' said the Major Domo, refusing to be hurried in her moment of triumph. 'I found them in the walk-in freezer in the kitchen, tucked away with all the other body parts.'

'That was clever,' I said.

'Thank you,' said the Major Domo.

'I meant the killer was, but you're welcome,' I said. 'We know who the killer is.'

'Who?' said the Major Domo. 'Tell me!'

'Baron,' said Penny. 'Your own Head of Security. That's how the killer was able to run rings round us. Because he knew all there was to know about the House's layout and guards.'

'But there's more to it than that,' I said. 'We're pretty sure Baron's working for someone else. Someone in this house. And we know for a fact that he's a shape-changer.'

The Major Domo put up a hand, asking me to stop for a moment so she could mentally get her breath. She didn't challenge anything I said. She didn't even seem particularly shocked. She just nodded slowly, taking it all in and deciding what to do next.

'Bastard!' she said finally. 'I trusted him. He seemed so hard-working, so eager to please. And his references were excellent! A shape-changer . . .' She smiled briefly. 'I suppose it makes more sense than a brains vampire . . . I should have known the Organization wouldn't take an interest in this case unless there was an unnatural element. All right. How are we going to find Baron? He could be pretending to be anyone.'

'Did you count the heads in the freezer?' I said.

She nodded quickly. 'The number's right. But I couldn't identify any of them. The damage to the faces was too extensive.'

'Deliberately inflicted,' I said, 'so we couldn't be sure. He wanted us to be confused as to who might be who. But I know where he's hiding. I know how he thinks. He'll have taken the place of one of the four surviving principals, because he believes we won't dare question their authority. I'll need your help to question them, Major Domo.'

'Of course,' she said. 'My man, my mess. It's my duty to help clear it up.'

'Then you'd better go and talk to the principals,' I said. 'Fill them in on who and what the killer is. We'll be along in a minute.'

She nodded quickly, and hurried off. Penny looked after her.

'She took that rather well, I thought.'

'She did, didn't she?' I said.

'We were brought in to find a fake principal,' said Penny. 'So . . . are there two fake principals now?'

'Beats the hell out of me,' I said. 'We'll just have to get at the truth through clever and subtle interrogation.'

'That could take a while,' said Penny.

By the time we got to the meeting room, the Major Domo had filled the outer corridor with heavily armed security guards. Who all snapped to attention as Penny and I approached. One of them diffidently announced they'd been given orders that no one was to be allowed in or out of the meeting room, apart from me and Penny. And then only if we were together. It was clear they hadn't been told why. I nodded approvingly. The Major Domo had been thinking about the implications of dealing with someone who could be anyone.

I knocked on the closed door and announced myself loudly. Penny added her voice, just to make it clear we were together. The Major Domo unlocked the door, looked us both over carefully, and then stepped back. The moment we were inside, she closed the door behind us. As though afraid someone might make a dash for it. The four principals weren't at the long table any more. They were sitting separately, on chairs some distance apart. January and March weren't even pretending to be interested in each other. August sat at the back of the room, quiet and grey as ever; the Major Domo went to stand beside him. December looked old and tired, as though he was having trouble keeping up with everything that was happening.

'Well?' he said querulously. 'Is it true? Is it true what the Major Domo says? That Baron is the killer?'

'Yes,' I said. 'And yes, he's a shape-changer. He can make himself look like anyone.'

The four principals looked at each other uneasily, but they all seemed to be taking the news in their stride. January saw the surprise in my face, and sniffed loudly.

'We've all had dealings with the hidden world, in our time,' she said flatly.

'Money is money,' said March. 'You can find profits in the strangest places. Gold is gold. Unless it's elf gold, of course.'

'My family made its fortune in the hidden world, originally,' said August.

'Shape-changing would explain a lot,' said December, 'I suppose.'

'But there's more to it than that,' I said. 'Baron was just a hired man, working for someone else. Someone in this house. And the only people with the authority and money to arrange that are in this room. Baron is here, too. Pretending to be one of you, so he can use a principal's authority to protect himself. As well as keep an eye on his employer, to make sure he, or she, won't betray him.'

The four principals looked startled, and shocked, for the first time.

'But that's not possible,' said January. 'None of us have any reason to want the rest of the Group dead.'

'How can you be sure?' said March, his hands twitching restlessly in his lap. 'We don't know each other outside Group meetings. Who knows what we're capable of? We all broke the rules; apart from December, of course. How can we be sure any of us really are who we claim to be?'

'We'd know from the way we all act, wouldn't we?' said August, blinking confusedly. 'I mean, someone could look like one of us but not know how to act like a principal.'

'I'd know if you weren't you,' said the Major Domo.

'Of course you would,' said August. 'Thank you, my dear.'

'Claiming the killer is a shape-changer,' said December, glaring at me, 'could just be an excuse. To explain why you haven't been able to catch him.'

'Why would any of us want to hire an assassin?' said January, sticking stubbornly to her point. She sounded honestly puzzled. 'It doesn't make sense. What would we have to gain?'

'Let me walk you through the basic motives,' I said. 'January and March first. You couldn't afford to be found out, because your private conspiracy could get you kicked out of the Baphomet Group. But that's not a good enough reason to kill all the other principals. And the first killings, of Jennifer and October, took place before your relationship was revealed.

'August, you've been very open about not wanting to be part of the Baphomet Group. But killing all the others wouldn't put an end to the Group or free you from your duties. The families would just appoint new replacements, and the Group would go on.

'And finally, December. You hated what the Group was becoming. But again, even if all the others died, they'd just be replaced by more of this new generation that you despise so much. And you'd be more outvoted than ever.'

I stopped talking, and waited.

'OK . . .' said Penny. 'Are you saying none of these four have any reason to be the killer?'

'No,' I said. 'It's just that the basic motives don't work here. This was never about money or position; it was always about hatred.' I looked round the room, at the suspicious January, the supercilious March, the confused August and the scowling December. 'But first, let's talk about the shape-changer. Because we need to deal with him before we can proceed to his employer. Baron is in this room. I recognize . . . something very distinctive about him, which he didn't think to change when he changed shape.'

I smiled around at the principals. 'Which of you left this room, even though I told you not to?'

Three of the principals immediately turned to stare at December. He bristled angrily in his chair.

'Oh, come on! I only went to the bathroom. It wasn't like I sneaked out! I told you where I was going. You can't expect a

man of my years to go for long without a toilet break. Stop
looking at me like that! I was only gone for a few minutes . . .'
    'A few minutes is all it would take,' I said. 'I wonder, if I
was to send some of the guards outside to search all the nearby
bathrooms, would they find December's body tucked away
somewhere?'
    'Oh hell!' said December, rising to his feet. And suddenly
he didn't look tired or old any more. He just seemed to shrug
and Baron was suddenly standing there, in his distinctive red-
leather jacket. He smiled around the room, as the principals
jumped to their feet and backed away from him. The Major
Domo moved quickly to place herself between Baron and
August, who was looking even more dumbfounded than usual.
January stabbed a quivering finger at Baron.
    'It's him!' she said loudly. 'It's him!'
    Baron ignored her, nodding cheerfully to me. 'Very clever,
Ishmael. You've found me. But it doesn't matter, because you're
going to let me go.'
    'Pretty sure that's not going to happen,' I said.
    'You'd be surprised at some of the things I know,' said Baron.
'Give me a moment, Ishmael. We need to speak privately, just
you and me. For old times' sake.'
    'You already tried that,' I said.
    'This is different. Come on, Ishmael! This doesn't have to
end in a massacre.'
    I looked around the room, shrugged, and moved off to one
side. Baron came over to join me. Penny looked uneasy, but
stayed put after I nodded reassuringly to her. Baron leaned in
close, his words little more than a murmur.
    'I did some checking into your past, while I had access to
the Beachcombers' files. They knew all sorts of things they
weren't supposed to. I was curious about you, about certain
things I'd seen you do. The point is I know what you are. I
know why you appeared out of nowhere in 1963, and why your
appearance hasn't changed since. Why you have to keep moving,
to stay hidden. Ishmael . . . I know where your starship is
buried. Let me leave here and I'll take you right to it. You can
reclaim your heritage. Who knows, maybe you can go home
again.'

'Even if I believed you,' I said, 'which I don't, I won't betray my job and my trust. That's the difference between you and me.'

Baron sighed heavily. 'You always were the sentimental one. I just thought . . . Well, we're back to where we were, then. You let me leave, or I kill everyone else in this room before you can stop me.'

'Including the one who's paying you?'

'His fee was contingent on my completing the job and not being found out,' said Baron. 'You've blown that. So to hell with him! And to hell with you!'

'Can I ask one question that's been bugging me?' I said.

'Just one? All right. For old times' sake.'

'How did you get the missing heads out of the principals' rooms and past all the guards without them noticing?'

'I made a pouch in my body and tucked them away inside. When I went back to being human, the heads were absorbed inside me.'

'I think I was better off not knowing,' I said.

'I could have told you that. Are we done now? Good.' He stepped back, and smiled around at the watching room. 'Guess what? You're all going to die.'

The Major Domo called out, the door burst open, and all the guards from the corridor came rushing in, guns at the ready. Baron spun round to face them, and every single guard opened fire at once. Bullets slammed into Baron over and over, but no blood flowed and the wounds healed almost immediately. The guards concentrated their fire on Baron's head, and he raised one arm to protect his face. And then, one by one, the guards' guns fell silent as they ran out of ammunition. Suddenly, it was very quiet in the room. Baron lowered his arm and smiled at the guards. The smile stretched unnaturally wide, showing row upon row of horribly sharp teeth.

I stepped forward, putting myself between the guards and Baron. His back arched and his head surged forward, the snapping teeth reaching for my throat. I grabbed hold of his head with both hands and ripped it right off his body. Black blood jetted from the stump of his neck, and the headless body crumpled bonelessly to the floor. I held Baron's head up so I could look into his eyes. He smiled briefly, and tried to say something.

I crushed his head between my hands. The skull shattered, and brains erupted all over my hands. I dropped the broken head to the floor, took out a handkerchief, and cleaned my hands carefully.

'That was for you, Jennifer.'

People were saying things all around me, but I wasn't listening. I'd just killed a man who might have been my friend. I put away my handkerchief and looked at Penny.

'I'm sorry you had to see that.'

'It's all right,' she said. 'I understand.' She looked like she did, even if it disturbed her.

I looked around the room, taking my time. Everyone was staring at me, white-faced and wild-eyed. Most of the guards were covering me with their guns, even though they were empty. The three remaining principals stared at me uncertainly. The Major Domo hovered beside August, ready to stand in front of him again if necessary. I gave them all my most reassuring smile.

'Relax. It's almost over.'

'How could you do that?' said March. He sounded like he might faint at any moment.

'Never mess with a trained Organization agent,' I said.

'But Baron was the only one who could have told us who he was working for!' said the Major Domo.

'Not necessarily,' I said. 'First, send the guards out of here. They don't need to hear this.'

The principals didn't look too sure about that, but the guards were already hurrying out of the room, glad of any excuse to leave. The last man out slammed the door behind him, and it was suddenly very quiet in the room. I smiled easily about me.

'Now we have only three suspects left, and only one motive that makes sense. I've been thinking about this for some time. And, as I was saying before I was so rudely interrupted, it all comes down to hatred. The bottled-up rage of a man forced to be what he never wanted to be.' I looked steadily at August. 'It had to be you. January and March might have conspired against the old order, but they still wanted the Baphomet Group to continue, on their own terms. Same with December. You're the only one who hated everything about it. And you were the only one to say that Baron went to meet February in his room before the gunfight. But none of the guards mentioned seeing him; and they would have noticed the Head of House Security. He changed to look like one of the escorts, and that's how he got to his first victim.'

January and March stared at August, who looked steadily back at them.

'You're wrong,' said the Major Domo. 'August, tell him he's got it wrong!'

'Oh do be quiet, Helen,' said August. He was still the same grey little man, but the look in his eyes silenced the Major Domo. He turned to face me. 'You've worked it all out, haven't you, Mister Jones? Despite all the obstacles I had Baron throw in your path. I never wanted to be a part of the Baphomet Group. Never wanted to run the family business. It was forced on me. All the things I could have done, could have been . . . One of the richest members of the financial elite, but my life wasn't my own. I put up with it for as long as I could, for the sake of my family . . . But perhaps it was just one meeting too many, one argument too many . . . I simply decided I'd had enough.

'I used my family's connections with the hidden world to hire Baron. And then it was easy enough to provide him with forged credentials and position him here. So he could kill all the people who'd made my life such a misery.' He stopped, to look at the Major Domo. 'Your company was very pleasant, Helen, but you were only ever a source of information. You told me everything that was happening in the House, and I told Baron. I couldn't have done this without you.'

'I thought you cared for me!' said the Major Domo.

'Sorry,' said August. 'After all, you're just a servant. Now do be quiet. I'm talking.' He paused a moment, to gather his thoughts, and then looked back at me. 'With so many of the Group dead, there will be chaos in the financial markets. Encouraged and manipulated by people I've already put in place. More than enough to wipe out all the other families. The Group will be discredited . . . and I will be free at last. Free to become someone who can be happy, at last.'

'I thought I made you happy,' said the Major Domo. 'You made me happy.'

'Do you really need me to say it, Helen? Very well, then. You were just a means to an end. Nothing more. Now, please hush.'

He deliberately turned his back on her, giving all his attention to me.

'Why kill Jennifer?' I said.

'Baron panicked,' said August. 'He was afraid she'd recognized who and what he was, so he silenced her. But then the Organization sent you.' He glared at Baron's headless body. 'If you hadn't killed him, I would have seen to it. I told him what needed to be done to throw you off the scent, but he never was subtle . . . All my marvellous plans derailed by one impulsive action!'

'Isn't it always the way?' I said.

August stared coldly at me. 'You must know that you can't touch me. Even your precious Organization can't touch me . . . I am protected by centuries of invested money and accumulated privilege. No one can do anything about all the things I've done.'

There was the sound of a single shot. August made a puzzled sound, and dropped to his knees. He bent slowly forward, revealing the Major Domo standing behind him with a gun in her hand. I remembered taking the gun away from Baron in the private bar and giving it to her. August cried out softly. Blood spilled from his mouth, and he fell forward on to his face and didn't move.

'You should have loved me,' said the Major Domo. 'I loved you.'

She lowered the gun and looked at me.

'Am I going to have any problems with the Organization?'

'I shouldn't think so,' I said. 'It's not like we could have put him on trial . . . This is as neat an ending as we were ever going to get.'

The Major Domo looked at January and March, who were already nodding.

'We'll make sure there's no problem with his family,' said January. 'Probably be glad to be rid of the ungrateful little wretch. As the last two surviving members of the Baphomet Group, we're free at last to make it into what we always thought it should be.'

'Exactly,' said March. 'New blood comes in, and the Group goes on. As it always will.'

'Praise Baphomet!' said January.

'Praise Baphomet!' said March.

Penny shot me a look and started to say something, but stopped when I shook my head. We were never going to know for sure.

'I should have realized it was August,' said the Major Domo. 'But I let him get too close to me. I couldn't see the monster inside the man.'

Penny nodded. 'People can always surprise you.'

EIGHT
Reflections

I t was morning, and the sun was out. I stood on the bank of Loch Ness, looking out over its still dark waters. Penny stood at my side, one arm slipped companionably through mine. Birds were singing cheerfully, while a brisk wind blew clouds across the sky. There wasn't a hint of mist anywhere. A handful of guards patrolled the grounds, careful to maintain a respectful distance.

'It's a pity we never got to see the monster,' said Penny, after a while.

'There were enough monsters in the House,' I said. 'Or more properly, in the people in the House.'

'Do you think Nessie's just a legend?' said Penny. 'Like the Coronach creature?'

I thought about it. 'Just because we haven't seen something, doesn't mean it might not be out there somewhere. There's room in the world for all sorts of things.'

A small boat came chugging calmly down the loch, apparently entirely unconcerned about what might exist in the depths beneath. Penny waved to it, and someone on deck waved back.

'So,' she said, 'there never was a fake principal.'

'Looks that way,' I said. 'Apart from Baron, right at the end.'

'An odd case all round,' said Penny. 'No one was who or what they seemed to be.'

'An entirely suitable case, then, for the mysterious Mister Jones,' said the Colonel.

We both looked round, as the tall military figure came striding across the grounds. He slammed to a halt beside us, held himself at parade rest, and looked out over the loch with a stern gaze, as though daring anything in it to misbehave.

'I thought it better to meet out here,' he said, in his usual clipped tones. 'The principals don't need to see my face. The two remaining principals, I should say. At least you kept some of them alive. The Organization . . . is not entirely displeased.'

'Good to know,' I said. 'I have a question.'

'Of course you do,' said the Colonel.

'Who told the Organization they thought one of the principals might be a duplicate? I never found any evidence of that. But if Jennifer Rifkin hadn't been called in . . .'

'Quite,' said the Colonel. 'The Major Domo alerted the Organization. She is one of us, after all.' He allowed himself a small smile at the look on my face. 'Not a field agent, of course, but one of many who serve our purposes out in the world.'

'That's why she wasn't thrown when we told her Baron was a shape-changer!' said Penny.

'Exactly,' said the Colonel. 'She was unhappy about Baron being forced on her as Head of House Security. And when she couldn't find out why, she started looking for a reason. She decided she didn't like the way one of the principals was acting, so she alerted us. And we sent Miss Rifkin.'

'And Baron killed her,' I said. 'She had no idea of the danger she was in.'

'My people are removing her body,' said the Colonel. 'And sorting through the various bagged body parts to assemble as much of the dead principals as we can, before returning them to their families.'

'Did the Major Domo ever say who she thought the fake was?' said Penny.

'No,' said the Colonel.

'Presumably not August,' I said.

'Indeed,' said the Colonel. 'But then we all have our blind spots.'

He looked up and down Loch Ness, decided he wasn't impressed, and walked away. I went back to looking out over the loch.

'Still waters run deep,' I said.

'You should know,' said Penny.

'I'm not a monster,' I said.

'Of course not,' said Penny. 'If you were a monster, how could you love me?'

'Because it's all about you.'

'You and me.'

We laughed quietly together, in the rising light of the morning.